AN INFIDEL IN PARADISE

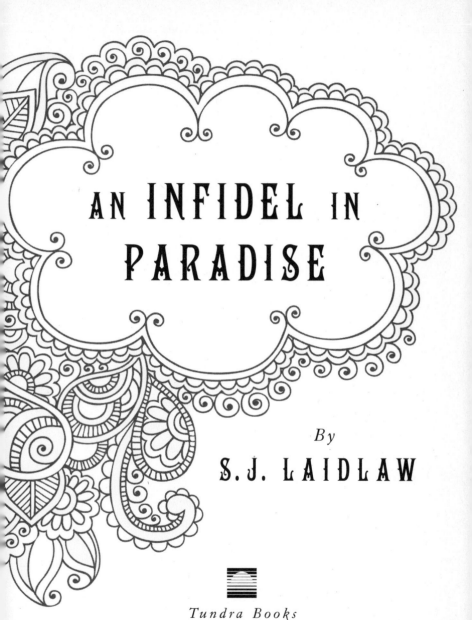

AN INFIDEL IN PARADISE

By

S.J. LAIDLAW

Tundra Books

Published in Canada by Tundra Books,
a division of Random House of Canada Limited,
One Toronto Street, Suite 300, Toronto, Ontario M5C 2V6

Published in the United States by Tundra Books of Northern New York,
P.O. Box 1030, Plattsburgh, New York 12901

Library of Congress Control Number: 2012938139

Library and Archives Canada Cataloguing in Publication

Laidlaw, S. J.
An infidel in paradise / S.J. Laidlaw.

ISBN 978-1-77049-304-9. – ISBN 978-1-77049-305-6 (EPUB)

I. Title.

PS8623.A394154 2013   JC813'.6   C2012-902852-5

We acknowledge the financial support of the Government of Canada through
the Canada Book Fund and that of the Government of Ontario through the
Ontario Media Development Corporation's Ontario Book Initiative. We
further acknowledge the support of the Canada Council for the Arts and the
Ontario Arts Council for our publishing program.

ONTARIO ARTS COUNCIL
CONSEIL DES ARTS DE L'ONTARIO

Edited by Sue Tate and Kelly Jones
Designed by Terri Nimmo

Printed and bound in the United States of America

www.tundrabooks.com

1 2 3 4 5 6   18 17 16 15 14 13

For Rafa and Gabe,
who grew up in many different worlds
but were always the center of mine.

CHAPTER 1

The snake is lying on the front porch like a present or a warning, blood pooled at its throat, glistening against the blackness of its leathery skin. The guard shot it at daybreak, execution-style. I'm glad it's dead – better it than me – but I can't bring myself to step over it. I imagine it suddenly arching up, its ghost fangs sinking into me. Not for the first time, it occurs to me that I shouldn't be here. I don't belong.

"Emma, we're late! What are you standing there for?" Mandy, my eight-year-old sister, has almost squeezed past me before she notices the snake. "Is that it?" she whispers.

Mandy is the master of stupid questions. Mom told us about the snake at breakfast, a twelve-foot cobra sunning itself on our own front path.

I don't bother answering. Together we contemplate the snake blocking our way. It's fatter than I expected. *What has it been eating?* Our front yard is a small rectangle of scorched grass with one spindly tree. It's hard to imagine a cute little nest of field mice. One large rat is more likely. Or several, with long yellow teeth. And superior hunting abilities. And a taste for human flesh.

Mandy clutches my hand. No doubt she's had the same thought. "It's gross," she says. "Throw it away."

Right, like I'm going to touch it.

"*You* throw it away." I try to sound nonchalant. "You're not scared, are you?" She increases her death grip on my hand. I think I hear bones cracking.

"Are you sure it's dead?"

"I don't know. Only one way to find out."

"No way!" She snatches away her hand, shrinking back like I might wrestle her to the snake. *Drama queen.*

"Daddy would have liked to see it," she says, a few steps behind me now.

I wince as her words slice into me. Taking a deep breath, I quickly hop over the snake. "So, are you coming, or what?"

Just then, our brother, Vince, appears in the doorway, his lanky frame towering over Mandy. He puts a reassuring hand on her shoulder.

"That's the snake," Mandy tells him, as if he couldn't work that one out.

"Really? Wow!" Vince always humors Mandy. It's irritating yet impressive at the same time. You have to admire his patience. "A real live cobra in our own front yard. How cool is that?"

It is so *not* cool, but I know what he's thinking. It's

the First Day. Another new school, another new country. It's not like we don't have enough to worry about.

"It's not cool. It's scary!" says Mandy.

"But exciting!" Vince thinks if he says something often enough, he can make it true. For weeks after Dad left, Vince insisted it was only temporary. "Pakistan is going to be great. How many countries do you think we could live in where we could get this close to a real cobra without leaving the house?"

"That's right, Mandy," I chime in. "Who needs movies, shopping, restaurants, and friends when we've got this kind of entertainment?"

Vince gives me a look, but I'm busy trimming my nails with my teeth. I'm down to the cuticles now. They're starting to bleed.

"I wish we could show it to Daddy," says Mandy.

Vince's jaw tightens. He takes Mandy's hand and flashes her a totally fake smile. "You can tell him about it the next time he calls."

"But who's going to take my First Day of School photo? Daddy always takes my First Day of School photo. It's our tradition."

"Maybe we'll have to start some new traditions." Vince is trying his best, but Mandy's no pushover. I give him a sympathetic smile, but he's too focused on Mandy to notice.

"I don't want new traditions," she whines.

"Come on, Chipmunk." It's Dad's name for her. Vince has recently started using it every time Mandy corners him. It'll stop working eventually, but for now she lets him take her hand and help her awkwardly over the snake.

"I could have used some help," he says quietly, pausing beside me.

"To lie to her?" I challenge, but I know he's right. If we're going to survive this day, much less this country, we have to help each other.

"You used to be a lot more fun," he says, which obliterates my remorse.

I round on him angrily. "I used to be able to walk to the mall, grab a pizza with my friends, catch the latest movie, shop in stores that actually sold clothes from this century, and walk home for a poolside chat with our loving father. A lot of things used to be more fun."

My chest is heaving as I wait for him to deny the truth of what I've said, but he's looking over my head toward the van. We should all be in it by now. I know he's wishing he didn't get into this, and he's not the only one. I don't want to be angry at Vince. He's just trying to make the best of a bad situation. But since the night Dad dropped his bombshell, I feel like my skin has become this fragile membrane, barely containing the anger that seethes beneath. It doesn't take much to pierce its surface, and then I lash out at the nearest victim. I'm always sorry afterward, but for those few seconds that I let the anger take over, the relief is exhilarating. Since Dad's departure, it's the closest I ever come to feeling good.

"That was Manila," he says finally. "We're in Islamabad now. You need to deal with it. It's not like it's our first move."

"It's our first one without Dad." I want to take back the words the second they escape. I've promised myself I won't miss him. He chose not to be with us. He's not worth my regrets.

"I want Daddy," whimpers Mandy.

"Do you see what you did?" demands Vince, meeting my eyes for the first time. I look away. Vince doesn't say anything more about it as he pushes past me and leads Mandy away, fast-talking about the joys of living at Terrorist Central.

I stand alone on the walkway for a few minutes, staring at nothing. I can hear the voices of the other embassy kids greeting my siblings and the sound of a door sliding open as they load into the van. There are four other kids on this compound, all of them too young to be of interest.

On Compound C, the other Canadian compound, there's a girl, Michelle, only one year older than me. She's a senior like Vince. I can already tell she has her eye on him. She hardly left his side last week at the welcome dinner, and she's phoned every day since, taking him shopping in Rawalpindi and out to eat at the local excuse for a fast-food restaurant, showing him off to her friends like a fashion accessory. It's not that I want to spend every minute with him, but we used to be close and — with all my friends thousands of miles away – I don't know if I can bear losing him as well. I feel the prick of tears, but no way am I crying on the First Day.

It's a short five-minute drive from Compound B, where we live, to Compound C. In fact, everything in the diplomatic enclave is within easy walking distance. Embassies from all over the world are crowded together with homes and apartments for embassy workers. Most embassies have a commissary, sports facilities, even a restaurant, so diplomats can last for days without ever going outside the surrounding walls.

We pick up Michelle, who sits unnecessarily close to my brother, and head for the gates out of the enclave. Half a dozen heavily armed soldiers are milling around at the entrance, smoking *bidis* and looking bored. One leans into our van and stares at each of us intently, as if he's trying to memorize our faces. I plan to roll my eyes at him when he gets to me, but when our eyes lock, I change my mind.

I can't explain it, but it's happened to me before. I see someone – in a crowded bazaar or on a railway platform in the middle of nowhere – and suddenly they're all I see. Everyone else, all the noise and confusion, drops away, like in the movies when they cut the sound and zoom in on the heroes. I don't know why it happens with some people and not others, but I feel this connection, like I know this person. Not their name or the boring details of their life, but really know them, their humanity, maybe their souls.

In this moment, the army fatigues, the rifle and pistol, the heavy mustache all seem like props. I stare at the man's gaunt, hawkish features and into his dark brown eyes. And I wait. I know he feels it too, and any moment he'll smile or maybe nod in recognition. But abruptly, The Hawk looks away, steps back, and waves us through like swatting flies. I look down at my palms. My bitten nails have left crescents of blood.

Just outside the gates, I see the beggar woman where she always sits, her acid-burned face peering out from under her veil like a reproach. I feel a rush of guilt that I forgot money for her today. Walking to the gate to give her a few rupees has been a daily ritual since I spotted her the day we arrived. According to Mom, she was burned by her own husband or in-laws. I've seen beggars before, but the agony this woman endured at the hands of her own family, before being abandoned at the side of the road like garbage, compels me to return day after day. And every time, as I trudge the wide, shaded boulevard to this spot, I fantasize that she won't be here. That someone – her husband, her parents – filled with remorse, will have come back for her, taken her home, begged her to give them a second chance to love her.

Mandy leans over the back of my seat. She and the other little kids have taken the two middle rows. Michelle and Vince are in the back, leaving me the whole front row to myself. I guess I should be pleased.

"How long till we get there?" Mandy asks.

"Forty minutes." I timed it when we came out to register.

"Why's it so far?" She's whining again.

She's right, though. It is a long trip. Like the diplomatic enclave, the school is deliberately built on the outskirts of the city. Unfortunately, it's on the opposite side, and we take the farm-tour to avoid main roads or anyplace we might encounter the "local population." We're like pariahs. Our entire existence is set up to minimize contact.

The first week here, I tried to leave the enclave to do some exploring on my own. In Manila I walked from my house to the mall all the time, but here I didn't get as far as the front gate before soldiers escorted me home like an escaped felon. I tried to tell them I was allowed to go where I wanted, but they didn't speak English and – to be honest – I'm not sure I have the same freedoms here. Mom spends half her time telling us what a great adventure we're going to have living in Pakistan and the other half telling us to stay inside the compound. You've got to wonder what kind of adventure she has in mind with a bunch of other Canadian kids in a space the size of a football field.

"Emma?" Mandy leans forward over my seat again.

I stare out the window.

"Emmaaaaaa?" She draws out the last syllable like a zombie gurgle. She knows I hate it when she does that. "Emmaaaaaaa." Now she's punctuating the gurgle with jabs to my shoulder. "Emma! I'm hungry. Can I eat my snack now?"

Mandy never used to ask my advice on anything, but since Dad left, she doesn't make a move without consulting me. It might be flattering if I didn't know exactly how misplaced her trust is. I let Dad slip away without lifting a finger to stop it. She was too little to pick up on the clues, and Vince's a guy; covert passions never make it onto his radar. But I knew something was wrong.

Dad always used to take a break from work to swim with us after school. I'd float in the pool and recount my day. Even if it had sucked, I felt better the second I hit the water. Dad wasn't great with the wisdom, but he listened, and Zenny, our maid, would come out with cold drinks. She'd sit with us too, cracking jokes that were so lame they were funny. Dad laughed harder than anyone. And then he didn't.

At first, I thought maybe he just wanted to be alone with us kids. A look would pass between them as she laid down the drinks, like he was warning her not to stay. They'd both look away too fast, and she'd make some excuse about needing to get back to the kitchen. I thought maybe she'd done something wrong, and he didn't want us to know.

Until I caught them.

It was late one night. Mom was still at work or at some event – typical for her. I'd said good night to Dad hours before, but I couldn't sleep. I came down to the kitchen, and there they were, not kissing or even touching, just sipping tea and talking.

They didn't see me. I slunk back to bed and never spoke of it. I told myself there was nothing to worry about. My dad wasn't capable of that kind of betrayal.

Like I said, Mandy really needs to find a more competent advisor.

"Don't you have snack time at school?" I say finally. "You should wait."

"But I'm hungry now."

I rummage in my bag, pull out an apple, and offer it to her. I'm not trying to be generous by doling out my own food, but I packed her lunch myself so I know she has only one sandwich and exactly four cookies, and I don't want her eating the cookies now. They're homemade chocolate chip and worth more here than a cure for leprosy – which is totally out of control, by the way, and I'm pretty sure there is a cure for that. Anyway, we brought the chocolate with us. You can't even buy chocolate chips here, and the local chocolate is about as appealing as dirt, so no way is she wasting the cookies.

The fact is, Mandy doesn't make friends easily, which seriously sucks when you consider she has to make all new friends every two or three years. So not to put too fine a point on it, but the cookies are bribes. I'd rather she didn't eat any of them herself, but at a minimum she has to give a couple away. I've gone over this with her about a billion times. I'm truly sorry that chocolate chip is her favorite and that she has to use them to bribe people to be her friends, but like Vince said, this is our life, Mandy needs to deal with it, just like the rest of us.

She's eyeing my apple like Snow White after the big sleep. I know she's debating whether to demand something better, but finally she takes it.

In other circumstances, I might have enjoyed this drive. Unlike our yard, the wheat fields show lingering life, a dried-out but hopeful green. In contrast, lumpish oxen erupt wartlike out of the brush every few feet, but their bovine complacency, as they chow down on their surroundings, is strangely reassuring. The occasional farmer seems non-threatening, pausing to gawk at our white faces hurtling past.

I'm used to being stared at. This is my seventh year in Asia, and I spent three in Africa before that. I won't say I like it, but I've come to view my own skin with a kind of detached reverence. I know it has a power, a life of its own. It gives me a status beyond my years. And it can get me killed.

We didn't have a school van in Thailand or the Philippines. It was always just the three of us with our driver. We'd fight over whose turn it was to sit in the front. Vince would always insist on giving Mandy a turn, even though she'd spend the entire trip turned around in her seat listening to us. Vince and I would talk about mutual friends, but we'd save the really juicy gossip for when Mandy wasn't around. Sometimes I'd rant about teachers. Often Vince would bore us to death with details on some random sport. It's weird how you don't know you're happy until you aren't anymore.

Every First Day, in every new school, Dad would slip a note in my lunch bag. That was *our* tradition. I always pretended like I didn't know he was doing it, but all morning, sitting in strange classrooms, surrounded by kids ogling me as if I had six legs and an exoskeleton, I'd think about that note. It didn't matter what it said. It was always some parent drivel anyway, about what a great kid I was. *Seriously, do parents really think we believe that junk?* But somehow it helped. Even if I didn't read it – and sometimes I wouldn't until I got home – I knew it was there. I knew he was there.

"How long?" Mandy has the tenacity of a tick. I wonder when she'll find the note. I don't know if Dad used to leave notes for her as well. I always thought it was just our thing, but I couldn't take the chance. I'd like to think I at least had some originality. When it came down to it, though, I spewed the same BS he did all those years. I tried to fake Mom's handwriting. Like Mom would ever do something like that.

"Almost there," I say.

I'm as desperate to finish this trip as she is, yet dreading our arrival. Suddenly the miles of empty brush give way to the high fortress walls of the school, as startling as a pyramid in the desert. We stop just outside the gates while two guards use a mirror attached to a long rod to check under our van for bombs. We're cleared through, and the driver pulls into the parking lot and stops. When the doors open, a sudden blast of heat sears my flesh. Lightheaded, I slide across the seat and try to hop down but catch my foot at the last minute. Seconds before my face would have hit the pavement, a firm hand encircles my upper arm and swings me up in a surprisingly graceful maneuver. I land against the chest of my rescuer, my free arm instinctively reaching up to grab his shoulder. All we need are ice skates and it would be a perfect ten.

I'm about to share this insight when I look up and any intelligible thought evaporates. I'm gawking into the face of a boy who is surely the product of genetic engineering. He is that beautiful.

CHAPTER 2

"Sorry," I mumble, looking into the thickly fringed green eyes of the gorgeous godlike creature while my heart does little cartwheels in my chest.

"Don't apologize. It's not like every day starts with a pretty girl falling into my arms." He smiles and it's like being zapped by a Taser, not that I've ever been zapped by a Taser, but I'm pretty sure this is what it would feel like. It's a good thing he's still holding me because I may just swoon in his arms. And I'd be only half-faking it.

"Mustapha!" A loud voice shatters our magic moment.

We both jump and take a few steps back as the beautiful boy drops his hands.

The girl striding purposefully toward us could be his twin. Tall and slender, she has the same pale olive skin and glittering green eyes. She puts a hand on his arm.

"Everyone's been looking for you," she says to him, completely ignoring me. "You have to see Saalima's

new cell phone. I'm going to ask Daddy to buy me one."
She flicks back a strand of glossy black hair, adjusts her
dupatta, which is already draped perfectly around her
neck, the ends fluttering down her back, and she eyes
him impatiently. She still hasn't acknowledged my
presence.

"Didn't your father just buy you a new phone last
spring?" He chuckles.

"That was months ago," she pouts. "Come on, you
have to see it." She pulls at his arm.

By this time, I've decided I must have become
invisible, so I'm startled when he turns back to me.

"I must go," he says, "but it was a pleasure. Try to
stay on your feet now." He beams one last heart-stopping
smile, but it's the girl who takes my breath away. She
shoots me a look of pure hatred before she escorts him
away.

By now, the other embassy kids are out of the van,
and Vince and Michelle are trying to get Mandy to
remember the name of her teacher.

"It's O'Grady," I say distractedly, still watching the
departure of the god-creature and Angry Girl.

"Oh, Mandy, you're so lucky," gushes Michelle.
"She's, like, the nicest teacher in the whole universe.
And I know exactly where her room is. Do you want
Vince and me to take you, sweetie?"

I give Vince a look. Taking Mandy to her class is
something we always do together on the First Day. We
walk Mandy. Then Vince walks me. It's another

tradition. Lame, but there it is. We pretend it's solidarity on her behalf, but really we just don't want to be stranded on our own.

Vince doesn't notice me trying to catch his eye. He's too busy gazing at Michelle like she's just announced a cure for zits.

"That would be great, Michelle," he says before Mandy can respond.

Mandy turns to me, and for a moment I think she might object, but Michelle grabs her hand and Vince takes the other, which is totally stupid since Mandy's eight, not three, and they march her away.

I stand there, not sure whether to follow. It's pretty obvious they don't need me and likely they don't want me. I try to remember the general layout of this huge sprawling campus and head in what I hope is the direction of the upper school.

I notice them as soon as I enter the upper-school courtyard. They're surrounded by friends, all local kids like themselves. The god-creature is chatting with a cute chubby boy. His hostile goddess is looking at me. I have the strangest feeling she's been watching out for me, which I know is totally paranoid. But she *is* staring at me – and not in a good way. I decide to head over to the fishpond so I can pretend I'm enjoying marine life and not obsessing on her.

The upper-school classrooms are arranged in a single-storey circle around a large stone courtyard. The pond is in the center, which actually makes it a pretty stupid place to go when my goal is to fade into the scenery, but it's minutes until the first bell, so I don't want to wander too far. I sit down on one of the stone benches overlooking the pond and watch trapped fish swimming around in circles.

I wonder if she's still watching me. I think I can feel her eyes, but I don't look up. I rifle through my bag, pull out my sandwich, and break off a piece, feeling a moment of guilt when I'm reminded it's tuna. I hope the fish won't be too grossed out by eating one of their own. I drop in a large chunk, which barely hits the surface of the water before the fish are attacking it with the enthusiasm of sharks at an Australian beach party. I guess they're not squeamish.

"What do you think you're doing?"

I jump. Seriously, the girl moves like a cat. I had no idea she'd come up behind me.

"I beg your pardon?" I ask. The sun glints off her hair like she's generating light. Is that real gold threaded through the long tunic of her *shalwar kameez*?

"You heard me." In spite of her words and death-ray eyes, her cultured voice, with its faint British accent, is smoothly melodic.

I stare at her for a moment, trying to figure out what she wants. *Should I apologize for flirting with her boyfriend?* I can feel people watching us. I wish I could disappear, or that she would. I look back down at the fish and break off another piece of bread. I don't get as far as dropping it in before she speaks again.

"Has it never occurred to you that you should ask before feeding the local wildlife, or do you always do exactly what you want when you're a guest in another country?"

Local wildlife? I look from the fish up to her looming over me and back down to the fish. *Is she kidding?* "Sorry. I, uh, didn't realize goldfish were a protected species here."

"Do you think you're funny?" Okay, I was being a little sarcastic, but give me a break – *wildlife?* It occurs to me this girl is not accustomed to having her authority questioned. The sensible thing to do now would be to back down. After all, she's right. It is her country. As if I need to be reminded.

"Is there a problem here?" asks a familiar voice.

I can't believe I was so focused on the ice princess that I didn't notice the approach of the god-who-walks-among-us. I look at him through my lashes before turning quickly back to the fish. I wonder if I could drown myself in less than two feet of water.

"No problem on my end," I say when it becomes apparent that completely ignoring them is not going to make them go away. I look up. I notice his eyes are a different color than hers, a much deeper green. I can't read his expression. I stare back down at my sandwich. There's still more than half left, which is good because I didn't bring any lunch money. I finger the crust for a minute before reaching out and dropping the entire thing in the water.

"Stop that at once!" she shrieks. My heart is racing now. Despite my current behavior, I hate confrontations. "Do you see what she's doing?" She turns to Mustapha. I wonder if I should expect to be taken out by a bolt of lightning right about now. It certainly seems to be what she's expecting.

"It's just bread, Aisha. I'm sure it won't hurt them." His voice is soothing, but I can hear a hint of something else and look up to catch a smile tugging at the corner of his mouth. It quickly disappears when I catch his eye, and his face is again impassive.

"But I told her not to. The fish won't eat it, and it will become a disgusting mess that someone else will have to clean up." I look at the fish and, to my chagrin, discover they're now innocently swimming around as if they didn't just do a *Jaws* imitation two minutes ago. My soggy wad of bread floats above them, ignored. *Traitors*.

"It's biodegradable," I offer.

"But I told you not to," she repeats, glaring at me. She's really stuck on this point. It crosses my mind to tell her I don't take orders from her, but I pretty much exhausted my supply of bravado when I dumped the bread.

"She's new, Aisha. She didn't know any better."

Did he just call me stupid?

"You saw her. She did it deliberately."

This girl definitely has control issues.

"You're new, right?" he asks.

Why won't they just go away?

"Actually, I was sitting behind you all last year in biology, didn't you notice?" *Well, what did he expect me to say?* With less than two hundred students in the upper school, I'm sure there isn't a kid in this courtyard who doesn't know I'm new.

"I didn't notice you, and I'm very certain I would have." He flashes his smile, and I stand up, trying to relieve the adrenaline suddenly coursing through my body. I'm disappointed that, even standing, I'm a couple of inches shorter than the ice princess and I barely reach Mustapha's shoulder.

I give him what I hope is a cool look. "Well, I guess I must be new, then." This is *so* not the time to flirt. *Why do boys never get stuff like that?*

"We should be going to class, Musa." Finally, the ice princess and I agree on something, but apparently "Musa" has other ideas. He barely acknowledges she's spoken, continuing to smile at me with a determination that makes me think he has control issues of his own.

"Don't let me stop you," I encourage.

"No hurry. We always have time to welcome guests."

I don't know if it's being reminded once again that I'm a guest in this country that I'm supposed to call home, or being treated like a criminal for feeding goldfish, or everything else – Dad leaving, Vince ditching me – but suddenly I've had enough. I move to walk past him, but he catches my arm.

"Mustapha Khan." He holds out his other hand. The ice princess sighs dramatically, but Mustapha's expression is unreadable as he waits for me to respond.

"We don't have time for this, Musa. Let her go find her friends." I look into the cold green eyes of the ice princess and wonder what friends she imagines I have on my First Day at a new school. Or if her meaning is simply to remind me that I'm not *their* friend.

"How are you enjoying Pakistan?" he asks.

The question catches me off guard, which it shouldn't. I've been asked variations of it a hundred times in more countries than I can count, and there's only one answer. Whatever poverty, violence, or hatred you might be confronting on a daily basis, people always want to hear that you found one tiny thing that made their homeland paradise.

My eyes travel from the hand curled around my arm up to the broad shoulders under a designer polo shirt, the strong chin, perfect teeth, high cheekbones, and intense, darkly fringed eyes. I wonder if this boy has ever lived through a single moment in his life feeling like an outsider. My mind races as I try to come up with a compliment, no matter how insincere, but my arm is hot under his touch and the ice princess clicks her tongue impatiently.

"Well," I begin, feeling the familiar anger wakening like a beast inside me, "there's not a single mall, movie theater, or Caramel Frappuccino within a thousand miles, but there are huge poisonous reptiles, beggars on every street corner, and all the atmosphere of a maximum-security penitentiary. I'm just surprised there's not more tourism."

We stare into each other's eyes, and, for the first time, I know exactly what he's thinking. The ice princess has stopped whining. She may have stopped breathing. Even the other kids in the courtyard have quieted down, though I think they're too far away to hear our conversation. He's no longer holding out a hand for me to shake, but the other one has tightened. My arm is going numb. I look down at it and back up to his face.

"I'm sorry you feel that way," he says dryly.

Finally, he lets go of my arm and nods to the ice princess, indicating they're leaving, but he stalks off a pace ahead of her. A few feet away, he stops and turns back.

"Welcome to our country," he says, throwing his hands wide in a mocking gesture that belies his words.

Just then, the bell rings, and I see Mustapha absorbed into a throng of laughing kids. One boy throws his arm around him, while on his other side, the ice princess leans in, saying something that makes him laugh. Suddenly, I feel weak with longing. Like a rat gnawing the inside of my stomach, my loneliness feels like a living thing, powerful and dangerous.

It's not that I want Mustapha, particularly. It's more than that. I want someone who knows me. My friends from Manila, Bangkok, or even Nairobi, just someone I don't have to explain myself to. It's like I'm an amnesia victim reawakened every two or three years, each time with my entire history wiped out. I have to constantly recreate myself, with the growing certainty that each time, pieces of me are lost. I become less who I am and more a creation, a holograph, projected onto yet another exotic landscape.

"Do you know where you're supposed to be?" Mustapha shouts across the courtyard, breaking into my thoughts. The unexpected kindness of this small gesture brings me close to tears.

"Almost never," I shout back, and I make my way to my first class.

CHAPTER 3

I follow the crowd into the dimly lit barnlike structure that houses the cafeteria. I swear it looks like one of those cell-block structures from some B-grade prison movie, which is completely appropriate for how I'm feeling about the next forty-five minutes of my life.

The morning went as well as you might expect, considering it began with pissing off the reigning king and queen of the school. Every freaking teacher made me stand up and introduce myself to the class. The worst was the psychology teacher. No matter how many different ways I told him I didn't have any "fun and exciting" stories to share about my former life, he kept right on asking.

I thought about telling him how my dad ditched our family for our former maid and how my normally sane brother had fallen under the spell of a heinous Hip-Hop Barbie. But, in the end, I decided to tell him about my dad's tragic accident, the one that left him in a vegetative state, hooked up to about a million machines in a hospital in Manila run by nuns, who still wear the old-fashioned black habits and float around with serene faces, talking in soft voices and praying over their patients.

Of course, the accident never happened. Dad's living on a beach in Boracay with Zenny, writing, and last I heard, he's happier than a pig in – well, enough said. But some stories are best left untold.

When my psychology teacher turned white as a sheet and demanded the entire class observe a moment of silence in honor of my dad, I thought that might be the lowest point of my day. But standing here alone, looking around for my brother in a crowd of kids who are all looking right back at me, I've decided I'm no longer trying to identify lowest points. I'm sure every one of these kids has heard about what I said this morning to the royal couple. I can only imagine what they're saying about me.

The cafeteria is a furnace. The windows along two walls are wide open, presumably to let in the breeze from outside, except that there is no breeze. A row of ceiling fans, fifteen feet up, push around blistering air and the licorice smell of cumin mixed with sweat. My stomach is churning, and I seriously regret layering a tank over my T-shirt as the wetness grows under my arms and across my chest. The loudness of the voices all around me seems purposeful, like the war cries of a hostile nation. If I had to imagine my own personal hell, this would be it.

I wouldn't even have come into the cafeteria, but Vince and I always eat together on the First Day. It's another tradition and one thing that makes moving around a little easier. Vince is always beside me, going through the same stuff.

But at our old schools, we agreed where to meet ahead of time. I figured we'd discuss it while we were taking Mandy to her classroom this morning, but then that didn't happen.

I try to look casual as I stand just inside the doors, scouring the room. The first familiar face I spot is Michelle's, and there's Vince right beside her. His table is packed with kids, and everyone is asking him questions. Hip-Hop Barbie is grinning – she doesn't realize how excruciating it is for him to talk about himself. I can see the pink flush under his tan from here. There's no space to squeeze in beside him, but I need to find a way to take the attention off him. Although events of the day so far would suggest I'm not the most socially adept kid on the planet, I've got mad skills compared to my brother.

I'm just about to hurl myself on the floor and fake a choking fit when suddenly he laughs. Not the predictable awkward laugh of the First Day, when you really don't get the joke, but a genuinely happy sound. It's arresting, and I'm shocked that every single kid in the entire room is not staring at him like I am. He's laughing like he does at home when I've done an impersonation of one of our teachers. He's laughing like he laughs with me, or at least used to.

"Take a picture, it lasts longer." I turn to see a petite, dark-eyed girl with olive skin, a gorgeous mane of black hair cascading down her back, and a mischievous, elf-like grin. From her accent, I'm guessing she's American.

"What?"

"The guy you're crushing on. If you want him, staring at him like a stalker is *so* not the way to go."

"I don't know what you're talking about." I really don't. *Who is this strange little elf?*

"Tousled blond hair, baby blues, great butt, the guy you've been drooling over for a solid five minutes. You are way not subtle."

I can't decide if I'm more shocked by her description of my brother or her assumption that I'm after him. "So, you think he's cute?" I ask.

"You kidding? He's hot, but if you want a shot at him, you're gonna have to get in line. And I gotta tell you, Michelle has him pretty much sewn up. She's the tall chick sitting next to him who can't keep her hands off him."

"You noticed that too?" I'm starting to like this girl.

"Oh yeah, but go ahead and make your move. You're new, blonde, hot. You'd make a cute couple. Take out that Michelle bitch. I'll support you."

"Great idea. Just one small hitch. He's my brother."

"Yeah, I knew that." She grins again, and it's such an unaffected, happy grin, I find myself grinning back at her. "I was just messing with you. Your brother is hot, though."

"Thanks, I guess." She really is an odd little thing. There's something fearless about her, like she doesn't know the rules. I want to protect her, or get out of her way.

"Come sit with me." She grabs my hand. "I'll introduce you to your new friends."

I want to snatch my hand back. I have a method for starting over in a new school. It's like figuring out your role in an ecosystem. The structure's already in place; all you need to do is keep a low profile until you decide where you fit in. This girl is moving way too fast. Before I have time to react, she's dragging me over to a table full of raucous girls in the middle of the room. I'm just thinking that if I could choose one table *not* to sit at, this would be it, when she barks out orders to at least half a dozen girls to shift — and a space opens up. She plops down on the bench, dragging me down with her.

"So, tell us about yourself." She glares around the table. "Shut up, girls," she orders and grins.

"You shut up," says a girl directly across from me, who I'm pretty sure is breaking dress code with her low-cut top and multiple piercings. "I'm Jazzy, and I should warn you, the sooner you learn not to take orders from Angie, the happier you'll be."

"Don't kid yourself," retorts Angie. "You couldn't dress yourself if you didn't have me picking out your clothes."

"Only because I've got more important things to do than read fashion magazines all day."

"Right, you're too busy trying to get Johan to notice you," says Angie.

"Get with the program, Angie." Jazzy sniffs. "Johan is so last year."

"Yeah, but you didn't get him last year. Don't tell me you're finally giving up?"

"Not giving up. Moving on. I don't even like him anymore."

"Oh, of course. We understand," says a girl on Jazzy's right. Her kohl-darkened eyes sparkle, and her multiple gold bangles tinkle together as she lightly pats Jazzy's shoulder. "Johan has only grown three inches over the summer and become even more handsome, but why would you care? You don't even notice him. Isn't that right?"

"Don't tease her, Leela," says a girl sitting beside me, the seams of her shalwar kameez straining as she leans across the table. "Perhaps Jazzy has decided to become more serious this year. You would do well to follow her example."

Leela's bangles clink again as she covers her mouth to stifle a smile. "I'm sorry, Jazzy. Tira's right. We must all be serious. What must this poor dear girl think of us?" She turns to me and flashes an exaggerated look of apology. "And we haven't even introduced ourselves." Leela goes round the table, rattling off names, most of which I promptly forget.

"Now, Emma, tell us all about yourself," Leela says. "Don't leave anything out. We want every detail. Isn't that right, girls?"

"Yeah, but you can leave out the bit about your dad's coma," says Angie, smirking. "We already heard about that." The entire table erupts in laughter.

Busted! I'm silent for a few long seconds, trying to think of something to say that will achieve the perfect balance of boring but not stupid. The goal is to discourage further interrogation without sounding like an idiot. I consider myself a bit of a master at this.

"I'm Canadian."

Angie is not impressed. "We know that."

"My mom runs the consular section at the embassy."

"Know that too."

"I have a birthmark on my right shoulder."

"Really, that's fascinating. We'd love to hear more about that, but first maybe you could tell us what exactly you said to Musa Khan this morning?"

"Musa who?" I ask innocently, hoping to buy a little time. In a perfect world, the bell would ring right now and we'd all have to rush back to class.

"Nice try, but you may as well tell us. Aisha's going around telling her version to anyone who'll listen. She has a lot of people convinced you're some snotty North American looking down your nose at everything. And, FYI, that's not someone you want to be in this country."

"Thanks for the news flash," I say grimly, staring down at the table.

"Look, it doesn't matter what you really said. Aisha's a queen biatch. She thinks every girl in this school is after Mustapha. Most of us she's not worried about, but with your looks, she's gotta be freaking out, and half the school saw you in his arms this morning. Even if you hadn't attacked their country, she'd be out to get you."

"I didn't mean what I said." *How long is the lunch break here?* My head is starting to throb.

"Of course you didn't." Leela reaches across the table and puts her hand on my arm, her bangles cascading down her wrist. It would be more comforting if I didn't get the definite impression she just likes to jingle her bangles.

"Still you must apologize," says Tahira. Though she and Leela are both wearing shalwar kameezes, Leela's *bindi* sets her apart. She's Indian and Tahira's local. I flush at what Tahira must think of me.

"What she should do is stay out of their way," argues Angie. "Anything she says will only be used against her."

"Definitely," agrees Jazzy. "Mustapha's in twelfth grade. She may not even run into him again."

"On the other hand," says Angie, "she could easily have him in one of her classes."

"Whether she has him in her class or not, she needs to apologize. Musa is from a good family. He will accept your apology, and that will be the end of it." Tahira is beginning to sound annoyed.

"Tira's right," says Leela. "No good can come from avoiding the issue."

They all begin talking at once. I'm pretty sure I could walk away right now and not one of them would notice.

"You're all missing the point." Angie shouts to be heard. "Aisha isn't trashing Emma because of what she said. She's trashing her because Mustapha isn't."

For a tiny girl, Angie has a shockingly loud voice. Everyone at the table stops talking at once. Unfortunately, so does everyone at every other table in a five-mile radius. *Is it inevitable that Aisha is only two tables over and now glaring at me with a heat that could melt glass?*

For a nanosecond, I think of making a penitent face, staring at the ground, and beaming "sorry" thoughts her way. But the entire school is watching, so when our eyes lock, I go with a friendly smile and a little wave I once saw Queen Elizabeth do on TV.

Jazzy bursts out laughing in the same moment Tahira gasps. Leela shakes her head and reaches for my hand as if there's still time to save the situation, and Angie abruptly stands up, pulling me with her.

"Lunch is over," says Angie. "Come on, Emma, I'll show you where to fix your makeup."

"But I'm not wearing makeup." I grab my bag as she drags me to my feet.

"Well, obviously that's one of the things we'll have to fix." Still holding me firmly at the elbow, she begins pushing me ahead of her, out the nearest door. She's muttering something under her breath, but in the general hubbub of other conversations, I can catch only a few words, which sound a lot like *head case* and *death wish*.

Inside the girls' bathroom, Angie leans on the door to keep other kids out. She has a pained expression on her face, and her eyes are closed. I think we're going to be late for class. Maybe if we're really late, there won't be time for me to introduce myself. I'm not even sure what my next class is, and I definitely have no idea where. I slip my bag off my shoulder and begin rummaging for my schedule. Finally, she opens her eyes and looks at me earnestly.

"Don't worry. We can still fix this."

This is a lie and we both know it, but at this very moment, what's really worrying me is her use of the word *we*. I hardly know this girl, and I wouldn't say up until now she's done a brilliant job of protecting my interests. She just told the entire freaking school that this Aisha girl is threatened by me. I'm pretty sure that is not going to help smooth things over.

"I know you're probably wondering why you should trust me."

Now that's just creepy. *How could she know that?*

"You live on Compound B, right?"

I don't answer, which apparently doesn't matter because she keeps talking.

"I'm right across the road on the American embassy compound. I'll come over after school, and we'll work out what you should do."

"Great," I say without enthusiasm. I sling my bag back over my shoulder and make a move for the door.

"Don't worry," she says with a grin, stepping aside and following me out. "I'll grow on you and we will fix this."

Just before we part ways in the middle of the courtyard, Angie grabs me again and pulls me in close for some final intel. "Mustapha and Aisha are kind of important people here."

"You don't say."

"You need to understand. They come from these rich families, and they're, like, promised to each other or something. I'm not totally sure what the deal is. But the thing is, you don't want them for enemies, if you know what I mean."

I nod my head, but I'm pretty sure the boat's sailed on that one.

CHAPTER 4

I get lost on the way to my last class and have to stop twice for directions. I'm looking for a large free-standing building that looks like a theater, beyond the lower-school classrooms. After twenty minutes of wandering, so overheated I feel like I'm going to pass out or vomit, I find myself standing outside a large freestanding building that looks nothing like a theater but decide to go in anyway. At this point, all I really care about is getting out of the heat. The sun has gone from aggressive to violent, and I would go into the boys' changing room right now for five minutes of air-conditioning.

Of course, my luck being what it is, the building I enter is not only hotter than outside but has the added agony of being humid as well. Even delirious with heatstroke, I realize I'm in some kind of greenhouse. The long corridor in front of me is a riot of color with flowering plants on both sides. The air is thick with perfume. I'm obviously in the wrong place, yet weirdly it's the first thing that's felt right all day. I know I'm late for class, but something pushes me forward through the maze of branches until I stop in front of a small flowering bush. There were hundreds like this in the Philippines, two in my own backyard.

I close my eyes, breathe in the smell from the flowers, and suddenly I'm transported out of this dry, dusty country back to Manila, with its lush greenery and towering palms. It's like I'm on the edge of a time portal. If I can just find a way to step through, I could be back in my garden, sitting on the patio swing overlooking the pool, sipping iced tea, and telling Zenny about my First Day of school. She'd want to know what everyone had worn, since we always agonized the night before about what I was going to wear. We'd share a laugh over the worst fashion disasters, and she'd reassure me I looked good, even if I didn't. Of course, in my fantasy, this would have to be before I found out she was sleeping with my dad.

"You shouldn't be in here."

I jump at the disembodied voice that sounds alarmingly close, though all I can see in every direction is leaves. A man steps into the corridor, emerging from the plants like a pod-person.

"What are you looking for?" His voice is stern, but the eyes in his deeply lined face are gentle.

"We had these at home." I finger one of the branches.

"In America? Are you sure? That's Medinilla. They

don't grow in cold places." I don't bother telling him I'm not American. Once you leave Canada, everyone on the entire planet assumes you're American. After a while, you just go with it.

"I meant the Philippines."

"*Achcha*, the perfect climate. You don't look Filipino."

"No."

"And now this is your home." He takes a step closer, and I look away.

I don't know how to answer. There are a million words in my head right now, but none of them cuts it. *Why is one place home and another place just isn't?* We have an awkward moment.

"How do you like Pakistan?"

I really want to say something nice. *After all these years, why am I suddenly overwhelmed by this question?* We have another awkward moment.

"Come." He gestures that I should follow and turns away into the greenery. I'm not sure I want to follow, but what else am I going to do? Taking a few steps after him, I see there's a narrow overgrown walkway through the branches. We walk for several minutes, twisting and turning deeper into the maze. It occurs to me this would be the perfect place to murder someone. No one would ever find the body, and you could use the rotting corpse for compost. *Why didn't I think of something nice to say about his stupid country?*

Suddenly he stops and points to a large flowering bush with frilly orange petals and hanging tendrils. "It is my favorite. The Red Bird of Paradise." He smiles proudly.

I definitely don't see the big deal, but I smile politely. I wonder if the heat's gotten to him as well.

"This can grow in your country."

"The Philippines?"

"Yes. And America. And Pakistan." He gives me a look like he's sharing something important. "Allow me to show you." He seems a little frustrated now and starts scrabbling in the dirt at the base of the plant. I surreptitiously look around for an exit. "Look!" he shouts triumphantly and yanks a long gnarly root out of the ground. "The roots are very deep. You see? The temperature can be very cold or very hot. The plant gets no water for many days. Still it will not die. One day you think it is dead; the next you have a flower."

"Can you tell me how to find the theater?"

He doesn't answer right away, and I fidget with my bag while he reburies his root. Turning away, he heads back the way we came. "Follow me. I will take you." His voice is über-polite, and I know I've disappointed him. I wonder how many more people I'm going to let down before this day finally ends.

We emerge from the greenhouse, both shielding our eyes against the blinding intensity of the late-day sun. "It is your first day, isn't it?" I don't even wonder how he knows. "How is it?"

"Great," I lie, finally having the wherewithal to put my game face on.

"It is always difficult in the beginning. You think no one will like you."

I know no one likes me. Well, maybe Angie. But that's not the point.

"Soon you will make a friend."

I have friends, or I had them anyway. I've made friends everywhere we've lived and had them wrenched away every time we moved. You could sink an ocean liner with all my friends. But not one of them is here.

"I think I got off to a bad start with some people," I say.

Where did that come from? I'm blurting out my life story to total strangers now?

"A known mistake is better than an unknown truth."

Oh God, another Yoda moment.

"So, what do I do about it?" *Rewind! What did I ask him that for? What the heck am I doing?* This man is not my friend. He doesn't even know me. But I hold my breath as I wait for him to answer.

"You make it right," he says, as if anything can ever be right again. I wonder what it would be like to live in his world.

"How?" We're crossing a field now. I wasn't even close to the theater.

"Allah will show the way. You just have to let him," he says calmly. I sigh and pass my hand over my eyes. It's been a really long day, and my head is throbbing again.

"This is the theater." We stop outside a large free-standing building that does indeed look like a theater. *"Aap ka naam kya hai?"*

This is the first thing he's said that I completely understand. Mom makes me take survival language lessons every time we change countries. I do my best to learn nothing so she'll finally take the hint and stop moving us, but no matter how hard I try, I always pick up the basics, just like she knows I will.

"Emma Grey," I tell him, looking up into his wizened face and wondering how many kids like me have passed through his life and what difference it makes who I am.

"I'm always in the greenhouse, Emma Grey. I am Mr. Akbar." He gives me a look so full of empathy that I feel tears welling up in my eyes and have to look down to blink them away.

"Okay, well, thanks." I wish he would leave so I can duck around the corner and cry in private. I cross my arms tightly over my chest, as if the emotion struggling to erupt is a physical thing I can mash down. But he continues to stand there, so I have no choice but to enter the theater. I don't even care anymore how late I am. I just want to get through the next hour without falling apart.

The theater, which must have nearly a thousand seats, is in almost total darkness, with only a few stage lights on at the front. I can see a bunch of kids milling around, engaged in some kind of activity that involves a lot of laughter. I make my way down the aisle toward them and only at the last minute – like opening a drawer and discovering a huge hairy spider – do I see Mustapha Khan is among them. If this is Allah's idea of showing me the way, he certainly has a sense of humor.

CHAPTER 5

"You must be Emma," says a man almost as round as he is tall. He strides toward me with his hand extended. I think he's going to shake my hand, but instead he grabs my arm, drawing me in like I might try to escape. "You've missed the introductions, but don't worry. Had some trouble finding us, did you?"

I mumble something that must sound like assent because he rambles on for several minutes about how confusing the campus is. I don't hear a word and I can't take my eyes off Mustapha, even though I know I need to stop staring. Finally, the cheerful cherub pauses and looks at me curiously. "I hear you and Mustapha already know each other. Why don't you join his group?"

Now *that* gets my attention. I tear my eyes away from Mustapha to look at the teacher. Inconveniently, I'm struck speechless, allowing just enough time for the voice that has been ringing in my head all day to call over, "Yes, Emma. Why don't you come join us?"

Can anyone else hear the challenge in his voice?

I look at the teacher for support, but he's smiling happily and gives me a small shove in Mustapha's direction. "There you go, then. He'll take good care of you." *Is he kidding?*

Mustapha certainly isn't. He's grinning with all the warmth of a tiger that's just caught sight of a gazelle. I try to remember what Mr. Akbar said about making things right, but it no longer seems relevant. My goal here is pure survival. Mustapha walks toward me because I've stalled somewhere beyond the shove but still a safe distance from him. I have no intention of going closer. Wordlessly, he takes my arm and leads me over to two other guys.

"This is Ali and Faarooq." He doesn't bother to introduce me. No doubt he's told them everything. *Is it my imagination, or is it two hundred degrees in here?*

"How's it going?" Ali smiles warmly, and I wonder for a minute if I'm mistaken, but Faarooq cuts in.

"Mustapha's told us all about you." Well, that's blunt. I look at him for some hint of warmth, but his eyes are as cold as his voice.

"So, what are we meant to be doing?" I croak, cursing myself for letting my nerves show.

"We have a week to prepare a five-minute skit," Mustapha answers.

I've got to work with them all week? It must be some kind of cosmic retribution, and I'm sure I deserve it, but I'm still hoping it won't be as bad as I fear.

"Any theme?" I ask shakily, still not doing a good job of keeping my emotions in check. No one answers. Faarooq and Mustapha exchange glances. I get a queasy feeling and wonder if it's too late to retract my question.

"Something to do with colliding cultures," says Mustapha, his lips twitching.

"Mustapha suggested it," Ali interjects. As if I needed to be told that.

"Well, that's just great," I snap, anxiety finally giving way to anger. "Have you come up with any ideas yet?"

"As a matter of fact, I *do* have one," Mustapha exclaims.

"Really. Well, I can't wait to hear it," I say coolly.

"Maybe we could do something about a foreigner who comes to a new country and goes around telling the people who live there how awful their country is."

"I don't know," says Faarooq, and for a second I think maybe he's on my side. "Would anyone really behave so rudely? I'm just not sure it's *believable*. What do you think, Emma?" I could get radiation poisoning from his smile.

Now would be the moment to apologize, but for me, the moment's long passed. The anger courses through my bloodstream like a drug, and I'm grateful for it.

"Maybe we should do something about male-female relationships," suggests Ali enthusiastically, oblivious to the tension.

"Well, that could certainly be part of it," says Mustapha, not taking his eyes off me. "What do you think, Emma?

Can you think of any possible cultural misunderstandings a guy and a girl could have?"

"I don't know, Mustapha," I say. It occurs to me it's the first time I've said his name out loud, and I find it curiously appealing. *Can you hate someone and be hot for them at the same time?* "I think you need to be more specific. Do you have a situation in mind?"

"I do have one, yes. But perhaps you also have an idea you'd like to share."

"Not at all. I can't think of a single thing."

"You surprise me. You seemed so quick with your opinions this morning."

We stare at each other for a long moment. My breath is coming in short bursts. I can hear his breathing as well and feel the heat coming off him in waves.

"How about arranged marriage?" Ali suggests. We all whip round to look at him, but he smiles back cheerfully. *Don't they do basic IQ tests to get into this school?* He continues, obviously proud of his brain wave. "We could do a play about this Pakistani guy who falls in love with this American girl, only his parents don't approve, and she has to go through this meeting with his father and his brother so they can vet her."

"That would never happen," cuts in Faarooq angrily. "It would be the boy's mother who checks out the girl."

"That's a great idea," Ali says excitedly. "I could dress up as the mother, and you could dress up as an aunt. It would be funny." I like this guy. He's dorky-looking, with a round face that matches his body, but it works for him. He's cute and not in a scary-Mustapha sort of way either.

"It's a stupid idea," says Faarooq sulkily.

Just then, the teacher announces the end of the class, and we agree that we'll work on a script next time, which is actually two days away because of block scheduling. I hope it'll give me time to come up with a way to make things right.

As we leave the class, someone comes up behind me, lightly tapping my shoulder. A charge rifles through me because I assume it's Mustapha, but it's not. Faarooq looms over me in the gloom at the back of the theater.

"Stay away from my sister," he says. Not waiting for a reply, he pushes past me and storms out. At this moment, I can't imagine any request I would be happier to oblige. I wouldn't go near his third cousin if she was handing out hundred dollar bills and Snickers bars. The only problem is, I have no idea who his sister is.

CHAPTER 6

I sit at my desk after school, staring at my laptop screen. Fifty-two unanswered e-mails. That's got to be some kind of record. I reread the most recent from Cassie, my best friend in Manila, and wonder how long my friends will keep writing before they catch on that I'm not writing back. Cassie's worried about me. I want to reassure her, but just thinking of the extravagant lies I would have to weave to convince her I'm okay exhausts me before I even begin. She's managed to call here twice, which is impressive because I didn't give her our new numbers. I made Vince lie and say I wasn't home. She'll figure it out eventually, but that won't necessarily stop her. Cassie's loyal to a fault. She'll keep trying to rescue me as long as there's breath left in her body. I used to think I'd do the same for her.

Now I'm not sure I even have what it takes to be her friend. She wants me to tell her whether she should go after a new boy at school. Marc, her current boyfriend, cheated on her over the summer. No shocker there. I always said he wasn't worthy of her. She says he's history, but I can tell she's still into him. I don't know what to tell her. *Should she give Marc a second chance because all guys are faithless dogs, or should she recognize Marc for the worm he is and cut him out of her life, like I did Dad?* I want to help her, but I'm not the one she should be asking. *What do I know about relationships?*

Her e-mail goes on about a Dolce & Gabbana dress she picked up on sale. Manila is the best place in the world for designer shopping. I close my eyes and imagine Cassie and me trolling through Power Plant, our favorite mall. We take a break at the French café that opened just before I left. I order an iced cappuccino, and Cassie gets amaretto cheesecake and milk. She doesn't care about calories or being cool, which is only a small part of what made us inseparable. I cared way too much about both, but when I was with Cassie, I always felt like I could be totally myself.

I return to reality with a jolt when I read on to discover that all of my Manila friends, plus Marc and the new boy, are going clubbing next weekend. This is a first for our group. We drank a bit at parties last year, but none of us looked old enough to get into clubs. I can't believe that the first time my friends go clubbing, I won't be there; even worse, they'll do it while I live in a country where alcohol is illegal and clubs are nonexistent.

Cassie's going to wear the new dress. Her big question

is whether to wear it braless. I try to picture it, spaghetti-strapped and shimmery, draped over Cassie's flat chest and wide hips. My most recent clothing dilemma was whether I could get away with wearing a sleeveless shirt outside the house. I learned it was against both local and school dress codes, but I don't think that tidbit of fashion wisdom is going to help with Cassie's decision.

For three paragraphs, she complains about our friend Livi giggling during the sex scene of a recent chick flick. Instead of commiserating, I get distracted trying to remember the last time I saw a chick flick, or any movie, for that matter. Mom whisked us out of Manila so fast I hardly had time to say good-bye to friends, much less see a movie or shop or eat a burger for the last time. *Would Cassie commiserate if I told her I'm living in a city that doesn't even have a movie theater and where public kissing is a criminal offense?*

I'm used to losing friends. I've moved enough times to know that long-distance relationships are hard to hang on to; the calls and e-mails dwindle over time; and people change and get closer to the friends they see every day. That's normal.

But this is different. It's not just that these e-mails are time capsules, talking about people and places I've left behind, it's as if they're talking about a completely different reality, one I can barely remember. I sift through the words, trying to find some common ground, some experience I can share that would shore up my connection to that world, but I come up empty.

Finally, I highlight the page full of messages from people who used to be my closest friends, and I hit "delete." I get a prompt asking if I really want to delete everything. Even the computer can't believe it. I confirm the command and shut it down before I can change my mind.

CHAPTER 7

"He's in your theater class?"

"Yeah, that's what I just said." It's Monday evening, and, as promised, Angie has come over to my compound to talk strategy about Mustapha. I swat a mosquito. *Do the evening ones carry malaria or dengue fever?* I always forget.

"And you're in his group."

"Yes."

"For the entire week."

"Would you please stop repeating everything? I don't need an instant replay. I lived it. Remember?"

"Sorry. It's just that it's such incredibly bad luck."

"You think?"

Angie walks back on her swing and lets go, whizzing up, rocking the whole swing set dangerously. I'm sitting on the swing beside her, but I keep my feet sensibly anchored to the ground. We're alone in the little kid playground between the Canadian staff housing and the servants' quarters. It's a perfect vantage point for babysitting, which is what I've been doing since our bearer, Guul (a.k.a. The Ghoul), our cook-nanny-roach-killer, went home an hour ago. Mandy and the other compound kids are playing a raucous game of hide-and-seek. The servants' quarters are out of bounds, but I'm sick of mediating their boundary disputes, so when Mandy races past us, obviously headed in that direction, I don't say anything.

Angie continues rocking us both with the power of her swinging. This equipment has got to be older than I am. I'm sure it would be illegal in Canada, but here, the parents are just grateful to have somewhere they can send their kids to get them out of the house. It's not a bad setup. There aren't many places in the world where you can let your kids play unsupervised, knowing that they're never more than a few feet from armed guards – not to mention dozens of servants and groundskeepers.

"Maybe we should look at this as a good thing," says Angie.

"What?"

"Well, you need to smooth things out with Mustapha, and now you have the perfect opportunity."

"Would that be before or after Faarooq lynches me?"

"You're having problems with Faarooq? Tahira's brother?"

"Is that who he is? He told me to stay away from his sister but forgot the small detail of telling me who she is."

"Don't mind him. Tahira's brothers don't approve of many people. They hate Leela."

The pretty girl at lunch with the bangle mania? She seemed nice enough. "Why do they hate Leela?"

"I don't know. It may be the whole India and Pakistan thing, the war and everything. And they probably think Leela has too much freedom for a girl who is sort of from their culture, if you know what I mean. I don't think they approve of any of us, but Leela's the only one I've seen them actually be rude to."

"How many brothers does Tahira have?"

"Three."

"No sisters?"

"No. That's part of the problem. They think the entire honor of their family rests on Tahira. She has to stay a virgin for, like, forever, and she can't do anything fun. If she even looks at a guy, it's a capital offense. They're always watching her."

"Huh." I don't know what to say. Obviously, I'm not the only one with problems.

One of the little kids runs up to us. "Have you seen Mandy?" he asks as he wipes the snot dripping from his nose with the back of his hand and scans the area.

"Haven't seen her," I lie.

"She didn't go in the servants' part again, did she?"

"Don't think so," I say.

He looks at me for a minute, but I continue to smile pleasantly. Finally, he heads back up to the Canadian housing.

"I think we should practice what you're going to say to Mustapha the next time you see him," says Angie.

"I think you should stop swinging before I hurl."

"Sorry. You sure have some lame-ass equipment here. You should come to the American compound. It's like state of the art. We even have three baseball diamonds."

I sigh.

"So I'll be Mustapha." She stands up and faces me. "You be you."

"Great casting. Now, what are my lines?"

"Just say it was your first day and you were nervous and you said some things you didn't mean and you're sorry."

"I don't know how I'd say that to him. Maybe you should be me," I say. "I'll play Mustapha."

"But you need to practice your part."

"That's why you should demonstrate it. So I get it right."

"Fine," she sighs. "Stand up."

We square off in front of the swings.

"Mustapha," Angie begins, giving me an earnest look. "I'm really sorry if I offended you the other day when I made those comments about your country. I was really nervous, it being my first day and all, and I really didn't mean what I said. I hope you can forgive me." She gives me this fake smile that is shockingly convincing.

"Okay, now you go," she says.

"I'm Mustapha?"

"Right."

"Okay," I drop my voice to a low snarl. "You're dead, bitch."

"Emma! Mustapha would not say that."

"I just did."

"Emma."

"I'm not Emma, I'm Mustapha."

"Okay, I think you should play yourself now. I'll be Mustapha."

"But I'm just getting into it." I smile innocently.

"I can see that." She gives me a reproving look. "Which is why now it's my turn."

"You're too short to play him." I plop back down on my swing and begin rocking, not taking my feet off the ground.

Angie walks over to the rusted metal monkey bars – another throwback to the last decade – climbs up a couple of rungs, and swivels round to face me, wrapping her arms around the ladder for support.

"Okay, now I'm taller. Go for it," she says.

I give her a look, but she waits patiently.

Finally, I clump over to the monkey bars. Even halfway up, she's only inches above my head. "Mustapha," I say a little more forcefully than I intended. "Do you remember the other day when we were by the fish-pond, and I was feeding the fish, and it was my first day of school, and you were on the other side of the compound, and the fish were really hungry, and it was crazy hot and –"

"Emma," Angie interrupts, "are you planning to get to the apology before the class ends?"

I glare at her.

She smiles back.

I heave a self-pitying sigh that only makes her smile harder, and I feel my own lips twitch as I take one last shot at it. "Mustapha, do you remember when your heinous girlfriend harassed me for giving the poor starving goldfish a tiny bit of bread, and then you grabbed me and wouldn't let me go and dug your fingers into my arm, and –"

"Emma."

"And then your heinous girlfriend said I didn't have any friends and –"

"Emma!"

I look down at her in surprise. *When did she climb down from the monkey bars?*

"What?" I snap in a voice known to mothers the world over, but it doesn't faze her a bit.

"I think maybe you should write him a note."

"I don't know what I'd say."

"Not a problem," she says way too quickly. "I'll dictate."

"Okay, but I think I was really getting the hang of the role-playing." I say this just to bug her, but she gives me such an encouraging smile that I feel almost guilty. "We better find Mandy first. It's past her bedtime."

CHAPTER 8

We head into the servants' area. It's actually the first time I've been in this part of the compound. It's inside the same high walls as our own housing, the two sections separated by an iron fence, but it's like walking into a different world. Long rows of tiny one- and two-room dwellings are separated only by narrow corridors. Every door is open, probably for light as much in welcome because each gloomy room has a single bare bulb hanging from the ceiling. I try not to openly gawk, feeling badly that we're intruding on the little privacy that must exist in this crowded warren, but the inhabitants don't share my reserve. Adults and children spill out of doorways to watch our progress. The braver ones shout phrases of English – "How are you?" and "What is your name?"

I know they're just being friendly, but I wish I could be invisible. It's exhausting spending your entire life in places where you're always the center of attention. And I know I'm unworthy, a donkey in a herd of zebras, not stared at for any deserving quality but only for my differentness, my weirdness. Just once I'd like to walk down a street without drawing attention. Angie smiles easily, returning greetings. I force myself to do the same.

We don't even have to shout for Mandy. They know immediately why we've come; a small boy steps forward and gestures for us to follow. He leads us down one long corridor and up another before coming to a stop outside an open doorway.

He leans in and says something, but the only word I understand is *Guul*, who suddenly appears, towering in the doorway. I look up into his sunken, pockmarked face, trying to make some connection, but he's typically dour as he wordlessly stands aside so we can enter.

Mandy is in the center of the room, sitting on a floor cushion. A cup of milky tea and a plate of samosas are on a low table in front of her. She grins up at me. A woman who must be The Ghoul's wife hovers nervously behind her. As my eyes adjust to the dim lighting, I notice three children lined up in one corner of the room, sitting on the bare cement, silently watching. Just one string charpoy leans against the far wall. I wonder if they all sleep together and how that's possible.

"I'm sorry," I say, though I'm not sure what I'm sorry for. "Mandy, let's go." My voice is too loud in the tiny room. Mandy jumps up immediately, looking at me with curiosity.

I turn to The Ghoul, who I haven't exchanged more

than a few words with in the two weeks since he's become a fixture in our house. "Thank you for looking after her. You didn't have to. Send her away next time." It comes out like an order. I blush and quickly back out of the doorway.

I don't talk as we walk back to the house, but Mandy chatters away about her "adventure" and Angie seems happy to listen, asking questions and commenting in all the right places. When we get home, I send Mandy upstairs to put on her pajamas.

Before Dad left, I never once put Mandy to bed. Dad's a writer, so he worked from home and was always around. On the rare evenings he accompanied Mom to one of her events, Zenny took over. In those days, Mandy's bedtime routine seemed fun. I'd often find an excuse to hang around. With Zenny, there was always laughter. She'd do these crazy impersonations of every Disney character ever created. Mandy was put to bed by the genie from *Aladdin*, the crab from *The Little Mermaid*, a different character every time. I figured Zenny must have learned her English from animated movies, the way she nailed the voices and knew so much dialogue by heart.

If Dad was putting Mandy to bed, I'd stay for the stories. He's a travel writer, but I always thought he should write kids' books. Funny, because now that he doesn't have kids, that's what he's doing. I wonder if he misses telling us stories or if it's just that he finally has the confidence, with Zenny telling him how great he is, instead of Mom reminding him she's the one with brains and talent.

Dad's bedtime stories would go on for weeks. He was right in the middle of one when he left. It was about a little girl named Mandy – we were always the heroes – who discovered she had the power to stop time, just like pushing the "pause" button on a DVD player. Ever since Dad left, I've wondered how that story turned out. *Would the girl ever discover a use for that power?* No question, there are moments in my life I would like to freeze, so I could take my time with them, savor them, but eventually you'd have to push "play" again. Things always move forward, whether you want them to or not.

"Come on," I say to Angie as I trudge up the stairs to my sister's bedroom.

Mandy is in bed under her covers when we walk in. I make my way toward her but have to skirt round the obstacle course of half-unpacked boxes that litter her bedroom – as they do the rest of the house, and will for weeks. I perch on the end of her bed, steeling myself for our nightly battle.

"I can't fall asleep if you don't tell me a story," says Mandy for the fifty-third night in a row.

"I can't *tell* you a story," I say. By now we both know our lines. "But I'll *read* you one."

"But you're good at making up stories," she whines.

This is true and we both know it. I was the storyteller on our family outings in Manila. Most weekends we went to the beach. Vince and I were learning to surf, and Dad never complained about driving, even though traffic was a nightmare. The only irritation was Mandy, who whined nonstop if she wasn't entertained. Dad had to concentrate on the road, so it fell to me to tell her stories. I often suggested we leave her at home, but secretly I liked telling stories, just like my dad. Sometimes I'd even continue a story he'd been telling Mandy at bedtime. If I didn't finish it, he'd pick up where I left off. I used to dream we'd write stories together when I grew up.

Stupid dream.

"I can't make up stories anymore, Mandy," I say firmly. I'm telling the truth, but she doesn't believe me.

Angie, who has followed me into Mandy's room, sits down at the desk and listens to our conversation with interest. I should have left her downstairs.

"I can't get tired unless you *tell* a story," repeats Mandy. In fifty-three days, she hasn't won this battle once, but she never gives up. She's a determined kid. Even when she's driving me crazy, I can't help but like that about her.

I go over to her bookcase and pick up the chapter book we were reading last night.

"I'm not listening," Mandy shouts. "I hate that story. It's stupid and boring!"

"Fine, then we'll leave, and you can go to bed with no story."

"I hate you!" Tears fill her eyes, and I feel my own start to prick. It's totally humiliating to have Angie watching all this, but it's like a soundtrack we play over and over. I can't figure out how to turn it off.

"I'll tell her a story," volunteers Angie.

We both stare at her.

"*You* know how to tell stories?" asks Mandy.

"You kidding? I'm an expert! How about *Little Red Riding Hood?*"

"I'm eight years old, Angie. I'm too old for fairy tales. And it has to be a *made-up* story."

"Trust me. You're never too old for this story, and it's totally made-up. But true at the same time."

Mandy and I look at her skeptically, but finally Mandy shrugs and snuggles deeper into her covers. "Okay," she says.

"So," Angie begins, "there was this little girl, Red, and one day she was riding in the hood —"

"You mean, she was Red Riding Hood." Mandy wiggles up on her pillow. She gives Angie a look as if Angie might be the stupidest person on the planet.

"Well, that's one version," says Angie smoothly, "but in this version, Little Red is out one day riding her very cool, low-slung, fifteen-speed, off-road Del Mondo racing bike in her hood when —"

"On her way to Grandma's house," interrupts Mandy, who is sitting right up in her bed now and eyeing Angie suspiciously.

"Right," Angie continues, "so Little Red is minding her own business, riding through the hood on the way to her grandma's —"

"Where are the muffins?" asks Mandy.

"What?" asks Angie.

I'm pleased to see Angie is getting the full experience of life with Mandy. Maybe I'll finally get some sympathy.

"She's taking muffins to her *sick* grandma," says Mandy.

"Of course," agrees Angie calmly. "Those are in her pannier bags on the back of her bike. So, as I was saying, she's riding through the hood when who should leap out in front of her but the wolf!"

"Yes!" shrieks Mandy, obviously pleased that Angie has finally got one detail of the story right. "A wolf jumps right out in front of her."

"Well," says Angie, "not so much *a* wolf as *the* wolf. You see, this particular wolf was the biggest player in the hood."

"What's a player?" asks Mandy.

"Are you sure this story's age-appropriate?" I ask.

"Emma," says Angie seriously, "I have two little sisters, and believe me, it is never too early to hear *this* story." She turns to Mandy. "A player is a guy who wants to get on the ride without buying a ticket."

"A lot of rides," I add helpfully.

"Right," agrees Angie. "Anyway, Little Red practically goes over her handlebars stopping her bike so that she doesn't run right into that wily wolf, and when she's finally resting there on the side of the road, sweating and panting, that wolf sidles right up to her, calm as you please, and says —" Suddenly Angie's voice drops to a deep, cajoling snarl. "'Little Red, you look good enough to eat. Why don't you and I go out to the deserted warehouse and see if we can't wake us up some sleeping dogs?'"

"What about Grandma?" asks Mandy.

"Exactly," says Angie. "That's just what Little Red said. 'I'm on my way to visit my sick grandma,' says Little Red, 'and I'm sure not wasting my time with a no-good wolf like you!'"

"So the wolf runs ahead and jumps into Grandma's bed!" says Mandy, leaning forward in excitement. No way is this going to help her fall asleep.

"That's exactly what he does," says Angie. "When Little Red shows up at her grandma's house, she finds the front door wide open. Of course, her first thought is that Grandma's been robbed and she doesn't know if maybe the robbers are still there, but Little Red from the hood ain't afraid of nothin', so she rushes right into that house and up the stairs to Grandma's room. And who does she find in her bed?"

"The wolf!" Mandy and I say in unison. Okay, so maybe I'm a little *too* into it, but I haven't heard a good bedtime story since Dad left, and this girl has skills.

"Yes! And Little Red marches right up to that smart-alecky, no-good wolf lying there in Grandma's bed, and she says, 'What the heck do you think you're doing?'"

"No," says Mandy. "She says, 'What big eyes you have.'"

"That's coming," says Angie. "So little Red says, 'What are you doing?' And the wolf says, cool as a

Popsicle on a hot day in July, 'Don't you recognize me, sugar? I'm your dear old grandma.' And Little Red looks deep into the wolf's eyes and she says, 'My grandma doesn't have big brown eyes like yours. A girl could drown in those eyes.' And the wolf says, 'I've only got eyes for you, baby.'"

"Now the ears," says Mandy.

"Right. So Little Red reaches over and tucks a lock of the wolf's hair behind his big wolfish ear and she says, 'I never noticed what big ears you have,' and the wolf says, 'The better to listen to everything you've got to tell me, darling.'"

"What about the teeth?"

"Yes, so then Little Red says, 'I never noticed before what big white teeth you have,' and the wolf spreads his lips in a big wolfish grin so Little Red can see every one of those teeth, and each one is whiter than the next."

"But what about Grandma?" says Mandy.

"Well, you know, Little Red wasn't thinking about Grandma right then as she leaned in close to get a better look at the wolf's big grinning mouth. She was thinking that this might just be the best-looking mouth she'd ever seen, and a girl could do worse than to spend some time in the company of a mouth like that. But just at that moment, she heard a banging from inside the closet. And she stopped and thought of Grandma. Then she remembered that the wolf might be more handsome than the devil, but he was still a wolf, and every girl knows that there's only one way to treat a wolf."

"Did she shoot him?" gasps my bloodthirsty sister hopefully.

"No, though he did deserve it, but that would have got Little Red into a whole mess of trouble, and most times, the best way to deal with a wolf is just to call his bluff – because that's all he's doing. That cool doesn't go very deep, and if you don't let it fool you and you let him know you aren't fooled, well, he'll either change his ways to hold on to you, or he'll turn tail and run."

"So, what did she do?" I ask.

"She told the wolf to get his sorry butt out of her grandma's bed and let her grandma out of the closet. Then she said that if he ever hoped to get with her, he would have to do at least a year of yard work for her grandma for free. And that was just for starters."

"Did he do it?" Mandy asks.

"I don't know," says Angie, looking at me. "I think your sister needs to finish this story."

"But I don't know how it ends," I say.

"Then the story stays unfinished until you do," says Angie.

"I'm never going to hear the end," says Mandy. I can't help but agree with her, but I keep my mouth shut.

"Don't give up on your sister, sweetie," says Angie confidently. "Sisters always come through. Sometimes it just takes awhile."

"Jeez, Angie," I groan. "Put it on a Hallmark card, why don't you."

She grins at me and doesn't look the least bit

embarrassed. Then she walks over to the bed and leans in to give Mandy a hug, and Mandy wraps her arms around Angie like she's the last thing floating in the open ocean during a hurricane. They stay like that long enough for me to wish I'd left the room when the story ended, but just as Mandy pulls away, I get a look at her face and something inside me shifts. A memory of a time when it wasn't so hard to give a hug – or accept one – flits through my consciousness, too quick for me to grab on to, but I feel the ache of it.

"Let's go, Emma," says Angie, walking out of the room. "We've got an apology to write."

"I'm coming," I say, but I don't leave right away. I pull Mandy's blanket up as she rolls over onto her stomach, just as I've seen her do every night since forever. Then I go check her AC and fiddle with the temperature for a minute.

"Will you finish the story, Emma?" Her voice comes out muffled from under her blanket.

I walk back over to her and lean down to turn out the bedside lamp. All I can see of her is the top of her head, white blonde hair spilling out across her pillow. I make a move to touch it, but my hand stops inches away. Dad used to do that – ruffle her hair every night before she went to sleep. I pull back, straighten up, and walk to the doorway to turn off the overhead light.

"Have a good sleep, Mandy," I say, and leave the room.

CHAPTER 9

I'm lying on the living room couch doing homework, with the TV on in the background, when Mom finally comes home close to midnight. She walks past me and turns off the TV.

"What the heck?" I object.

"You shouldn't have the TV on when you're doing homework, and you should sit up properly at a table." She leans over my notebook. "How can your teachers even read your writing? It's atrocious."

"It's doesn't matter, Mom. We take it up in class."

"It does matter," Mom snaps. "It's about developing good habits. And why are you up so late? You should have finished your homework hours ago."

I slam my books shut, toss them on the coffee table, and stand up.

"I'm going to my room."

Mom steps in front of me, blocking my way. "You have a chance to start over here, Emma. I was hoping you might take school more seriously this year."

"A chance to start over?" I scoff. "Is that what we're calling it now?"

"Your eleventh grade marks are what universities will look at. You can't afford to mess up this year."

"Maybe you should have thought of that before you cut our posting short in Manila. I was doing well there."

"I wouldn't call a B average doing well," says Mom.

I cross my arms tightly over my chest, struggling not to say something we'll both regret. "There're other things besides grades, Mom."

"Not in your junior year," Mom retorts, but like me, her voice strains under the weight of all the things she's not saying.

"What about junior prom, Mom?" I know I should stop there, but I barrel on. "Or spending time with kids who have known me for more than a minute? Or having a father?"

She exhales heavily and steps around me, leaving a free passage if I want to escape. I think she's hoping I'll go, but I stand my ground, watching as she shrugs off her tailored jacket, folds it carefully, and places it over the back of an armchair. For the first time, I notice how thin she's become. She's always been petite, but it's as if every ounce of flesh has melted off her body, leaving nothing but bones. I try to remember the last time I saw anything more than coffee pass her lips.

She turns back to me and seems almost startled to find me still in the doorway. "It's late, Emma."

She's dismissing me, but I don't move. "Why did we have to leave Manila early?" I persist. "Why did you do this to us?"

"I'm sorry." She stops, waiting for me to leave, as if her apology should be enough, as if it even comes close. "I know this move has been hard on you," she continues, finally. "But surely you understand why we couldn't keep living there the way things were – not with him, not with them. . . ."

She massages her forehead and gives me a beseeching look. It occurs to me she might have a headache, and I almost relent, tell her it's okay, but it's so not okay I don't know where to begin.

"You should blame your father, not me," she says bitterly. But she catches herself and takes a deep breath. "This has been hard on all of us. We're all making adjustments. I just need you to be a team player."

"What do you know about being a team player?" I demand. "You're never here! I'm the one at the dinner table, listening to Mandy's problems. I could count on one hand the number of times you've put her to bed since the move."

"I know and I'm sorry about that too," she says, sounding genuinely regretful. "But if you can just be patient. I was lucky to get this job at such late notice. They didn't have to offer me another posting, and it's even a promotion. It's my first time being a program manager. I need a few weeks to establish myself with my staff, then things will settle down. I promise it will get better."

"Mandy needs you now, Mom." I don't add that I need her too. I'm not admitting that, even to myself.

Mom looks past me and doesn't answer for several minutes. I don't know if she's thinking about what I said or just trying to wait me out. I am pretty exhausted, actually, and it's unlikely this conversation's going to make her change her ways. Despite her current excuse, she's always been a workaholic. The truth is, when I first found out about Dad's affair, there was a part of me that wasn't surprised. I think he was lonely. I know there was more to it than that, but I really believe that was part of it.

"I'm under a lot of pressure." Mom breaks into my thoughts. "You live in these big houses with servants, go to expensive private schools. You have a lifestyle most kids only dream about, but you never think about who makes it all possible. It was certainly never your father. Now he's gone. Is it too much to expect you to help a little?"

I tune out halfway through her diatribe. I've heard this one or versions of it too many times. I wonder how Dad felt when she went on about how hard she worked to support us. She never said it directly, but even Mandy could read the subtext. It's true, Dad never made much money off of his writing, but she never said anything appreciative about all the things he *did* do. She was too busy playing the martyr.

"Yes," I snap, my temper out of control now. "It *is* asking too much to expect me to pick up your slack. I didn't ask to come here. None of us did. You never checked with us about moving. You just dragged us along like you always do."

"You know why we had to leave, Emma. It was the only way I could separate your father from that woman."

"But you didn't separate them!" I shout. I can feel tears starting, but I blink them back. "You just forced him to choose, and he didn't choose us!"

"Do you think I could have predicted that?" Mom demands, exasperated. "I supported him for years, and he left me for a woman with a sixth-grade education. I asked him to come with us. We could have made a fresh start. It would have been the best thing for all of us, and he'd have a new country to write about. Why wouldn't he come?"

"Gee, I don't know, Mom," I say. "Maybe he felt like being in charge of his own life for a change."

"You don't understand anything," Mom says sadly, sinking down into the couch I vacated.

She picks up the remote and clicks on the TV, flipping around till she gets to an English news channel. I glare at her for a minute, but she ignores me, so I scoop up my books and head out of the room. I stop in the doorway and look back, but she's engrossed in other battles, giving every appearance of having forgotten our own.

"I understand you're a selfish bitch," I say under my breath.

She's on her feet like a shot, her face crimson with rage. "You're grounded!"

"Grounded?" I laugh humorlessly. "How can you ground me when I have no life to begin with? It's not like I have anywhere to go."

"Well, you can go to your room for starters." Her hands are balled into fists and she's breathing heavily, but her voice is controlled, her face a hard cold mask.

"My pleasure," I say, keeping my own voice steady. I don't shed a tear until I'm in my room with the door closed.

CHAPTER 10

"**Y**ou have to give it to him today," says Angie for the millionth time.

It's Wednesday lunch, and I'm sitting in the cafeteria with what I'm beginning to think of as the usual gang. Angie has not only told everyone about the note but has been passing around multiple versions of it for the past two days. She thinks this will pressure me into giving it to Mustapha, just so I won't have to hear it dissected and revised one more freaking time. I hate that she knows me that well already.

"I really think you should start off with a salutation," says Leela. Not for the first time. She looks down at the note again. "It's more polite, isn't it? You shouldn't go right into the apology. At least say 'How are you? Best wishes to your family.' It's rude not to ask about his family. Don't you agree, Tira?"

Tahira takes the note and reads it again, as if it might have changed since she read it three minutes ago. These girls don't get enough entertainment. Cineplex would make a killing here.

"You're right, Leela," she says. "She can't apologize for insulting him and then insult him again by not inquiring about his health and family."

"Forget the family," says Angie. "She doesn't even know the family."

"What difference does that make?" demands Leela.

"No difference at all," says Tahira. "You wouldn't buy fabric in the market without asking after the merchant's family. Are you saying Musa Khan deserves less courtesy than a trader in the market?"

"The only thing I ever ask a merchant is 'How much?'" chimes in Jazzy.

"And you wonder why you're always overcharged," says Tahira.

"And she shouldn't have typed it," says Leela. "A personal note should be handwritten."

"Good point," agrees Tahira.

"She handwrote the first four versions," says Angie pointedly.

"Five," I correct.

"Well, she should have handwritten it again," says Tahira.

"Although she does have terrible handwriting," Leela muses.

"All Americans do," says Tahira.

"Probably because they type everything," says Leela.

"Oh my God," I say.

Angie snatches the note from Tahira and passes it across the table to me. "Put it away, Emma, and give it to him today."

I roll my eyes at her as I shove it in my pocket. Rewrapping my untouched sandwich and shoving it in my bag, I jump up, mumbling an excuse as I head for the door. I don't realize Angie's behind me until, emerging from the building, I stop for a minute to let my eyes adjust to the blinding brightness of the midday sun. We walk over to the fishpond, which, in spite of its history, I'm inexplicably drawn to, and we sit side by side on the stone wall facing the fish.

"Have you spoken to him since Monday?" she asks.

"No, I've seen him around, but I just try to avoid him."

"I noticed him talking to your brother yesterday."

"Yeah. Me too, but Vince didn't say anything about it. I think they have some classes together."

"Yeah, probably. Are you nervous?"

"No."

"Liar."

We sit in silence for a few minutes.

"Can you hang out after school?" she asks.

"No, I have to go straight home. I'm grounded."

"Why?"

"Long story."

Another long pause; I can tell she's waiting. I watch my favorite fish. It's mottled white, orange, and black, the only one not a solid color. I wonder what it feels like to be a misfit in fish world.

"I look after my sister every day," I say. "Vince disappears with Michelle, and my mom just disappears, but she says I'm not a team player."

"That's not fair. Is that why you're grounded?"

"I said some things."

"Like?"

"I don't know. I might have called my mom a selfish bitch."

Silence. I look over at her, and she's grinning.

"You think it's funny?"

"Sorry, but you *might* have called her a bitch?"

"Okay, I did call her a bitch, but I really didn't mean for her to hear me. I was, like, halfway out the door and I just said it quietly. Is it my fault if she's got superhuman hearing?"

"So, why is your mom a selfish bitch?"

"She's not. I shouldn't have said it. It's just that she's never around, and I know she thinks she did the right thing bringing us here, and she works hard, but sometimes it feels like . . ."

I stop, pull my sandwich out of my bag, and unwrap it. I look around the courtyard before I break off a small piece and throw it to the fish. They thrash around, fighting each other to get some, so I throw in more. I'm not trying to provoke another confrontation with anyone, I just like feeding them. I don't know why. It's the same feeling I get when I make Mandy's lunch, or pour her a bowl of cereal at bedtime, or put out corn for the little green parrots that come into our yard, even though The Ghoul says I shouldn't encourage them. It's weird that I find it so satisfying watching food disappear because I've pretty much given up eating. For weeks now, I've had this boulder in my stomach that doesn't leave space for food. It may be the only thing Mom and I have in common.

"It feels like what, Emma?"

I turn to find Angie watching me, her face serious.

"What?" I ask.

"You said your mom's never around and it feels like . . . ?"

"It feels like we're going to be late for class," I say, shoving the remains of my sandwich back in my bag. Angie's a nice girl, but I hardly know her, and it's way too soon to start spilling every twisted detail of my messed-up life. The courtyard is starting to fill with students. I stand up.

"Good luck with Mustapha," says Angie, but she looks sad. I quickly turn away and try to focus on which classroom I'm heading for. I'm still not used to the way the classes alternate every other day at this school, and it's only my second day on this schedule.

I've taken just a couple of steps when Angie calls to me. I look back and find she's still where I left her.

"If you want my opinion, I think you're one heck of a team player," she says before turning away. I stand there for a few seconds, watching her retreating form until she disappears into a classroom. Angie is probably the sappiest girl I've ever met, but as I walk away, I feel a lightness that, for once, has nothing to do with losing my temper or letting off steam.

CHAPTER 11

I get to the theater early. I think maybe it will give me an edge if I have a chance to catch my breath and cool off from the heat before he arrives, but I realize my mistake almost immediately. With each passing minute, I get more nervous. My heart has expanded into my throat, cutting off my air supply. I take short, shallow breaths as my whole body throbs with each beat.

By the time he finally does walk in, with Ali and Faarooq and at least four other kids who orbit him like he's the sun, I've pretty much decided to ask for a nurse's pass so I can take my heart failure to a more appropriate location.

Unfortunately, the cherub, who is even more enthusiastic than two days ago, chooses that moment to get things started. He bounces to the middle of the room and shouts gaily to Mustapha and crew.

"Quickly, now! We have a fun exercise to get to know each other better." I cringe at the word *fun*, which every kid knows is teacher-speak for "excruciatingly embarrassing."

"How many of you have played Blind Trust before?" he asks, ignoring the groans of the few kids who have and the wary looks of the rest. "You need to take a scarf," he continues, holding aloft a fistful of dark scarves. "And choose a partner, someone you don't know very well. You're going to take turns blindfolding each other and leading each other around the school."

Ali and Faarooq race down the aisle to grab a scarf, jostling each other as they run back to Mustapha and begin debating whom he should partner with. He laughs good-naturedly and takes Ali's scarf. For a moment, I think the battle's resolved, but he says something to them and walks away. He seems to be coming in my direction, and I look around, thinking he must be targeting someone else, but he's heading for me with the resolve of a cruise missile.

"Hello, Emma," he says, flashing his devastating smile.

"Hello, Mustapha," I say, sliding one hand into my pocket to check if the note is still there or has suddenly imploded from the intense heat suffusing my body.

"Are you ready to follow me blindly?" he asks. I stare at him blankly until he holds up the scarf.

"I don't really think that's a good idea," I say, trying to sound calm and reasonable. "Do you?"

"Probably not," he agrees.

We both look around the room at other kids pairing off. I notice we're the only mixed-gender couple. I wonder if this is another huge cultural blunder, but I can't be blamed this time. I finger the note again. Now would be the perfect time to give it to him. We're alone. I haven't said anything stupid yet, and I'm only moderately irritated with him.

"Close your eyes," he says, interrupting my planning. I look back at him. In the dim lighting of the theater, his face is half-shadowed as he looks down at me.

"I don't think so."

"It's just a game. You're not scared of me, are you?" He's still smiling benignly, but the atmosphere in the room has changed. I'm pretty sure it's leaking oxygen. Any minute now, masks will drop from the ceiling.

"Mr. Baker will be disappointed if you refuse to join in." I startle at the mention of the teacher's name. I'd almost forgotten where we were. "Come on, close your eyes," he croons. "You can trust me."

We stare at each other for a long minute. I don't know why I finally close my eyes and let him tie the scarf over them. I regret it the minute the darkness becomes absolute.

"You know, I don't need to be blindfolded to get lost on this campus," I quip, trying to ease the pressure that has magnified exponentially with the darkness.

"You won't get lost. I'm going to guide you." Strangely, his disembodied voice is more comforting than I would have expected, and his hand on my elbow as he nudges me forward feels steady. I'm suddenly aware of his smell — soap and cinnamon.

I can tell we're heading out of the theater because the floor gradually slopes up underfoot. The giggling of various classmates surrounds us but seems far away. Light creeps under the blindfold as we emerge into the heat. Mustapha keeps leading me forward but is strangely silent, as if he's preoccupied with his own thoughts. I have the feeling he has a destination in mind. As we walk along, I can no longer hear other students and try to get my bearings under the blindfold. I think we must be crossing the parking lot because we've walked on pavement without stepping up or down for quite a while. Sweat is collecting in all the places you don't want to be sweating when you're blindfolded and with a boy.

"It must be time to take off the blindfold," I say, wishing I hadn't agreed to play this game.

"Soon," he says, picking up the pace and dragging me with him.

"Where are we going?"

"You'll see," he says, missing the irony.

Finally, he tells me to step up, and we're walking on grass. It's harder going, less even, and I stumble once, but he catches me. It's cooler now and I can feel shade.

"We're here," he says, eventually letting go of my arm. "You can take it off now."

I pull off the blindfold. We're at one far corner of the campus, in a field next to a wall. I look around, trying to figure out what I'm supposed to be seeing. It's obvious from his quiet watchfulness that this place has some significance, but I can't for the life of me figure out what it is.

"So?" I say finally.

He points to a pile of stones.

"A man died here," he says. "A guard. Students aren't supposed to know where it happened. They want us to forget. The administration keeps having the stones removed, but they always find their way back."

"When did it happen?"

"A long time ago, ten years maybe. There was rioting in the city. That happens a lot. People get angry about the foreigners, the infidels, and they look for someone to take out their anger on. The school's an obvious target. It wasn't as well-guarded back then, and the walls were lower. They've raised them eight feet since and put the broken glass on top. No students were hurt; the teachers hid them. But one guard was beaten to death right here."

We're silent for several minutes as we contemplate the pile of stones.

"Why are you showing me this?" I say after a time.

"Because you need to understand."

"Understand what?" I turn to look at him.

"You can't make fun of things." His gaze is intent. "You need to be careful, show more respect."

I'm disappointed. He thinks it's that simple. I'm just culturally insensitive, an ignorant kid who needs to be schooled in foreign relations. I know he doesn't know about my dad or how hard it was to leave my friends in

Manila, and maybe he wouldn't forgive me even if he did know, but still I expected more compassion from him. I hoped for more.

"So, that's it, then?" I ask. "You brought me here to do what? Teach me a lesson? Warn me?" My voice cracks.

He looks at me steadily but doesn't answer.

I look away. "Well, lesson learned," I say, still not looking at him. "I'll see you back in class." I turn to walk away.

"Emma," he catches my arm, but lightly, and immediately drops his hand when I turn to glare at him.

"Don't you want to blindfold me now?" His tone is friendly, but his eyes are searching. It's the first time I've seen his confidence waver.

"I don't think that's necessary," I say. "You're already blind."

I feel the tears starting as I leave him and begin making my way across the field. I want to go home, but not home to any one geographical location. I want to go back to a moment in time when I felt surrounded by people who knew me and loved me. I want to recapture that feeling of belonging, but right now, in this field where a man died trying to save kids like me, kids who don't really belong anywhere, I wonder if that moment ever existed.

We're a long way from the theater, and I hope I'm heading in the right direction. As I had thought, we're on the far side of the parking lot, but I can't see any of our classmates and suspect class resumed long ago. I keep walking and have covered some significant ground before I hear Mustapha's voice again.

"Emma!" he shouts.

I stop and look back. He hasn't moved from the stones. He's going to be seriously late.

"If I am blind," his deep voice resonates across the field, "shouldn't you guide me?"

"You think I know the way?" I shake my head at his ignorance and turn to resume my journey. I look back once more when I reach the edge of the parking lot. He still hasn't moved and he's still watching me, though from this distance, I can't read his expression. I don't think we'll be practicing our play today. I take the note out of my pocket and rip it into a dozen pieces, letting them flutter to the ground. A large cockroach scuttles toward me, disturbed or perhaps enticed by the flurry of paper. For a moment, I think of the appealing coolness of the theater, but I can see the greenhouse from where I'm standing, and without giving it much thought, I turn my steps in that direction.

CHAPTER 12

I don't see Mr. Akbar at first. He blends into the foliage like a creature of the forest. Only when I catch the movement of leaves on the far side of the greenhouse do I see a triangle of his khaki uniform.

"Mr. Akbar?" I say, not loudly. I feel embarrassed to disturb him and wonder if I should find a bathroom to hide out in until the end of class.

"Emma, how nice of you to come," he says, working his way through the foliage toward me. "How is your first week going?"

"I'm sorry," I say, my mind a few paces behind. "I don't mean to bother you. I should go." I start to back away, but he smiles and starts speaking again.

"I was just about to have *chai*. Would you be kind enough to join me?"

I hesitate. In spite of the heat, I can't think of anything I would rather do than have a cup of tea, here, with this man. I gratefully follow him through the plants to the very back of the greenhouse, where I find he has a small wrought iron table and two chairs. They seem out of place in this country, like something out of a Victorian garden, but at the same time, they suit him perfectly. I collapse into one of the chairs. A feeling of peace comes over me as I watch him crouch on the ground and lift an iron kettle off a low shelf, placing it on a small brazier already blistering with coals. He takes a clear packet off the same shelf, and the smells of cinnamon, cloves, and ginger fill the damp air as he shakes a measure of spices into the boiling water. We sit in silence for a good while, watching the steam evaporate.

"People add the tea at different times," says Mr. Akbar. "There's no right or wrong way to do it. Would you like to add the tea now?"

"I don't know how you like it," I say hesitantly.

"The trick is to discover how *you* like it." Mr. Akbar crouches to the shelf and hands me a second packet with loose tea leaves.

"How much should I add?"

"Just the right amount," he says with a smile. "Don't worry. You won't go wrong."

I use a cloth that's sitting on the ground next to the kettle to remove the lid. I'm sure I'm wrecking it as I shake some of the dark leaves into the spicy brew. I glance at Mr. Akbar, but he's looking off into the distance as if suddenly entranced by one of his flowering trees. I shake in a few more leaves and replace the lid. I resume my seat, and we sit in silence for a while longer.

Water keeps evaporating, and I watch the purposeful meandering of a small insect up the leaf of a nearby plant.

"Some people take it off the heat and let it sit," says Mr. Akbar, breaking the silence. "But, of course, it's up to you."

I crouch down again and take the kettle off the brazier, placing it on a rough-hewn patio stone. I look up at Mr. Akbar and catch him smiling at me before returning his gaze to his plants. I take my seat again and continue to watch my bug. He hasn't moved much since I left him. I wonder if he's a good bug or a bad bug, and I imagine him spending his entire existence in Mr. Akbar's greenhouse, thinking it's the whole universe. Perhaps he has extended family on a neighboring plant and he visits them on special occasions.

"The milk is on the shelf there." I jump a little when Mr. Akbar speaks. "It's already open."

I take the can of condensed milk and look at him for directions.

"You could pour it in the kettle and put it back on to boil, if you like," he says. "That's one way of doing it."

I watch as the creamy milk swirls into the inky blackness of the tea. I don't ask how much to add, but pour until it looks right to me. I put the kettle back on the brazier and resume sitting. I don't see my bug at first and look around for several minutes before I catch sight of him on the stalk, making his way down to the earth.

"How much sugar to add is really a matter of opinion," says Mr. Akbar. "And, of course, a matter of the waistline for some, but you and I don't have those worries."

I crouch down to the kettle again, taking it off the heat. Mr. Akbar puts teacups and a jar of sugar on the table, hunting for a spoon while I pour the tea. I watch as he adds two heaping teaspoons of sugar to his cup and takes a sip, swirling it around in his mouth.

"I think this is the best tea I have ever had," he says.

I add a teaspoon of sugar to my own cup and take a tentative sip. I smile in agreement.

CHAPTER 13

We all watch Guul as he brings in another plate of food. I offered to help, twice, but he looked at me as if I was suggesting he's not moving fast enough. In fact, he's moving too fast. Soon the table will be full and he'll retire to the kitchen, taking with him the only thing we can pretend to focus on to avoid the total weirdness of our mother at the dinner table on a weeknight. No one knows where to look. It's such a singular event, even Mandy is stunned into silence. And, of course, we all know why she's here.

It's what I said to her about never being around. But her presence is not an acknowledgment of the problem; it's a continuation of the argument. Her sullenness hangs over us like a storm cloud. I said she's never around, so she's proving me wrong and leaving no one in doubt how inconvenient it is. She's a busy woman, with far too many responsibilities to have time for family dinner.

The silence echoes off the walls as Mom smoothes the napkin in her lap and stares out the window at our tiny backyard. If we opened the French doors, we could probably hear the family next door sitting down to their own dinner. The houses are that close, an identical line of seven rectangular blocks, each separated by ten feet of grass and an eight-foot wall.

I wonder if the uniformity is meant to be reassuring. Even the furniture, although it belongs to the mission and will stay with this house when we move on, is identical to the furniture in Canadian embassies the world over. When Vince explained this to me many years ago, I didn't believe him. I carved my name on the underside of my desk in Kenya, convinced my very own desk would show up when we moved to Thailand. I was triumphant when I walked into my new bedroom and there was my desk, but when I looked underneath, the surface was clean, unmarked by my trespass, as if my previous life had no more substance than a play performed in multiple settings with interchangeable actors. With such order and predictability, it seems impossible that individual lives can unravel so chaotically.

"How was school?" Mom asks finally, still gazing at the ten feet of dead space. It's not clear whom she's speaking to. There's a long pause as my siblings and I exchange looks.

"Emma?" she says, turning to me.

I stare back at her. *What do I say?* A beautiful boy showed me where a man died trying to protect racist misfit kids like me and warned me to watch my step. Perhaps I could tell her I feel like I'm disappearing. I feel like the threads of my life have become so tangled and broken that I can no longer see the pattern of me.

"Fine," I say.

There's another long silence. Dad would never have let me get away with that. He would know that *fine* is a word designed entirely to communicate its opposite. He would probe deeper, dig out the pellets of truth, like a surgeon removing shrapnel so the wounds could heal.

"Vincent?" My mom moves on.

"Fine," says Vince. I look at him sharply. *What's wrong in his world? A fight with Hip-Hop Barbie?*

Mom sighs like maybe she does get it and lifts up her fork to push food around on her plate.

"Kirsty McDonough is having a party, but I'm not invited," says Mandy glumly.

We all turn to her, but no one speaks. I'm not sure if Mom's trying to work out a solution to Mandy's crisis or calculating how much longer she has to sit with us.

"Why didn't she invite you?" asks Mom, trying to sound sympathetic.

"She's mean," says Mandy predictably. "She invited everyone on the compound but me."

"Where is she from?" asks Mom, perking up a bit.

"I don't know."

Mom looks at her. She's disappointed in Mandy's failure to collect relevant details. She's not used to people presenting her with problems that haven't been fully researched. How can she do her job with only partial facts? She waits. Perhaps Mandy will suddenly remember some mitigating detail that will show she's not wasting Mom's time.

"I don't know," repeats Mandy, her bottom lip pushing out.

"Well, you need to find out," says Mom firmly. "I'll contact her parents and sort this out, but you need to follow up. Get me a phone number."

"Oh my God," I say.

"Do you have something to say, Emma?" asks Mom. Obviously I have something to say. I just said it.

"Well?" she prompts.

"You can't contact the kid's parents," I say, struggling to keep my voice even. "Do you want to make Mandy even more unpopular than she is now?"

"Emma, your sister is not unpopular!" Mom snaps, giving Mandy a reassuring look. "If you can't say something positive, don't say anything at all."

This time, the silence goes on forever. I sculpt mashed potato towers and smash them down with my fork. Mandy shovels in food with surprising determination for a kid whose entire social life is about to be torpedoed. She must have some kind of basic survival instinct. Even Vince, who finished his whole meal the night Dad left us, has been buttering the same bread roll for longer than it took to knead the dough and bake it. Mom is back to staring out the window. Guul pokes his head around the door, checking to see if we've all left the table or died en masse from virulent food poisoning.

"How's your job going?" asks Vince suddenly, giving us a collective jump.

"I have to go to Karachi tomorrow," says Mom with evident relief at the change in subject. "There's a consular issue."

"Death or drugs?" asks Vince.

"Drugs. A twenty-year-old kid caught with opium from Afghanistan."

"In prison?" he asks.

"Yes, they haven't let anyone see him yet, but I met with the minister today and he assures me they'll let me in."

"Will you rescue him, Mommy?" asks Mandy trustingly, reminding me of a time when I was actually proud of Mom's work.

"I don't have the power to do that," says Mom, sounding genuinely regretful. "I'll check on him, make sure he's being treated fairly. I'll take him a care package, food and blankets, and see whom he wants me to contact. I'm sure his family will want news of him. But if he did what he's accused of, there's not much more I can do."

"I wish you could save him," Mandy sighs.

"I do too," says Mom, her eyes lit with more passion than she's shown all evening. "He's so young, not much older than you, Vince. Maybe we could look through our books tonight and find some for me to take down to him. I'm sure he'd appreciate that."

"Wait just a minute," I say. "Am I the only one who finds it a little hard to get worked up over a drug dealer?"

"Conditions in the prisons here are horrific," replies Mom. "Any caring person would find it heartbreaking to see a young man throw his life away like this."

"But he's the one who threw it away. He made a choice. No one forced him to make a quick buck selling heroin to little kids." The anger is back, ferocious and unbridled. The second the words leave my mouth, I can think of a thousand arguments against what I'm saying. Hell, at my school in Manila, I spearheaded a letter-writing campaign to demand more humane prison conditions after Mom came back with horror stories from one of her visits. But at this moment, everything Mom says makes me want to scream.

"He has no one, Emma. He's alone in a strange country, where he doesn't speak the language or understand the culture. He's surrounded by people who are hostile to him. You have no idea what that's like." My mom looks annoyed and disappointed at the same time.

"I have no idea what that's like?" I shriek. "Is that what you think? That I have no idea what it's like to be all alone in a hostile place with no one who knows me? No one who cares about me? You think I don't know what that's like?"

"Lower your voice, Emma!"

"I feel that way every day, Mom." My voice is

cracking. I don't want to hurt her, but my words tumble out with their own momentum. "Every single day I feel alone."

Vince and Mandy shuffle uncomfortably and stare at their plates.

"How can you say that? I love you and I'm right here, Emma. I'm not the one who left. Sometimes, I really don't understand what you want from me." Her voice catches, and suddenly I'm taken back to a year or so ago. She's in her bedroom with Dad, and they're having one of their *private discussions*. We kids have been directed outside, but Vince and I have a pact. One of us always stays behind to listen. We need to know how bad it is. We think if we monitor it, we can somehow prevent the crisis from getting out of control, like watching the brinkmanship of two nuclear powers.

This was a bad one. Dad said he couldn't live with her anymore. He needed a wife, a companion, not just a breadwinner. Mom said she'd given him everything, a home, freedom to write without the pressure of having to earn, and children. She added *children* like we were just three more items in the ledger of her sacrifices. He said it wasn't enough, and she said, "I don't know what you want from me." Just like that. Just like she says it to me, in that sad confused voice.

I glance at my mom's face. The wounded look, like I've struck her, and in that moment, I know she's telling the truth. She really doesn't know.

"I'm going for a run," I say, getting up from the table and leaving the room before anyone can stop me. But no one tries. They're as relieved to see me go as I am to leave, and I wonder how long my family has been happier without me. *Do they see my anger always simmering beneath the surface and worry about when it will next burst out? Do they fear me as much as I fear myself?*

I don't bother with the pretense of changing into my sweats. I've never been a runner. Even my mom knows that. But I am practically running as I bolt out of the house in jeans and a T-shirt, stopping only briefly at the guardhouse while the gates are opened.

Exiting the compound, I take two sharp lefts, skirting the perimeter between the outer wall and the tennis court. The court, like the pool and weight room on Compound C, is our government's effort to make up for sending us to a hostile, impoverished country. *Nice try.*

I lean against the fence and stare in at the empty court. It occurs to me I don't have a plan beyond getting out of the house. I open the gate and let myself into the empty cage. Guilt and remorse, my familiar friends, are already seeping into my body like heat off the concrete. If I could, I would take back everything I said – yet if it happened all over, I know I would say the very same things.

A movement catches my eye beyond the far end of the court. The French compound is just behind us, but there's a stretch of no-man's-land between the two compounds that is used mainly as a garbage dump. Waste disposal, like so much here, is makeshift. I don't know if the massive festering mound between our two compounds is an agreed-upon dump or simply a convenience that no one bothers to object to, but right now, there are two kids climbing all over it.

My first impulse is to shout at them to get down. I'm sure it's rife with disease and rats. But I don't know how to scold in Urdu, so I walk to the end of the court for a closer look. It's a boy and a girl. The boy is maybe a couple of years younger than me. The girl's face is smeared with grime, and her baggy tunic doesn't give anything away, but I'd put her age close to Mandy's.

They eye me warily as I approach, yet they don't stop what they're doing. The boy scrambles across the mound, picking through it and occasionally throwing pieces of garbage down to the girl, which she shoves into a large canvas bag. I try to figure out what they're collecting, but there seems no logic to it. Tin cans, scraps of wire, even a moldering chicken's foot all make their way into her bag.

"*Assalam Alekum,*" I call to them, if only to reassure them that I'm friendly.

The girl is still watching me like she'd like to run away, but she can't leave the boy, and he's single-minded in his work.

"*Wa Alekum Salam,*" she answers softly, glancing at me from under her lashes before she turns away, blushing, as if mortified by her own boldness. The boy gives her a disapproving look before resuming his scavenging. She leans into the refuse and claws out a pop bottle, perhaps hoping to redeem herself.

"*Kya aap Angrezi?*" I ask. I don't really expect they speak English, but I want to keep the conversation going.

She shakes her head, glancing at the boy to see if he's noticed.

This time, he says something to her. It's clear he's telling her to ignore me, and she looks suitably chastened. I have a sudden insight that he's her brother. He bullies her out of habit and affection. I'm not sure what to say next. I don't want to get her into more trouble, but I'd like to know what they're doing. Of course, what I want is irrelevant because I don't have the words to ask, so I continue to watch them in silence.

The bag is bulging by the time the boy climbs down off the mound. He slings it over his shoulder and picks up a rusty bike that I only now notice is lying on the ground nearby. He waits while the girl hops onto the handlebars.

"*Khuda Hafiz,*" I say.

The boy mounts the bike and begins pedaling over the rough gravel out to the road. As they reach the corner of the French compound, the girl looks back and gives just the hint of a wave. I raise my own hand, but they've already disappeared from view.

Heading home, I contemplate lives so fragile they're

built on the discarded remnants of my own. Suddenly my problems seem trivial, and although they don't disappear, the burden is lightened – like grief is a single poisoned chalice, and as I share it with these children, my own portion is less.

CHAPTER 14

I'm halfway to the whiteboard before I realize I don't have my assigned question completed in my notebook. I check again to make sure, and there it is, question nineteen, dutifully recorded, missing an answer. It's so unfair. I completed the first eighteen questions. *Why do we have to do the same formula nineteen freaking times, anyway?* I read about this study once that said doing homework actually makes kids stupider. Apparently, they discovered repetition kills our creativity. *You think?* What kills me is that they had to pay some fancy PhD to discover what any half-witted kid could have told them for free.

If I had any guts, I would turn to Mr. Derry right now, in front of the entire math class, and tell him he killed half my brain cells with the first eighteen questions and I simply didn't have enough left to complete question nineteen. And, given that I'm only in standard math, he really should not be messing with my limited mental resources. I bet if I did that, the entire class would stand up and cheer, or maybe even organize a spontaneous parade in my honor. Of course, to be honest, the kids in this room would do pretty much anything to get out of eighty minutes of math. This class is where the mathematically challenged congregate to get a hard-won pass on their exam so they can go on to lives that will never include math again. Ever.

I glance over at Mr. Derry. He's standing off to the side with that hopeful, excited look that teachers get when they see their budding prodigies spewing out the garbage they have methodically shoveled into them, step-by-boring-step. *Can I really burst his bubble and tell him I didn't complete my homework? That solving* x *wasn't sufficiently compelling last night to distract me from listening to Mom hiss into the phone to Dad that if he thought he could do a better job parenting me, she'd stick me on the next plane because it sure wasn't what she'd signed on for?* Nor could quadratic equations, although admittedly complicated, distract me from puzzling over what exactly Mom meant by "not what she'd signed on for." She didn't say she'd put *all* of us on a plane. Sometime in the early hours of the morning, I concluded, with mathematical precision, that the solution to the equation of Mom, clearly, did not equal me.

"Emma," says Mr. Derry, breaking into my thoughts. "Is there a problem?"

Oh yeah. There's a problem.

"No, sir," I say and begin copying the question onto the board. Maybe I can work it out on the spot.

Yeah, right, and maybe aliens will beam me up to their spacecraft and replace my brain with one that actually solves quadratic equations in under twenty minutes.

Sweat pops out on my forehead. If I expire right now from heatstroke and my life flashes before my eyes, my overwhelming memory of this country will be the place where I sweat. Constantly.

I start working on the next line. There's only one kid left at the board. It's Johan, the cute Swedish boy Jazzy had a thing for – and probably still does. He appears to be struggling as much as I am. He pushes back the platinum-blond lock that has fallen over his forehead as he steps back to review his work. Satisfied, he replaces the whiteboard marker on the ledge and walks past me to return to his seat, bumping into me in a move that is shockingly uncoordinated, unless he's trying to feel me up. It takes me a minute to realize he's slipped me his notebook. I look down at it, marveling at his neat penmanship. I should have had *him* writing the note to Mustapha.

I don't have high hopes that his solution is correct, but chances are mine is wrong anyway, so I gratefully copy his answer onto the board. The teacher, bursting with the joy of a board full of numbers, doesn't notice when I take a circuitous trip back to my desk that allows me to return Johan his book.

"Thanks," I whisper.

He smiles in response, and I notice for the first time how truly gorgeous he is – perfect white teeth, chiseled features, sea-blue eyes. I totally see why Jazzy's stuck on him, but beyond the casual admiration of this perfect specimen of burgeoning manhood, I feel nothing. Not a flutter of interest. *Strange.*

Mr. Derry begins talking through the work on the board while I slide into my seat and stare at the back of Johan's head. *It would be really inconvenient to like the same guy as Jazzy, but shouldn't I feel something for a guy this hot?* In Manila, I totally crushed on guys like this. Even for the thirty seconds I had my own boyfriend, I would still get a rush when a really cute boy smiled at me.

My thoughts are interrupted by a knock at the door. Mr. Derry motions for a student to open it, and one of the local staff, wearing the blue shalwar kameez uniform, walks in with a note. That's one thing about schools in developing countries, there's no shortage of workers for every job you can think of. But this school seems to have more staff than students. It's positively bristling with guards, groundskeepers, carpenters, plumbers, electricians, cleaners, cooks, and – apparently – messengers. I guess with the security issues, they can't risk bringing in an outsider every time they want to pass messages not suitable to announce over the PA. I wonder what kind of information cannot be publicly announced. *A plane waiting at the airport to whisk me out of my mother's life?*

While Mr. Derry has a quiet word with the messenger, the class takes the opportunity to have a few quiet words of their own, and pretty soon, several kids are out of their desks, including Jazzy, who's made her way over to Johan. Jazzy's the only person I know in this class, the other girls having made it into higher math. I'm a little disappointed she doesn't come over to me.

Mr. Derry finishes with the messenger and spends several minutes trying to restore order. This is no easy task. It's not that everyone in here is an airhead, though if there were airheads, this is definitely where they'd be, but even kids who are generally good students (like me, for example) turn into the worst sort of miscreant when you put a math book in front of them. It's like the mental energy required for even minimal attention to numbers saps whatever intelligence we have.

Finally, the class settles, and Mr. Derry, with a deep sigh, tells us the rest of the class is canceled and we all have to proceed directly to the theater.

"It's nothing to worry about," he says, "but there are some demonstrations in town." He doesn't say what kind of demonstrations. But we all know that if they weren't anti-Western demonstrations, he would tell us more, because that would be unusual.

"We're going to get you all home safely," he continues. "A few mullahs are stirring things up at the Friday prayers. Nothing to worry about, but we need to make our way to the theater in an orderly fashion."

He looks pointedly at several boys, and Jazzy. "Wait there for further instructions. It's really no cause for concern."

Is that the third or fourth time he's told us not to worry? I look around at my classmates and wonder how many are also thinking of a desolate pile of stones in an unforgotten corner of the school.

The playful energy of moments before has dissipated as students quietly shuffle out of their seats and head for the door. I try to make my way over to Jazzy, but she's made a beeline for Johan again, so I end up leaving the classroom on my own. I look for Angie in the courtyard, but with every class emptying at the same time, I can't see her in the crowd.

"What did you get out of?" Mustapha materializes at my side like I'm harboring some internal tracking device.

"Math," I say, noticing that my pulse has just sped up and my heart's doing little backflips against my rib cage.

"Oh, bad luck," he says. I can't tell if he's serious. I look up at his face, and a sudden rush of heat explodes somewhere south of my forty-ninth parallel. He grins. I'm doomed.

"Musa!"

We both look back to see the ice princess gliding toward us in a shimmering ensemble, gold accenting every extremity and woven into the fabric of her clothes. *How much does she spend on those dresses?*

"Aisha," Mustapha says. And in that single word, I hear a hint of something that surprises me. *Annoyance? Disappointment?*

"This is so tedious," she says. "Just because there are a few demonstrations, we all have to waste our time in the theater. Why can't they let us go home and just keep the foreigners? It's not like we have anything to do with this. They're only making *us* a target by putting us together with *them*." She wrinkles her nose in my direction.

"It's not their fault either, Aisha," Mustapha says.

"Well, it sort of is, darling," Aisha purrs. "After all, no one asked them to come here."

"No one asked you to come to an international school either," I say, admiring my restraint in not totally going off on her.

"Mustapha," she pouts, turning her back to me. "I thought you said she wasn't that bad."

"Well, I heard rumors you weren't a total ice bitch," I say sweetly, relinquishing the moral high ground. "I guess we're both victims of inaccurate intel."

She whips round to give me a toxic glare, and Mustapha steps between us.

"There's nothing to worry about," says Mustapha firmly, though at this point, I'm not sure if he's referring to the demonstrations or the fact that Aisha and I are heading for a throwdown.

"I need to find my friends," I say directly to Aisha. I wonder if she remembers dismissing me with that very directive only four days ago. I'm glad that this time I'm the one who says it and there are people I can actually go find, even if it's too early to call them friends.

"Emma –" Mustapha begins.

"Don't let us keep you," Aisha interrupts, giving me a fake smile and little finger wave.

"When you didn't come back to class on Wednesday," Mustapha continues, "the guys and I wrote a script." He slings his book bag off his shoulder and pulls out a stapled sheaf of papers, which he hands to me.

I take it and skim down the first page.

"Your country is a primitive, vermin-infested police state," I read aloud. I glare at him. "I'm not saying that."

"Actually, I believe you already did," says Aisha with a smirk.

"We also decided we need an extra practice," says Mustapha, like he didn't hear my objection. "So we're meeting at my house tomorrow."

"Have fun with that," I say.

"We need you there too." Mustapha gives Aisha an uncomfortable look, and I suddenly realize why he wasn't happy when she came up to us. "You're in our group," he says, as much to her as to me.

"What?" snaps Aisha.

"We have to practice," Mustapha repeats.

"Mustapha –" Aisha begins.

"Sorry," I cut her off. I don't bother to sound sincere. "I'm grounded. There's no way my mom will let me out on a Saturday."

"Could you call her and ask?" Mustapha persists.

"You know, I would try," I lie, pleased with my quick thinking, "but she's out of town."

Mustapha looks like he's going to say more, but I don't give him the chance. I hustle away in search of Angie.

CHAPTER 15

The lower and middle grades are already seated under the watchful eyes of their teachers when I enter the theater. I search the crowd till I catch sight of Mandy, seated near the front. Like the rest of her classmates, she has a book on her lap, but she's not reading. She's not talking to the kids next to her either, even though most of the class is whispering. I try to catch the eye of her teacher, willing her to notice my sister. Mandy's not a kid to sit quietly when there's socializing going on unless something is wrong. I've seen enough of how the other kids treat her on the van to know she's not fitting in, but I don't know if it's just that or something more.

"Emma!" I look across the theater and feel a rush of relief to see Angie standing up, waving her arms.

Teachers are herding upper schoolers to the back rows of the theater, well away from the little kids and my sister. I push through my unruly peers, all similarly engaged in finding friends. There's at least fifteen minutes of chaos before everyone is settled. Leela and

Tahira join Angie and me. Jazzy's several rows away, sitting with Johan. I lean over to ask Angie if we're allowed to get out of our seats. I still have one eye on Mandy, and even though I can only see the back of her, I know she's upset. I don't get two words out before a teacher shushes me and points to the front, where the superintendent is taking the stage.

He stands in front of the microphone and raises his hands for silence. The lower-school teachers start a rhythmic clap. Amazingly, their little charges all join in and stop talking. The middle and upper schoolers are way too cool for this, but we get the point and quiet down.

The superintendent runs through a bunch of boring rules and tells the upper schoolers to set a good example, simultaneously pointing out how much better behaved the little kids are with all their books and clapping, like they thought that stuff up themselves. He gets annoyed that we aren't sitting with our classes, since our teachers are supposed to take roll call, but he doesn't suggest anyone move. He probably figures if he lets us get up again, we'll never get settled. Obviously, this guy's been around a while.

"I have to check on my sisters," says Angie as soon as the superintendent leaves the stage.

"I was just thinking the same thing," I say and jump up, following unnecessarily close behind her. I know I'm not supposed to be scared, but I keep thinking of the pile of stones. I'm also thinking how sorry my mom would be if I was hacked to death by religious fanatics and how she'd regret planning to send me away. I almost wish something would happen, which is just stupid. She'd be way too busy mourning my siblings to spend a nanosecond missing me.

"Stick with me," says Angie, giving me a knowing look.

I try not to look too relieved. It's not like this is my first time living in a dangerous country. We never had lockdowns in Manila or days when we couldn't go home, but we did live in a gated community. There were occasional bombings in town, random violence. But it was just that. Random. There were no hostile stares as we wandered the city, no public demonstrations demanding we be wiped out. Manila was dangerous, yet violence — when it did occur — seemed out of the ordinary. But standing here, among these other kids hiding out in the school theater, our voices echo like the distant rumblings of an avalanche, and I can't get past the feeling that we're directly in its path.

I'm right behind Angie as she squeezes out of our row. We pass a teacher on the end, who frowns at us, but Angie tells him we need to check on our sisters and he just shrugs.

Unlike the upper schoolers, who are a jumble at the back of the theater, the other two schools are seated by class, in orderly rows, with the youngest at the front. So as we work our way down from the back, we come upon Angie's oldest sister first.

"Hey, Casey." Angie waves across several students, and a girl with a glossy mane of black hair squeals with delight and begins pushing her way out of the row to stand in the aisle with us.

"Casey, this is Emma." I can tell by the way she introduces me with no explanation that I've already been the subject of conversation. Strangely, it doesn't feel that creepy, though I do wonder what she's been saying. "Casey's my mini-me," says Angie, putting her arm around her sister and giving her a squeeze. "Don't we look alike?"

I have to admit, the resemblance is astounding. Casey's a couple of inches shorter but has identical beautiful elfin looks.

"Our mom looks like us too," adds Casey. "We call ourselves the Three Musketeers." They both grin, as if this isn't a totally embarrassing admission.

"Oh," I say and look away, pretending my interest has been caught by something at the back of the theater. *Is it inevitable that my eyes are drawn to him? But who is he sitting with? Oh my God!*

I feel Angie clutching my elbow. "Emma, are you okay?" she asks worriedly.

I turn to her, and I can tell by the way her brow furrows that I do not *look* okay. I incline my head, indicating the direction she should look. I can't bring myself to look again, but I watch her eyes sweep the rows behind us and I see surprise, followed quickly by anxiety flit across her face.

"Oh my God!" she says.

"My thoughts exactly."

"Your brother is sitting with Mustapha."

"I know."

"They're chatting. And *laughing*!"

"I *know*."

She takes a deep breath and pastes an unconvincing smile on her face. "Look on the bright side," she chirps.

"Bright side?"

"It's taken your mind off . . ." She hesitates, obviously reluctant to voice my fears. "It's just that now you're not dwelling on, well, you know," she finishes lamely.

"Getting hacked to death?" I ask. "I guess it's true that being trapped in a theater with five hundred other kids while angry mobs march the streets demanding our executions is scarier than my brother getting chummy with the guy who keeps embarrassing me."

"Exactly!" she enthuses. "I knew you could put a positive spin on this!"

She turns back to Casey, who's been watching us curiously. No doubt this will be another thing they'll discuss behind my back.

"You okay, Casey?" asks Angie, looking her sister over like she might be oozing blood somewhere.

"Sure," says her mini-me in a voice that manages to be brave and plaintive at the same time. "But it's only the first week of school. I thought we might at least get through a week without one of these stupid lockdowns." She sighs dramatically, which I find reassuring. She's obviously more bored than scared.

Angie gives her a hug. "I'm sitting right back there,"

she says, pointing to our seats. "So come get me if you need anything."

"Stop worrying about me," says Casey, even though she was totally begging for it. "She's like the worst worrier," she explains, grinning affectionately at her sister.

Angie throws her arm across my shoulders, which – given the short time we've know each other – should make me uncomfortable, but instead it gives me an embarrassing glowy feeling, and, awkwardly attached, we continue down, pausing at Mandy's row. She's at the opposite end from where we're standing, so we agree to continue down to the kindergartners first and loop around to the outside aisle. When we reach the front row, a tiny girl leaps out of her seat and hurls herself in our direction. Angie drops to her knees and catches her just in time to prevent a painful landing. She settles back on her haunches and pulls her sister onto her lap.

"Penny, this is Emma," she says. "Remember I told you about her?"

The little girl looks up at me with huge eyes. "Are you still lonely?" she asks, playing with a lock of her sister's hair.

So I guess I have some idea of what Angie's been saying. I stare back at her sister.

"How can she be lonely?" jokes Angie. "She's got me, doesn't she?"

Her sister nods solemnly and continues twisting Angie's hair around her finger. I notice her own hair is neatly braided, complete with plaid ribbons that match her jumper.

"When can we go home?" Penny sighs.

"Pretty boring, huh?" says Angie.

Penny nods and burrows her head into Angie's chest.

"It may be awhile," says Angie gently, wrapping her arms around her sister and giving her a squeeze.

"She needs to take her seat," says a teacher.

Angie nods and rises, pulling her sister to her feet. Taking Penny's hand, she walks her back to where she was seated and makes sure Penny knows where we're sitting. I wonder what good it will do either of them to know where their sister is when religious extremists burst through the door armed with machetes and blind hatred, yet they both look happier than when we arrived.

I walk to the center of the theater, directly in front of Mandy but several rows below her. She's still staring fixedly ahead, not taking part in the whispering and giggling around her.

"She looks scared," says Angie, coming to stand next to me.

"Maybe," I say, hoping she's wrong. As useless as I may be at friendship advice, I know even less how to cope with violent extremists. "What do I say to her?"

"You don't really need to say anything," says Angie. "But you can tell her there's nothing to worry about."

"But I don't know if that's true."

"Doesn't matter."

"She's been lied to enough." I give Angie a meaningful look. She looks back at me.

"It's not a lie if you make it true. She has you to protect her."

I consider telling Angie I'm no one's hope for salvation. I couldn't even protect our family from a five-foot-nothing Filipina maid with an infectious laugh and a gift for mimicry.

"All right," I say. "I'll do my best."

Together we walk up the stairs. Mandy looks surprised to see me standing at the end of her row, but there's another emotion as well that I can't quite read. *Relief?*

She pops up immediately and begins pushing out of her row, completely ignoring her teacher's insistence that she sit down.

"It's my sister!" Mandy says, and even at a distance, I can hear the pride in her voice.

Reaching the end of the row, Mandy launches herself at me, clutching me in a bear hug that is totally not the way we behave in public, or anywhere else for that matter. Other than Dad, who was big on hugs, we're more of a friendly squeeze kind of family. I look around to see who might be watching, but the only eye that I catch is Angie's. She smiles encouragingly.

"What's going on?" Mandy burbles. "Why are they keeping us here? I want to go home. Is someone going to kill us? When can we go home?"

I can't think of a single thing to say, so I pat her back for a minute, just like Dad would. I expect her to push me away, knowing like I do the treachery that cloaks itself in affection, but she just clings harder, and so we stand there for an eternity, arms around each other. Like morons.

"Hey, Mandy," says Angie, crouching down to reach eye level. "How's it going?"

"I'm scared," says Mandy, breathing heavily against my belly. I suddenly feel dampness and realize she's crying. She burrows her face more deeply into me as I angle her away from her classmates so they don't see. The last thing she needs is a reputation as a crybaby.

I look over her head at Angie, hoping she's got some words of comfort, because I'm still trying to quell my own visions of machete-wielding jihadists bursting through the doors.

"There's nothing to worry about," says Angie. "This happens a lot. You'll get used to it."

Mandy pulls away from me and turns to Angie, shamelessly exposing her tearstained face to the entire third grade. "Why does this happen?"

"There are people here who are very poor and unhappy. They want someone to blame for their troubles," Angie recites smoothly.

"Do they blame us?" asks Mandy.

I know the answer, but I find myself waiting to hear what Angie will say.

"Some do," she says. "But most don't, and that's what you have to remember. Most people you meet here are kind and want to live peacefully, just like us."

Mandy nods her head slowly, mulling this over, while I give Angie a grateful look – and not just for the explanation. I know I'm not a great sister, but she makes me feel like maybe there's hope.

Mandy's teacher demands she return to her seat, but it's several more minutes before I can convince Mandy to let go of me. The truth is, I take my time. It's comforting having her hot sweaty arms wrapped around me. If a bloodthirsty mob bursts through the doors right at this moment, I'm exactly where I want to be.

CHAPTER 16

Angie and I take our seats next to Leela and Tahira and, for the next hour, listen to every minute detail of Tahira's brother's upcoming nuptials. Since Tahira's future sister-in-law is also her cousin, she's involved in planning for the bride as well as the groom. I've pretty much tuned out by the time she gets to the number of rubies in her cousin's *bindya*, but I rally briefly when she and Leela get into a heated debate over offsetting the rubies with crystals rather than diamonds. Leela's indignant on the bride's behalf. She's unmoved by the fourteen individually selected rubies, and there's a tense moment when Tahira accuses Leela of being a snob.

Angie changes the subject, asking Leela what a bindya is, and while Leela struggles briefly with her desire to maintain an outraged silence, her innate helpfulness gets the better of her. She not only explains the bindya, but she prattles on about *jhoomers* – nose gems, necklaces, earrings, bangles, and various other optional gems and attachments. I'm pretty sure there are less ornaments on a Christmas tree, but I keep that thought to myself.

Two hours into the lockdown, the AC goes off. Despite the fact that there's too much noise to hear the hum of machinery, everyone in the theater knows the instant it shuts down. When the superintendent takes the stage, he doesn't even have to tell us to be quiet. We're waiting for an explanation.

"It's on a timer," he says calmly. He flinches a bit when he admits it shuts off automatically at the end of the school day. He doesn't want us to notice that the end of the school day has passed and we should be at home enjoying our freedom. His concern about enlightening us is wasted. There's not a kid in the room who doesn't know we should've been on the vans forty minutes ago. He promises he's already dispatched engineers to restore the AC and tells us for the millionth time that there's nothing to worry about.

Thirty minutes later, still no AC, and some workers, possibly the engineers, open the doors at the back of the theater. This turns out to be a mistake. As the stifling air from outside mixes with the oppressive heat inside, we all share a sudden revelation that the theater is actually cooler than the outdoor temperature. There's some confusion as a couple of teachers jump up to shut the doors, and a couple more argue that it's too late, we've already lost the last bit of climate-controlled air, so we may as well get some fresh air. A debate ensues as science teachers square off against humanities teachers. Voices are raised, but most kids are so hot and fed up they don't bother to watch. Finally, the superintendent steps in and the doors are closed again – "Security," he says. I wondered when that would occur to someone. I guess that's why he's the big boss.

Another thirty minutes crawl by. Tahira stopped entertaining us with her stories some time ago, but I only now realize she's stopped talking. She's halfheartedly fanning one side of her flushed face with a notebook while Leela, who has materialized an actual fan, is briskly fanning the other.

"She's feeling faint," Leela explains when I catch her eye.

"We should take her to the bathroom," says Angie. "Wet some paper towel and cool her down."

We all jump up, Leela helping Tahira.

"Sit down!" barks the nearest teacher, who is an alarming shade of burgundy herself and looks like she should be joining us.

"We need to take her to the bathroom," explains Leela. "She's sick."

"One of you can go with her," says the teacher, sweat pouring down her face from the exertion of bossing us around.

I think of arguing, but Angie is already wilting back into her seat, so I sit down and move my legs to allow Tahira and Leela to squeeze past. Angie and I sit in silence. A few rows down, Jazzy's conversation with

Johan has also withered. She's no longer leaning into him with predatory intent. In fact, she's slumped away from him. Perhaps the inadvisability of going after a guy when you smell like a sewer has finally dawned on her, though he'd have no way of identifying her stench above everyone else's. I shake my watch, even though I know it's working perfectly, and look at Angie, uncharacteristically quiet beside me. Her eyes are closed and her head has fallen awkwardly to one side.

Gently, I try to rearrange her head so it rests on the seatback. I'm amazed she doesn't wake up, and all of a sudden, I'm flooded with memories of the Philippines. After long days of picnics at the beach or hiking in the hills, Mandy would fall asleep on the car ride home, and Dad would carry her into the house without waking her. I'd always run ahead, opening doors, and I'd pull off her shoes as Dad would gently lay her on the bed. Then we'd go downstairs, where Zenny would have cold drinks and some fresh baked snacks waiting. Vince would race off to the TV room, but Dad and I would sit in the garden, under the long shadows of the palms, until dusk turned into night.

Where was Mom? Why did she so rarely come with us? Was work really so pressing that she couldn't spend an afternoon with her family, couldn't even be there when we got home? I wonder if Dad and Zenny go on outings now. *Does he think of us when they're driving home, when he enters their house empty-handed? Do they sit in the garden as night falls and relive the casual moments of their day, not realizing how precious each one is?* The familiar ache begins in the pit of my stomach and I feel tears gathering, but my wallowing in self-pity is short-circuited by another commotion at the back of the theater. I turn to see Leela arguing fiercely with a teacher.

"She needs air," Leela insists as she tries to shoulder past two burly PE teachers, half-carrying Tahira.

I jump to my feet. Angie, suddenly alert, is at my side as we hustle out of the row, ignoring the irate commands of several teachers who tell us to sit back down. Faarooq, Mustapha, and a boy I take to be another of Tahira's brothers beat us to the back of the theater. My brother is no longer in sight. Faarooq has taken Tahira's arm and is trying to pull her out of Leela's grasp, but with more strength than she looks capable of, Tahira is gripping Leela's free hand. The teachers look worried and determined at the same time as they block the doorway.

"We've sent someone to get the nurse," says the older of the two teachers. "You all need to calm down."

"I think I'm going to faint," says Tahira seconds before she slumps against Leela, almost knocking her to the ground. Leela relinquishes her grip as Faarooq eases his sister to the floor, but Leela drops to the ground and it's her lap Faarooq rests his sister's head on.

"I think you need to elevate her feet," I say, suddenly noticing Aisha lurking just behind Mustapha. Her bored expression transforms instantly into contempt.

"What do you know about it?" she challenges.

The nurse arrives before we can get any further and presses a bag of ice to Tahira's forehead.

"Put her head on the ground and lift her feet," she instructs Faarooq.

Aisha snorts in irritation, but I'm too busy watching Tahira for signs of life to enjoy my victory.

Tahira's eyes flutter open.

"We need to cool her down," says the nurse.

"We could put her in our car with the AC on," suggests Faarooq.

The nurse nods in agreement, and Mustapha moves in to help Faarooq lift Tahira.

"I'm okay," she mumbles, her already-red face turning several shades darker.

"Do you think we could get her home safely?" Faarooq asks Mustapha, ignoring the teachers who, like me, are all foreigners.

"Let's see how she feels when she's had a chance to cool down a bit."

One of the teachers who was formerly barring the exit starts to say something but thinks better of it. For the first time, I realize they're as ill equipped to deal with the jihadists as I am. Sweat beads on my forehead as I start to feel queasy myself.

As a hand slips into my own, I jump. "It's going to be okay, Emma," says Leela, giving my hand a soft squeeze. "All these *badmaash* will get hungry soon and go home for their dinners. You'll see. We'll be out of here in no time."

Faarooq and Mustapha half-carry Tahira as they make their way to the door, with Leela right behind. I'm annoyed to see Aisha following as well but don't even bother trying to make my own escape. The PE teachers are still on either side of the open doorway, and I don't have to be told that they would never let me get past them. The double standard feels both unjust and reasonable. As if they're reading my mind, they shut the door firmly behind Tahira's entourage and move to stand in front of it again. Behind us, the microphone crackles from the stage, and I turn to see the superintendent waiting patiently for silence. I expect another excuse about the air-conditioning.

"I've been informed that the demonstrations are breaking up," he begins, but he gets no further because raucous cheers drown out his speech. Over the chaos, it's just possible to hear him instructing us to let the lower grades exit the theater first, but the upper schoolers are already halfway to the doors, and I think even he realizes it's safer to get the big bodies out of the way so they don't trample the little ones.

As much as I'm dying to get outside, I wait at the back of the theater for my sister. I'm watching the exiting tides, which is why I don't notice Mustapha until he's right beside me.

"What are you doing back in here?" I demand, sounding more indignant than intended.

He looks startled but quickly recovers. "I came back to see you," he says smoothly.

"Is Tahira okay?"

"She's fine. They've left for home already." He pauses, which gives me enough time to think I may not want to hear what he has to say next. "It's a shame we missed our class today."

Nothing to worry about after all. He's just making idle conversation.

"Yes, it's very disappointing," I say, infusing my voice with so much regret you'd think I planned a career in the theater.

"Lucky we'd already arranged to meet at my house tomorrow," he continues cheerfully.

My heartbeat suddenly kicks into overdrive, and my mouth goes dry. I know we've already established I'm not going to his house tomorrow. *So why is he grinning?*

"I'm sorry," I say warily. "As I said before, I'm grounded and I can't get my mom on the phone."

"Well, unbelievable luck," he says with a smirk. "Your brother got her on his cell, and it turns out she thinks it's a wonderful idea."

"My brother?" I repeat as the depth of Vince's treachery sinks in. He is *so* dead.

"Yes, Vince, your brother. You remember him?" Mustapha teases. "And do you know, it turns out your mother's not out of town after all?"

"Really?" I say, trying to buy time to come up with some other excuse.

I don't realize Mandy's standing next to me until she leans against me. I look down at her and, without thinking, put my arm around her. It's becoming a habit.

"Will you walk me to the van, Em?" she asks hopefully, and I give her a squeeze. She smiles so happily I have a moment to regret being such a lousy sister before Mustapha redirects my anxiety.

"My mother's looking forward to meeting you."

He's discussed me with his family? First Angie and now him. Do people in this country have nothing else to talk about?

"I have to go," I say abruptly.

"Of course." He nods in understanding and squats down till he's eye level with Mandy. "It's been a long day, hasn't it?" he says, flashing his earth-stopping smile. She smiles back, then turns her head into me while peeking at him flirtatiously out of the corner of her eye.

Is there any living, breathing female he does not *have that effect on?*

"So I'll see you tomorrow, my house, ten o'clock. I gave the address to your brother," he says, standing up again, and with that, saunters out.

Mandy and I follow him out of the theater. He hasn't taken more than a few steps before he's swarmed by his entourage. I notice Aisha in the group at the same moment she notices me, and we share a hate-filled glare, though truthfully I'm not sure I do hate her. It can't be easy trying to control a boyfriend like Mustapha. Mandy and I stop to let them get some distance from us and watch as Mustapha recedes across the parking lot, laughing and chatting with his friends.

"He's handsome," says Mandy after a time.

"As the wolf," I say pointedly. She shoots me a look, and I know she's remembering Angie's story. We share a moment of pure girl-connection.

CHAPTER 17

Dad's on the phone, but I refuse to speak to him. Mandy appears at my door every fifteen seconds to give me soulful looks and mouth pleas to try and change my mind. It's not going to happen. I rearrange the pillow behind my back and turn to the book in my lap, though I haven't turned a page in thirty minutes.

This is the fifth night in a row he's called, every night since the first day of school. It's always the same drill: a short chat with Vince (awkward), a shorter chat with Mom if she's home (painfully awkward), an interminable chat with Mandy, and then he asks for me. *Isn't it illegal to phone that often?* I think we could charge him with harassment or something. If I did speak to him, which I won't, I'd tell him to get a life and stop bugging us.

Mandy's at the door again. I should just shut it, but I'm eavesdropping on Vince's conversation with Dad. Eavesdropping is my new way of communicating with Vince. I listen to him talk to Michelle, though most of that is better ignored. I listen to him talk to Mom. I'm pretty sure half of that is lies because he's always going on about how great everything is. I listen to him talk to Mandy, which is unbelievably boring, but I listen anyway.

"Please," she mouths from my doorway.

"Get lost," I mouth back. I may get in trouble for that, but who cares. I'm grounded *and* I have to go to Mustapha's. It's totally unfair.

Angie invited me over for dinner tonight, but apparently the grounding does cover that, and I also lost the use of my cell phone, so I have to wait for the land-line to call and tell her I'm going to Mustapha's tomorrow after all. Angie will definitely want to give me some advice. She's still convinced Mustapha has some burning passion for me. I think it's far more likely he realizes his effect on me and is sadistically toying with me because I insulted his country.

Now Vince is at my door. Maybe the phone's free.

"Dad's on the phone. He wants to speak to you."

"Really? What a surprise." I angrily flip an unread page of my book.

"This isn't all his fault. You need to stop blaming him." He takes a step into my room but hesitates just inside the door.

"Are you going to tell me Mom was doing the gardener now?" I challenge. I'm full-on raging, and it feels good. I hope my voice carries all the way down the hall. I want Dad to hear, though truthfully I don't blame it all on him. I'm at least as angry at Mom.

"No, I'm just saying you know what was going on between them. They had a lot of problems."

"And more than one solution," I fire back. "He didn't have to screw the maid."

"Zenny, her name's Zenny. And you liked her too, Em. We all did."

"Well, I don't like her much now," I say fiercely, but my voice comes out raspy like I'm holding back tears. Vince is right. I did like Zenny. A lot. *But doesn't he realize that it just makes it worse?*

"I know you feel Dad abandoned us, but Mom made the decision to move us here, and he had no way of supporting us if we stayed behind in the Philippines. He barely makes enough to support him and Zenny."

"I never said I wanted to stay behind with him." I never said it, but it's true. More than that, I wanted him to fight to keep me. He knew I couldn't get along with Mom. I always took his side whenever they argued. I defended him. *How could he let her take me without a murmur of disagreement?*

Vince continues as if I haven't spoken. "He didn't stop loving us. But our lives are with Mom, and he couldn't live with her anymore. They've been unhappy such a long time. He deserves a life with someone who loves him."

I stare at Vince, wondering what he's really thinking. *Is he really okay with all this? Or does he have his own internal dialogue, angry words he'll never voice?* Perhaps our ears are so attuned to the clambering inside us we're no longer capable of really hearing each other. "We loved him," I point out. "Why wasn't that enough?" I bow my head. The words on the pages of my book swim before my eyes.

"He misses you, Em. You know you were his favorite."

"Well, I think we can all agree that now Zenny is his favorite," I say, still not looking up.

"What's happened to you, Emma? You've changed."

I don't answer.

"You know, you're getting more like Mom every day," he says.

He's gone before I can respond, but I wouldn't know what to say anyway. I swipe away tears and listen to him make excuses to Dad. Moments later, he's saying good-bye. I grab the edge of my bed to stop myself from running to the phone and ripping it out of his hand, just to hear Dad's voice. But Dad's already gone. That's what I have to remind myself. He left two months ago. It's like removing a bandage. Better to do it quickly, once and for all.

Vince is back in my doorway.

"Do you want to talk?" I can see it's hard for him to ask. He wants me to say no.

It's funny, we used to talk all the time. Vince is a good listener, for a boy. Like Dad, he's not strong on giving advice, but he keeps secrets way better than I do, and up till we moved here, I never doubted he had my back. But we haven't had a real conversation since the night Mom lost it.

We were still living in Manila. It was a few weeks after Dad left, and she came home late, like she always did. Mandy was asleep, and Vince and I were watching TV in the family room.

I knew something was up when she didn't come in to tell us she was home. She wandered around for a while. We could hear footsteps like she was pacing. Just before something hit the wall and shattered, she started moaning. It was a primal sound, inhuman, and yet it more starkly conveyed her agony than any words she could have spoken. I looked at Vince, but he kept staring at the TV, even though Mom's moans drowned out the sound. For the first time, I wondered what our lives would be like without Mom. Dad had flown the coop. *If Mom fell apart, who was left?* I remember the first tug of fear as I leaned across Vince and picked up the remote. Our eyes met for a second as I turned up the volume. We watched TV until the early hours of the morning, when we were sure Mom had exhausted herself and fallen asleep. We never spoke about it. Not then, not ever.

I look at my brother now, standing uncomfortably in the doorway, shifting from one foot to the other. I want to say something to bring him closer, but the territory that divides us could be mined; it's that dangerous. If I could only turn back the clock, rewrite our history, but it's too late. Actions can't be undone and some can never be forgiven.

"It's okay," I say, forcing myself to look him in the eye. "I'm fine." He holds my gaze as guilt and remorse gather in the air between us, like a low pressure front moving in. I don't know if I'm relieved or disappointed when finally he turns away and disappears down the hall.

I get up to phone Angie. I don't really feel like calling her anymore, but I know once I hear her voice, she'll make me want to talk. She has some freaky mind-meld power that way, and I need the distraction.

"What's up, girlfriend?" Angie comes on the phone, and I immediately feel better. Like I said, mind-meld.

"I'm going to Mustapha's tomorrow," I say, walking back to my room with the phone's handset and shutting the door behind me.

"No freaking way!" she shouts. I'm pleased with her reaction. At least someone gets it. "You can't go," she continues. "How did this happen?"

"He spoke to Vince, and now my mom is making me go because it's a school thing."

"That scheming bastard!"

"I know."

"Can't you fake being sick or something?"

"My mom would never fall for it."

"Okay, we just have to stay calm and think this through." I love how she takes over my problem. I know she can't really fix anything, but for a moment, it feels like I'm not alone. I think of telling her about my dad.

"The main thing is, you have to make sure you're never alone with him."

"Ali and Faarooq'll be there."

"Don't count on them to protect you. Guys always

stick together. They're probably already plotting some excuse to leave you two alone. I've got it!" Angie shrieks. I wince and hold the receiver a safer distance from my ear.

"What have you got?"

"I'm coming with you."

"You can't. Mom's sending me with our driver. She'll never let me take you."

"Don't worry. Leave it to me. Just watch for me when you come out of your gates. What does your car look like?" I tell her and we hang up. I'm still not clear what the plan is, but I feel strangely reassured. I really think Angie may be able to save the day. She has odd powers, that girl.

CHAPTER 18

I look for her the second we come out of our gates. All morning I've been certain something's going to go wrong – her parents won't let her out of the house, or she'll realize I'm not worth wasting her time on and decide not to come. I pull down the sun visor and check my makeup in the tiny mirror. I'm wearing mascara and eyeliner! I'm not trying to look good for Mustapha or anything. I just don't want another lecture from Angie about "making the most of what the good Lord gave me." Most people here think the only thing the Lord gave me is a smart mouth and a bad attitude, but maybe Angie sees more.

We pass the Egyptian embassy. It's been completely rebuilt since being blown up a few years ago. The explosion was so big, it blew out the windows on our compound as well, embedding glass in furniture, which all had to be replaced. There's still no sign of Angie, and I'm beginning to panic. Maybe I missed her.

Although the diplomatic enclave is densely populated, it's surprisingly leafy and overgrown. There are pockets of scrubby green space separating most of the compounds, and even in daytime, the streets are shadowed in huge trees.

Suddenly I catch sight of her. I needn't have worried. Her smile is like a beacon. I'm surprised I didn't see it a hundred feet back. She waves both arms with wild enthusiasm, and I grin and wave back, even though I'm only a couple of feet from her now. I feel like a total dork.

I already told Ahmed, our driver, that we're picking up a friend. He looked at me suspiciously, but he didn't say anything. I was afraid he'd refuse because he didn't have permission from my mom. Miguel, my driver in the Philippines, would never do anything without my parents' authorization. He was like a driver-bodyguard-babysitter all in one. He'd drive me to a mall, follow me till I met up with my friends, and be there within minutes when I called him to come get me. I always suspected he never left. Perhaps he followed me around all day, ducking into corners when I turned to look. It used to bug the hell out of me at the time, but I miss it. *Weird*.

"You look *so hot*! Mustapha's going to die when he sees you." Angie jumps in the car, spilling over with excitement.

I turn around to smile at her in the backseat. She seems unconcerned that we're on the way to witness my total and absolute humiliation at the hands of boys who hate me. I feel a small glimmer of hope.

"So, are you nervous?" she asks. "Don't be nervous. I won't let you out of my sight. Just be polite and friendly. But not too friendly. You're there to do a job. We go in. You practice your play. We get out. No problem. Nothing to worry about. What can go wrong, right? Nothing. That's what. Nothing can go wrong. And if it does, I'm right there to protect you."

Okay, now I'm worried. She's as nervous as I am. She knows they're going to annihilate me. She's already working out how she's going to drag my limp, lifeless carcass away from there.

"Have you memorized your lines?" she says, breaking into my fierce attempts to remember every action movie I've ever seen, where people hurl themselves from moving cars and get up without a scratch on them. *Is it crouch and roll or roll and crouch? How are you supposed to jump if you're crouching? And what do you do with your arms? Is it different for girls? Do I protect my brain or my boobs? It doesn't take a genius to know which are going to get me farther in life.*

"Emma? Your lines?"

"Oh, sorry. Yeah, I guess." I still haven't told her what the script is about.

"Now remember, if he tries to get you alone, just make up an excuse." I try to focus on what Angie's saying. "Be firm but polite. Whatever you do, don't lose your temper – and try not to be rude."

"I'm never rude!" Of course, I know I'm lying. I wouldn't be in this mess if I didn't shoot my mouth off the first chance I got, but it stings that Angie says it like it's a permanent character flaw.

Angie doesn't say anything.

"You've known me for only a week. How can you say I'm rude? I know I was rude to Mustapha, but that was a one-time thing, an accident, and I was provoked."

More silence from the backseat.

I look out the window. In Manila, no one ever would have thought I was rude. I cared about people's feelings. I was thoughtful and funny. Not biting and sarcastic, but funny. Angie doesn't know me. But my mind wanders to my ongoing battle with Mom, my overwhelming rage at Dad, and the fifty-two deleted e-mails. Maybe it's me who doesn't know me.

I break the silence first. "I'll try to be nice."

"That's all I'm saying. You are nice. Just let them see that."

I turn round in my seat to examine her face. She looks back at me seriously. She's not just being kind. She may think I'm rude, but she believes I have hidden niceness. I hope she's right, although I'm not so sure. Sometimes I think if I ever did have genuine human warmth or compassion, it was lost when I entered this country, like abandoned luggage at the airport. It never made it through Customs. It's already been disposed of. I face forward and sink down in my seat.

"Emma, turn around again."

I don't want her to see my face right now. I stare out the window, but I don't see the scenery whizzing past.

"Turn around, Emma."

We drive in silence for several minutes.

"Emma, I'm sorry. Okay?"

Why is she sorry? I'm the bitch. Does she think I don't know that?

"It's okay," I say, but I don't look at her. I can't. If I do, I'll start crying or turn into a pillar of salt or something. "I know I'm a bitch."

"Well, that's all right, then. As long as you know." I hear the laughter in her voice, and I do turn around. She's grinning and it's infectious.

I grin back.

"I've always been partial to bitches," she says. "Some of my best friends are bitches."

"Maybe that's because you're a bitch yourself."

"Could be . . . I'm not ruling that out."

We're still smiling like fools, and I think if I was in the backseat right now and she tried to hug me, I wouldn't pull away. It's a stop-time moment. If I could, I would capture it so I could come back to it, savor it. It's the first moment in this country I've wanted to hold on to. The first moment I haven't wanted to get through as quickly as I could so I could start the business of forgetting.

We've been driving alongside high stone walls for several minutes now, and I'm on the point of asking Ahmed what's behind them. I'm thinking military installation or terrorist training ground. Suddenly he pulls into a short driveway leading to an ornate iron gate. A guard emerges from the guardhouse, and I'm surprised to see he isn't wearing the government-issue fatigues, though he is armed to the teeth with an automatic rifle slung over his shoulder and a wicked-cool pistol on his belt. He's better equipped than our guards, which kind of confirms my first suspicion about the terrorist training ground. After a brief chat with Ahmed, the guard opens the gates for us.

It occurs to me Ahmed could make a packet of money turning Angie and me over to terrorists – American and Canadian diplomat kids. The press would be all over it. The terrorists could keep us hostage for years and just trot us out every so often to keep up the pressure. It would never get old. We'd keep getting thinner and thinner and look more and more desperate. People would write articles, like about how we're going to be messed up for life even if we do get out, and they'd speculate on whether we'd been tortured or abused. Our parents would go on television and make tearful pleas for our release. Somehow, even in fantasyland, I can't imagine my mom crying to get me back, but maybe Angie's mom could do that and my mom could be all angry and threatening. Maybe the trauma would bring my parents back together, and my dad would feel bad for ever ditching us and missing the last few months with me, and he'd beg for my forgiveness right on TV.

I don't notice we've stopped until Ahmed comes around to open my door. He doesn't normally do that. It's not like I'm a princess or anything. He looks at me curiously as I slowly climb out of the car.

We've pulled up beside a small mansion. A minute ago, I wouldn't have referred to this as a *small* mansion, but I can see a much larger one in the distance, beyond what looks like a stable with a dozen or so horses milling around it. Not too far off in the other direction is a swimming pool. I'd bet my allowance it's Olympic size.

As if he's been watching for us, Mustapha emerges from the mansion and strides toward us. He's wearing a loose white *kurta* over jeans, and his smile is blinding. For a second I start to smile back – until he brushes right past me, leaving just a hint of cinnamon, and goes to Angie, taking her hand with a warmth that makes me want to slap her, a momentary betrayal that I immediately regret.

"Angie, what a nice surprise. Emma didn't tell me you were coming."

I could point out that I didn't even know I was coming until yesterday, but I figure we're going to be arguing soon enough. Better to save my energy.

"I hope you don't mind," Angie simpers, all giggly and flirty. I don't blame her. He just has that effect on girls.

"Not at all. You can be our first audience and give us suggestions. We could use the help." He leans in and fake-whispers in a voice clearly loud enough for me to hear. "Emma seems to be having trouble with some of her lines."

Be nice, I remind myself. If he's going to spend the whole day antagonizing me, though, it's not going to go well. I don't want to get angry, but if I've learned anything about myself in the recent past, it's that I don't have great self-control. If he pushes my buttons, I'll go off on him and say mean things and feel elated for the first five seconds and terrible for eternity. It won't be my fault, or not entirely, but it will still feel like my fault.

"Emma!"

He's standing right in front of me. He's speaking to me. *Why is he so good-looking? It's totally not fair.*

"Emma, come inside. My mother wants to meet you."

I used to be good with parents. My old friends always said their parents would tell them to be more like me, polite and well-behaved. I *used* to be a lot of things.

Angie's wandered off in the direction of the house; so much for sticking together. Mustapha waits for me to start moving before he follows.

We walk into a large, dimly lit entrance hall. The ceiling sweeps up to the second storey, and I see there's a massive chandelier that's probably pretty impressive when it's turned on.

He comes up behind me. "Go through there to the right." He gestures to one of several doors. I can feel his breath on my head.

Where's Angie?

CHAPTER 19

I walk through the doorway but stop abruptly just inside. The first thing I notice is a stone fireplace that's so massive you could walk right into it and roast a full-size deer with room to spare. And I'm not just randomly thinking about deer, because the second thing I notice are dozens of glass eyes staring at me from every direction. To say it's disturbing would be an understatement. I've never seen so many dead animals outside a museum. There are two tigers posed on either side of a sofa, which I figure is two more than anyone needs in their living room; at least six gazelle-like things; plus several mouse deer posed au naturel, nosing under the ottoman for grass. *And is that a lion?* I didn't think they even had lions in Asia, but there it is, lounging right on the hearth, with a full mane of hair and its head thrown back, yawning and enjoying a cozy afternoon by the fire.

"My grandfather was a bit of a hunter," says Mustapha.

"You think?" I say, unable to take my eyes off the

carnage. "Do you hunt?" I'm not sure I want to hear his answer.

"Not often. There's not a lot left to kill."

I whip around to see if he's joking and think I catch the faintest twinkle in his eyes.

"How disappointing for you," I say dryly. I look around the room again and realize the one thing missing is Angie.

"We go through there," says Mustapha, pointing to a door on the far wall, and I hustle through the gauntlet of dead animals, hoping Angie is on the other side.

Instead, I find myself in another cavernous room, with glass-enclosed bookcases that reach up to the ceiling against every wall. There are a couple of large armchairs in the corners, but a huge leather-topped table that looks like it came from a palace dominates the room. In spite of its size, there's something about this room that's strangely soothing, though it may be just the lack of dead bodies. I want to check out the books, but Mustapha nudges me onward.

"Almost there," he says. As I skirt past the table, I run my hand along the backs of some of the twenty-or-so ornately carved chairs that are pushed up against it.

Finally, we're in a room that you might find in an ordinary house. An ordinary house owned by very, very rich people but not so big you could roll up the carpets and play softball, so I feel a little less like I've stumbled into an alternate reality peopled by giants with bloodlust.

The room is some kind of sitting room, though the two embroidered sofalike things and half a dozen matching chairs don't look at all comfortable to sit on. Which is perfect, really, because the inlaid ebony coffee table and matching side tables are way too fancy to actually put coffee on. I figure this is one of those rooms loved by socialites and interior designers the world over, reserved exclusively for photo ops and visiting dignitaries.

A man in a crisp white shalwar kameez, obviously a servant, is standing against one wall, but after nodding politely, he disappears. Otherwise, the room is empty. Still no Angie.

"Sit down," says Mustapha, but he doesn't sit as he eyes the doorway the servant disappeared through and fidgets with the sleeve of his shirt. I continue to stand, taking note of the exits.

"Where are the others?" I ask.

"My mother wants to meet you."

I'm reminded that he said that earlier. I should have been paying closer attention.

I don't have time to respond because, at that moment, an extraordinarily beautiful woman sweeps into the room followed by the servant I saw earlier. I glance quickly at Mustapha, who manages to look both relieved and anxious at the same time.

"Emma, it's so lovely to meet you. I'm Mrs. Khan." She comes straight to me and takes both my hands in her own. "Musa hasn't stopped talking about you all week." She has the same clear green eyes as her son and a smile that makes you want to smile back, though right now, that's the last thing I feel like doing.

I shoot a look at Mustapha, who's turned an alarming shade of burgundy.

"Come sit down," says his mother, pulling me onto a sofa beside her. "You'll join me for tea, won't you?"

I don't answer since it's clearly not a question. The servant also seems to know the drill because he slips out of the room without instruction.

"Stop hovering, Mustapha," scolds his mother. "Don't you have other guests to attend to?"

A look of sheer panic flits across his face as he debates how to answer.

"Go on," says his mother firmly. "Emma and I want to enjoy our tea in peace. I'll send her to you when we're done."

"But we need to practice our play," objects Mustapha without conviction. We all know he's lost this battle.

"Emma will be along shortly," says his mother, making a shooing gesture with slim manicured fingers.

Mustapha gives me a final look before he leaves.

The tea arrives almost immediately, making me wonder if the servant was standing outside the door with it the whole time. A tray displays a variety of cakes and pastries, and I politely take one as instructed, even though there's no way it's going anywhere near my stomach, which is currently roiling uncomfortably. *What has Mustapha been saying about me to his mother?*

"So, Emma," Mrs. Khan begins and then hesitates like she's just realized she has nothing whatsoever to say to me. And there's this awkward silence while I madly try to think of something I can talk about, even though this is clearly *so* not my responsibility. The servant pours tea into a dainty cup and saucer and hands it to me. I carefully place the pastry next to the cup.

"You have a very beautiful home," I blurt finally, surprising us both with my good manners.

"Thank you. That's very kind of you," says Mrs. Khan. She does look genuinely pleased and more than a little relieved, which makes me worry again what Mustapha's told her.

We both stir sugar and milk into our tea, and the sound of silver on fine porcelain echoes through the room. I'm sure she's running down a list of my alleged crimes in her head, and I try to think of something else I can say that will make her smile and think well of me.

"I like your . . . ," I begin. But then it occurs to me I haven't figured out how I'm going to finish this sentence. I raise my cup and shift uncomfortably on the edge of the sofa-thing. The tea is scalding. The excessive amount of milk I added has only served to make the cup dangerously full, but I can't return it to the saucer because the pastry has slid into the middle of the plate. Perhaps I could nudge it aside with my brimming cup. I gaze longingly at the coffee table, which, like every surface in the room, has million-dollar artwork inlaid into it.

I try not to think about the blisters rising on my fingers.

Mrs. Khan waits politely for me to finish, an expectant look on her face. I have to say something.

"Dead animals," I finish, realizing immediately it was *not* the thing to say. Truthfully, the death room has not really left my head since I saw it, and I've been doing amazingly well up till now not mentioning it.

Mrs. Khan gives me a startled look.

"I mean," I continue hastily, "they're so . . ." An image of a stuffed mouse deer, its adorable striped face and hopeful white chest emerging from behind an armchair, suddenly floods my consciousness. "Lifelike," I say, which is totally stupid because they're not statues. They actually were alive.

Mrs. Khan looks at me quizzically, so I feel obliged to try again, though I'm pretty sure I'm on an adrenaline rush now because any idiot would know it's time to shut up. "You know, they look very alive for formerly living things that . . . aren't," I explain, sweat popping out on my forehead.

Mrs. Khan breaks into a wide smile and suddenly looks exactly like her son. "They really are hideous, aren't they? After my father-in-law passed away, I tried to convince my husband to get rid of them, but, of course, that was all the more reason not to part with them. He's never picked up a gun himself, but they remind him of his father."

"Does Mustapha hunt?" I ask, fairly certain I know the answer.

"Mustapha?" She looks surprised. "Mustapha won't even let us kill insects. He's forever carrying spiders out to the garden." She stops for a moment and says something in Urdu to the servant, who's been silently watching us from his position beside the door. He opens one of the side table drawers and rushes forward with a coaster. I hastily put down my cup, sloshing half of it onto the table, which provokes frantic mopping by the servant. Mrs. Khan pretends there's nothing amiss, and I pretend I didn't wish I was dead.

"I can't imagine why Mustapha even took you into that room," continues his mother. "It would have been much more direct just to come down the hallway."

"Really," I say. "That certainly is a mystery."

His mother gives me a sharp look and then cracks another Mustapha smile.

"Did you know he's engaged to Aisha?" she asks.

The abrupt change of topic catches me off guard, and I pick up a linen tea napkin and begin pressing it into tight folds to hide my confusion. Zenny taught me napkin folding. I used to do it for all my mom's dinners and receptions. I begin fashioning a cat's paw. It took me weeks to learn this one, but Zenny insisted on naming every failed attempt, claiming they were more attractive than the original. Later, I started making my own designs. She enthused over every one.

"Mustapha's and Aisha's fathers were childhood friends," she says. I begin working on a napkin bull, complete with horns.

"It seemed like fate when we had Musa and they had Aisha so soon after. We agreed on the betrothal shortly after Aisha's birth. Of course, we wouldn't force them to marry if it wasn't their choice, but they're well suited, don't you think?"

She waits for me to answer, but adding feet is difficult with such a small napkin. I have to concentrate.

Finally, she gives up. "Musa's father and I were a love match. It was quite the scandal at the time, but we still asked permission from our families. We wouldn't have married without permission."

I use the edge of the teaspoon to work down small folds for the feet.

"You see, the important thing for us is the support of our families. I think that's why marriage in our culture is usually successful and marriage in Western cultures usually isn't. Without family support, there's no one to help when a couple runs into problems and no one to hold them accountable either. It's too easy to just give up."

My bull is finished, but it's missing eyes. I rest it on my knee, wondering what it would be like to go through life as a blind bull. I really want to give it eyes.

I look up to see Mrs. Khan watching me. She gives me such a kind smile that I have to look away.

"There's a woman who sits at the gates of our compound, begging," I say, still staring at my bull, who cannot stare back. "Her face looks like it's melted. In fact, it has melted. My mom said the woman's in-laws poured acid on her because they weren't happy with her dowry. They scarred her for life and threw her out of the house because they didn't get enough money for her." I look up then, and our eyes meet.

"That does happen," says Mustapha's mother. "But good families don't behave that way. You know, we have a lot of poor, uneducated people here."

I look around the beautiful room, at the opulent furnishings, the servant in the corner, and I drop my eyes to my blind bull.

"My parents are separated," I say, curling its horns like the ones on the bulls I see by the roadside every day on the way to school.

"Musa told me," she says quietly.

I stand up. "Thank you for the tea." I place my blind bull on the table in front of her.

"It's beautiful," she says.

"Not quite," I demur, but I don't tell her what's missing. She asks the servant to take me to Mustapha and thanks me for a pleasant chat.

CHAPTER 20

"Where were you?" Angie hurls herself at me as the servant shows me into the room. I stumble slightly but lean into her embrace for just a second. Mustapha raises an amused eyebrow, but I really don't care.

"Well, finally we can get down to work," he says, as if it's my fault we've been delayed.

We're in some kind of entertainment room. Ali and Faarooq are sprawled on the floor, playing a video game on one of the largest flat screens I've ever seen. Beyond them is a pool table, air-hockey, Ping-Pong, and various smaller tables, presumably for board games.

Ali briefly turns away from the game to wave at me but then cries out in frustration as Faarooq seizes the opportunity to deal a deathblow to his character. He doesn't have long to mourn, however, because his character reappears immediately, one life gone, but ready to start another. If only it were that simple.

"Faarooq," Mustapha commands, "we need to practice now."

I expect an argument, but Faarooq pushes "pause" and sets down the controller. Ali stands and stretches, his polo shirt hiking up over his round belly. He pulls is back down and flops on a large overstuffed sofa. Angie takes my hand like she's afraid I'll disappear again and drags me over to an armchair facing the sofa. We squeeze into it together, which is surprisingly comfortable thanks to Angie's elfin proportions.

"Has everyone learned their lines?" Mustapha asks, but I'm the only one he's looking at.

"It's a stupid script," I say. Angie makes a small disapproving noise, but I ignore her. "It wasn't fair of you to write a script when I was absent."

"Well," says Mustapha, a teasing grin on his face as he walks over to the sofa and flops down next to Ali, "you weren't technically absent. You were skipping class."

"That's beside the point," I snap.

"No, that *is* the point when it affects our grade." Faarooq sits up, folding his long legs in front of him like a spider.

"Maybe we should write a new script," says Ali, glancing at Angie for approval.

Mustapha looks from Ali to Angie and back again before he gives me a small wink. I'm pretty sure my heart stops for several seconds.

"We're not starting all over," says Faarooq, glaring at me.

I drag my eyes away from Mustapha to glare back at him.

"What's the script about?" asks Angie.

"A racist American girl," Faarooq says with a smirk.

"How many times do I have to tell you I am not American?" I don't bother correcting the racist dig.

"Well, it's not about you, is it?" says Faarooq.

"Yeah, right." I begin chewing the cuticle on my index finger.

"Did you guys have any other ideas?" Angie asks in a conciliatory voice.

"I had one," says Ali. "This Pakistani guy is in love with this American. Sorry, Emma, I mean Canadian."

Does this have to be the one time he gets that detail right?

"That sounds like fun," enthuses Angie, and Ali gives her such a love-struck look I feel sorry for him. She is so out of his league.

"So they have to get permission from his mother and maiden aunt," he continues boldly, ignoring the huffing coming from Faarooq's direction.

"What a great idea," Angie exclaims, ignoring the huffing coming from my direction. I've changed my mind on Ali's chances, though; these two are made for each other.

"We've already decided on our script," insists Faarooq.

"I don't know," says Mustapha. "I think Ali's idea sounds like fun."

There's a tense silence as Mustapha and Faarooq look at each other.

Faarooq looks away first. "Fine," he says.

The next two hours pass quickly as we pull together a story. It turns out Ali has hidden talents, and he immediately takes charge, scripting and directing at the same time. Angie is an enthusiastic audience, laughing and making suggestions from the sidelines, and even Faarooq cracks a smile when Ali, playing the mother, quizzes me on my cooking skills. Turns out, cinnamon toast and cheese omelets don't cut it in the local marriage market.

Mustapha seems intent on being the perfect host. I have to keep reminding myself he has a girlfriend and a scary mother, but resisting Mustapha when he's trying to be charming is as easy as outrunning a tsunami. Every smile is like another wave crashing over me. In the end, all I can do is tread water and hope I don't get smacked in the head with a fish. So it's totally understandable that I don't recognize a trap when our practice is winding down and he asks if we'd all like to see his horses.

It takes us a good ten minutes, at a brisk pace, to cross the grounds to the stables. We pass at least five groundskeepers, but all I'm thinking about is why Mustapha's family doesn't buy a freaking golf cart. I'm all for the beauty of nature, but I'm about to pass out from heatstroke by the time we get to the paddock, which explains why his second maneuver slides right by me. I don't even notice that Faarooq's dropped way behind, and Ali has taken Angie in hand and disappeared into the barn. I'm too busy resting against a fence pole, trying not to vomit.

"You're still adjusting to the heat," says Mustapha.

Several smart retorts flit through my head, but at this moment, I just can't be bothered. I rest as my breath returns to normal.

"I wanted to talk to you alone," he says.

It's like a douse of cold water. I straighten and look around for Angie. Even Faarooq might be welcome, but I see we are indeed alone. *Uh-oh.* I look at him warily.

"We got off to a bad start," he continues.

He waits for me to say something, but I don't know where he's going with this and I'm not going to risk saying something that could make things worse.

"What you said the other day about being new and feeling that Aisha didn't like you . . ."

I have to literally bite my tongue to refrain from interjecting my own thoughts on Aisha.

"I hadn't seen it from your point of view." He pauses again and looks at me with his forest green eyes.

It occurs to me that if I let myself get drawn into those eyes, I sure as hell better leave a trail of bread crumbs.

"So I want to start over."

It takes me a moment to realize he's holding out his hand and a good half a minute more before I figure out what he wants me to do with it. I take it and watch his earnest expression transform into a smile that lights a fire behind those eyes. I realize there's no longer any point in worrying where I'm headed, because I'm already lost. And I smile back.

CHAPTER 21

Against my advice, Mom spent most of yesterday tracking down the girl who didn't invite Mandy to her party and the rest figuring out how to inveigle an invitation. Today, Sunday, is the big day, and Mandy got her invite this morning. But instead of putting on her best jeans and skipping out the door, present in hand and a grateful smile on her face, she stomped up to her room and locked herself in. Mom has spent a good twenty minutes threatening and cajoling from the outside, but like I've said many times, Mandy is one stubborn little kid and no way was that door going to open.

What Mom doesn't understand is that her good intentions decimated Mandy's already shaky social status. Mandy might have an invitation, but if she went to that party, she'd better be a piñata because she'd be in for one hell of a beating. Far better to wait till Monday when at least lessons would provide an occasional distraction from the shunning, gossiping, and name-calling.

I listen to Mom go on at Mandy until I can't listen anymore, then I come out of my room and tell Mom the way it is. I try to be respectful. She was only trying to help, but it doesn't change the fact that all the kids from Mandy's class, not to mention the kids from our own compound, have made my sister their new target. It would have been so much better if Mandy had stayed invisible.

"She can't go to the party, Mom," I explain in my most reasonable voice. "The other kids are angry at her for squealing to you. They don't want her there." We stand outside Mandy's door, and I'm sure she's listening to every word. I just hope she appreciates me taking a bullet for her because Mom is really annoyed.

"But she was invited," Mom insists, willfully missing the point. "I spoke to Kirsty's mother. She said it was just an oversight and Mandy was welcome to come."

"Kirsty's mother might have said yes," I say calmly, "but trust me, she is not invited. She'd be as welcome at that party as a toothache."

"Stop being so dramatic," Mom groans, annoyed. She raps again on Mandy's door. "The point is, she can't hide in her room every time she has a problem. That's no way to get through life."

"She's not trying to get through life, Mom, just the weekend, and – with any luck – third grade." I'm leaning against the wall opposite Mandy's room, wanting nothing more than to slink back to my own.

"I didn't raise you children to run from your problems." Mom's voice rises passionately.

I want to say that she didn't raise us at all and that the one who did hightailed it out of our lives the first time he got a better offer, but even I know that wouldn't help Mandy's case, so I appeal to Mom's sympathy.

"They're calling her Moandy," I whisper. It's not like Mandy doesn't know what they're calling her, but she doesn't have to hear it from me.

"I don't get it." Mom's brow furrows.

"You know. Mandy, *Moan*-dy."

"She should just ignore them," Mom reasons. "After all, it's such a silly name."

I sigh. "They're little kids, Mom. The rapier wit doesn't kick in till puberty."

"Who's calling her Moandy?" she asks, slumping against Mandy's door, the weight of the problem finally sinking in.

"Everyone, the kids on the compound. *Every*one."

"The other *Canadian* kids are calling her that?" She sounds so shocked I have to smile. Sometimes you've got to wonder how parents get through the day without feeling disappointed a million times.

"Yeah, Mom." I shake my head like it amazes me too. "I know it's hard to believe, but even our fellow countrymen aren't being nice."

Mom's face suddenly clears like a storm passing. "Well, that's easy to solve. I'll speak to their fathers. I work with all of them. Heck, I'm the boss of half of them."

"Oh my God!" I finally lose my patience. "Mom! *Hamsters* learn faster than you. Little painted turtles that end up under radiators every time they escape learn faster than you."

"There's no need to be rude, Emma," says Mom, scowling. She straightens and throws up her arms in exasperation. "So, what am I supposed to do?" she demands. But it's one of those rhetorical questions that precedes a parental rant, so I keep quiet and wait it out. "Am I supposed to just sit back and let her be miserable?" she shouts. "Am I *not* supposed to do anything to help her? Should I simply let her give up without a fight and hide in her room all day?"

She pauses, but I give it a second to see if she's finished. When she doesn't continue, I state the obvious. "That's exactly what you're supposed to do, Mom. Just let her work it out in her own time. Leave it alone."

"Well, I can certainly see I'm not needed here," Mom huffs, but I have a horrible feeling she's close to tears.

I try to think of something to make her feel better. "You gave it your best shot, Mom. You were just trying to help."

"But I never get it right, do I?" She is definitely close to crying, and I know I should just leave it alone.

"Maybe if you just listened to us more —"

"That's it, isn't it?" Tears stream down her face, and she doesn't even bother to hide them. "You'll never forgive me. Everything I do just makes things worse. Well, you know what? Since you're so smart, you can babysit." She pushes past me, furiously wiping her eyes as she storms down the hall to her bedroom.

"I'm going to the office," she shouts before slamming her bedroom door.

I go into my own room and listen to her banging around for several minutes as she gathers up work to take with her. She doesn't speak to either of us; she just slams out of the house like she can't get away fast enough.

I lie on my bed and stare at the ceiling, wondering what Vince is up to. He left early to hang out with Michelle at the other compound. He spends most of his time over there. I can't say I blame him.

It's hard to believe that Sundays used to be my favorite day of the week. It was Zenny's day off, so Dad and I always cooked breakfast. We'd make way too much food – pancakes, fresh fruit, sausages, eggs. Mom would bitch about the mess in the kitchen, but she would sit down and eat with us. It was the only day of the week we ate together like a family. Mom was never home early enough on workdays, and she often had some crisis come up on the weekends. But Sunday mornings were sacrosanct. We sat around the table, sometimes for hours. There was talking and laughter. *When did it change?*

When did the conversations become stiff with undercurrents of anger and blame? When did Mom's absences become more frequent and Zenny start making excuses to stick around? When did the seed of Dad's unhappiness germinate and grow so large it blocked out everything we were? And how could I not have seen it?

How could I have thought Zenny was warm and kind and not suspect for one minute that she was stealing my father?

The phone rings. I retrieve the handset from the hallway and carry it into my room, grateful for the distraction. I flop back down on my bed.

"What're you up to?" Angie's voice lifts my spirits. "Can you come over or are you still grounded?"

"Actually, I'm not sure if I'm grounded, but I can't leave the house anyway. I'm babysitting."

"Bring Mandy. She can hang with my little sisters."

"Thanks, but I don't think I can get her out of her room." My attention is caught by a flash of green on the balcony. I sit up.

"Oh, it's like that, is it? Don't worry. I'll be right over."

She hangs up before I can respond, so I stand up and walk over to the sliding glass door that leads out to the balcony. The balcony runs the length of the second floor, and a lime-green mustached parakeet is perched on the railing. I'm enchanted. I've lived in Asia for seven years, but not until Pakistan did I ever see parrots in the wild. I slowly back away from the glass and out of the room so I don't frighten it, and I walk down the hall to Mandy's door. I lean in and listen, but there's no sound.

"Mandy," I call softly. "There's the cutest little parakeet out on the balcony."

"I don't care." Her voice is hoarse, like she's been crying.

"I'm going to get some food for it. What do think he might eat?"

"Go away."

"Come on, Mandy. You know you're better with animals than I am." This is a total lie. Mandy's hyper. She terrifies anything small and annoys the hell out of anything too big to get out of her way.

"He might like toast," she says and pauses for a minute. "With cinnamon."

"What a great idea." I hope she can't tell I'm smiling. "Since I'm making it anyway, could I make you some as well?"

There's a deep sigh on the other side of the door and another long pause. "Okay," she says finally.

By the time Angie arrives, Mandy and I are sitting at the kitchen table eating cinnamon toast with milky tea. The parrot is long gone.

"Mandy, how are you, sweetie?" Angie gives my sister a big hug before she comes over and hugs me. Strangely, it feels like the most natural thing in the world.

"Do you want some toast?" I ask, getting up to pop some more bread in the toaster. It's nice sitting in the kitchen. It's a small narrow room, more a service kitchen than a regular eat-in kitchen, but it's still more homey than the dining room where we normally eat. It's weird that I never feel comfortable being in here when Guul's working, since I used to spend hours with Zenny in our Manila kitchen.

"So, what are we going to do today?" Angie asks, looking from Mandy to me.

"You guys don't have to babysit me," says Mandy. "I just want to go back to my room."

"You can't do that," exclaims Angie. "We have big plans, right, Emma?"

"Sure," I say, though I can't think of a single thing that would take the sting out of being Moandy-Mandy.

"Do you want to come over to my house?" asks Angie. "My sisters are dying to meet you."

"No," says Mandy forcefully, licking cinnamon sugar off her fingers. "I just want to stay home."

"All right," says Angie, undaunted. "We could play a game. What games do you like?"

"I don't feel like playing," says Mandy quietly. "I just want to be by myself." She stands up and starts to head out of the room. I barely resist the urge to tackle her, I'm that desperate not to let her sink back into her own misery. I can't explain it. I didn't used to give Mandy's happiness much thought. But happiness didn't used to be such a rare commodity that I had to think about ways to capture and preserve it.

"Secret City!" I shout. It comes into my head like a flash, and I can't believe I didn't think of it before.

"What?" says Angie, a small perplexed smile on her face.

But Mandy doesn't say anything at all. She just stops in the doorway and turns to look at me, her eyes shining. We hold each other's gaze, and so many memories pass between us it's like we're beating with one heart.

"Secret City," she breathes.

And though Angie doesn't understand, she hears the wonder and excitement in my sister's voice and leaps to her feet. "Secret City it is, then!" she crows, gleefully clapping her hands.

Families that move a lot, like us, can't always have traditions like normal people. Favorite places, rituals, activities, and even trusted friends are left behind each time we move. We can't put up the Christmas tree in the same corner or hang stockings over the same fireplace. Chances are, there won't be a fireplace and there may not be Christmas trees. But that only makes the traditions we *can* maintain all the more precious.

Dad built our first Secret City. I was only three, but I remember it. For rotational kids, it's an idea that's so obvious you wonder why everyone doesn't think of it yet so inspired it takes on mythic proportions. We create a city with the one thing we can be sure will follow us to every new home: hundreds of sturdy empty packing boxes in all shapes and sizes.

In Nairobi, we created a rabbit warren of two- and three-storey ramshackle homes ambling throughout our yard. We were smaller then and light enough to sit on the top floors, and we spent days out there, insisting Asabe, the nanny, bring our meals out on a tray. In Thailand, we filled the living room. Our cardboard homes sprouted turrets and elaborate casement windows as we took over the design work from Dad and became more adept at cutting and building. In Manila, we started in Mandy and my shared bedroom, building walls and roofs over our beds, adding curtained windows, and we traveled by tunnel through the bathroom that connected to Vince's room, where he'd built an elaborate fort, complete with tinfoil moats and plastic crocodiles.

It's been three years since we built our last Secret City. It was always our first activity after the movers left. It kept us occupied in the first few weeks, helping us over the transition. Suddenly I remember something else. I remember how neighborhood kids flocked to it. A lot of our earliest friendships were Secret City inductees.

"You realize," I say to Mandy, "not just anyone can play in your Secret City. It has to be a really special friend, someone you can count on." And a smile passes between us as we start building our most tantalizing Secret City yet, with Angie as our first recruit.

CHAPTER 22

"For the last time, he is *not* in love with me!" I glare at Angie and tear off another piece of naan, ready to throw it at her if she says one more word about my now-legendary conversation with Mustapha over the weekend.

She grins and uses her own naan to mop up the last of her *daal*.

It's only Monday lunch, but word has already gotten around our little group that Mustapha and I have agreed to be friends. Only, every time Angie says *friends*, she insists on sketching quotation marks in the air.

"Right," she says. "I keep forgetting you're just friends." There go the hands, and another piece of naan soars across the table, hitting her squarely in the forehead. Leela retrieves it from where it's landed on the floor and adds it to the growing pile in front of her.

"You really must stop teasing her," scolds Leela, though she's obviously struggling to put on a stern face. "She's wasting food and she's not eating again."

"You should have seen them when we came out of the barn, though," says Angie. "They were holding hands. If we hadn't interrupted, they would have been kissing for sure."

"It's about time," interjects Jazzy.

"We were shaking hands, not holding them." I tear off another projectile. "I think you're just trying to distract us from the fact that you and Ali disappeared into the barn all by yourselves. What was that about?"

"That's a good point," says Tahira primly. "It was very wicked of you to leave Emma alone and even worse to go into the barn alone with a boy. Did you even think of your reputation?"

"Of course she thought of it," crows Jazzy. "She thought, 'I'm sixteen! Screw the virgin rep, it's time to get laid!'"

"Jazzy, keep your voice down!" hiss Leela and Tahira almost in unison.

"I'm not denying anything," says Angie. "Ali's a cutie."

"Of course," says Tahira. "But you would not have sex with him!" It's not clear whether this is a statement or an order.

"The point is, I admit I'd go out with Ali if he asked me," says Angie.

"You'd go out with anyone if they asked," says Jazzy. "You're just desperate for some action."

"Yeah, and how's it going with Johan?" asks Angie.

"The guy's completely clueless," sighs Jazzy. "I don't think he even realizes I'm flirting with him."

"Maybe you need to work on your game," says Angie.

I'm pleased to see the heat's off me as I shovel a chunk of lamb into my mouth.

"I've got plenty of game," insists Jazzy. "I've got game to spare!"

"Speaking of game . . ."

We all jump as a deep, very male voice breaks into our conversation.

For a group of girls who do little else but talk about boys, you'd think one of us could have noticed when the species was approaching. He stands at the end of our table, grinning mischievously. I gulp, momentarily forgetting I have a huge wad of meat in my mouth, and I start choking. Tahira, who's sitting next to me, pats my back while leaning forward to try to shield my indignity from Mustapha. Leela coos sympathetically and hands across a pile of napkins, which she never seems to be without. Jazzy laughs, earning her a much-deserved jab from Angie, and not one of us has the presence of mind to actually *say* anything.

"Speaking of game," repeats Mustapha when it's obvious we've all been simultaneously struck mute, "we have our first cricket match after school today, and I was wondering if any of you ladies might like to come out and cheer us on."

He's addressing the whole table, but as Tahira moves back so I can have a clear view, I see he's looking directly at me.

"Have you ever watched cricket, Emma?" he asks.

I clear my throat, which is still sore from the whole near-death experience. "No," I croak.

"Well, you should come out. We're playing Pindi International. They're our biggest rivals." He shifts his weight and looks around the table, his smile starting to look a little frozen as we all stare back at him.

He shifts his weight again, and in that instant, I realize Mustapha Khan, school heartthrob, the god-creature, is nervous. My grinchy heart expands two sizes. "I'll try to come," I say, and I'm rewarded with a smile that could make plants grow.

"That's great." He turns away and practically jogs back to his table of mates.

"Okay, that was just pathetic." Jazzy is the first one to speak. "Why would you want to waste your time watching a stupid cricket match? Do you see what I mean about boys being clueless?"

"I believe Johan's on that team," says Leela.

"That's right," agrees Tahira. "Ali is as well."

"It's decided, then," says Angie firmly, getting up and piling her plate and cutlery onto her tray. "We're all staying after school to watch cricket."

"Fine," says Jazzy, picking up her tray and stepping over the bench. "But we are so lame."

The rest of the day passes quickly. Angie finally gives up teasing me about Mustapha when I return every comment with a few of my own about her budding romance with Ali. By three o'clock, we've assembled in the bleachers beside the cricket pitch and are watching the boys take the field. Tahira painstakingly tries to explain the game to me, with frequent corrections from Leela, but I don't really listen to either of them as the match progresses.

It turns out, watching cricket really is a singularly boring experience, but watching Mustapha for a solid ninety minutes is not. He lopes around the field and smashes the ridiculous little ball as gracefully and beautifully as a thoroughbred in action. The only stain on an otherwise perfect afternoon is Aisha, who's found the precise spot in the bleachers where she can glare at me and watch the field at the same time. She's also close enough that her voice carries as she prattles on about her and Mustapha's plans for the future. And I'm sure it was intentional.

Our team wins, and though she's farther from the field than me, Aisha manages to swoop down to Mustapha's side to be the first to congratulate him. In spite of her presence, I follow my friends down and stand by while Angie tells Ali he was the best player, which is a lie, and Jazzy tells Johan he looks hot in cricket whites, which is not.

"What did you think of the game, Emma?" asks Mustapha, apparently unaware of the ice princess shooting death rays from his right flank.

"It wasn't the worst ninety minutes of my life," I say pleasantly.

"Really." He laughs. "So, it was better than what? A trip to the dentist?"

"Sure," I grin. "Or a math exam. It was definitely better than a math exam. Maybe not English, but definitely math." *Are we flirting?*

"I think all this flattery is going to go to my head," he says.

He looks as if he wants to say more, but Aisha reminds him he has an appointment to meet his father, like she's his personal social secretary, and after apologizing for rushing away, he allows her to shepherd him off the field.

"Don't worry," says Angie. Ali has departed with Mustapha, and she's come up beside me to watch them as they disappear in the direction of the car park. "He clearly likes you better. It's just going to take awhile to dig her hooks out of him."

"We're just *friends*, Angie." I turn to look at her and I see the gleam of elfin wisdom. I know I'm not fooling anyone. We may be just friends, but that doesn't stop me from wanting more.

"Give it time," she says.

"Sure. Do want to come over to Secret City today?"

"Can I bring my sisters?"

"Absolutely. But it might be crowded. Every kid on the compound is begging Mandy to let them come over."

"Revenge is sweet." She holds her hand up and we high-five.

"Isn't it?" I say with a grin.

CHAPTER 23

I can't figure out what the noise is when I wake in the middle of the night to a muffled ringing. As my head gradually clears, I roll out of bed and fumble around in the dark, looking for my cell phone.

"Hello," I mumble.

"Emma, it's me Angie. Wake up!"

"What time is it?" I wonder if I've overslept, but I can't see any light from the window.

"Come out on the balcony."

She sounds totally awake. Much *too* awake. I hold my cell phone away from my face to look at the time, accidentally drop it, and have to scrabble through a pile of clothes on the ground to find it. I'm wishing I wasn't so uncomfortable letting The Ghoul into my room. It's true he barely speaks to me and never looks right at me, but maybe that's not enough reason to stop him from tidying my room. It hasn't seen a broom since I got here, and most of my clothes, which I hastily unpacked because we needed the boxes for Secret City, are still in piles on the floor.

"Emma, are you still there? Come outside."

I follow the sound of Angie's voice, triumphantly rescuing my phone from a pile of dirty clothes.

"Ha!" I exclaim.

"What?"

"I found my phone," I mutter, checking the time. "Angie, it's two o'clock!"

"I know. Keep your voice down. You don't want to wake up your family."

"Why are you phoning me at two o'clock?" I try not to sound too indignant.

"I need to talk to you."

"I don't think the guards will let me out of the gate this late."

"I think you can get over the wall."

"What?"

"If you go outside, walk down to the end of the balcony, past your brother's room. There's only a few feet between the end of the balcony and the wall. If you hurl yourself off the balcony and out a bit, I think you'll sail right over."

"Where *are* you?" I walk over to the glass doors that lead out to the balcony and peer into the darkness. But all I can see from here is a small patch of yard.

"Here. Just outside your wall."

I step out on the balcony and, as quietly as possible, hurry down to the end nearest the outside wall. Sure enough, Angie is standing just on the other side.

"What are you doing there?" I hiss.

"I think we've covered this, Emma," she whispers. "Will you jump already?"

"Hang on." I look down at the wicked shards of glass cemented along the top of the wall.

Returning to my room, I hurriedly pull on my jeans and a T-shirt and a sweatshirt over that. If I'm going to land on broken glass, I want some protection. Grabbing my thickest blanket, I head back to the end of the balcony.

"This is totally crazy," I grumble as I throw the blanket over the top of the wall and climb up on the railing. I take a deep breath and climb over. Not letting go of the metal, I slide myself down till I'm hanging from the ledge. My feet dangle just below the top of the wall. Resting one foot gingerly on the blanket-covered shards of glass, I swing the other leg to the outside of the wall and feel Angie's hand just barely reaching my calf.

"I've got you," she lies. "Stop being such a wuss."

"It's a shame about you being unnaturally short," I say.

"Drop. I'll catch you."

If the definition of *catch* is to provide a small bony surface to land on as your face and hands scrape to the point of bleeding down eight feet of cement, then Angie totally comes through on her promise. We lie panting in a tangled heap on the ground while I slowly flex my hands and feet to test for irreparable damage.

"Ow."

"Get off me," she groans.

Slowly we struggle to our feet.

"So, what now?" I ask.

"We're going for a walk. There's a place I want to take you. We'll talk there. The only problem is, we have to get past the front of your compound, so we need to cut through the brush on the far side of the road so your guards don't see us."

"Okay," I say, not sure what the big deal is.

"Watch out for snakes."

"Oh." I remember the huge cobra from my first day of school and shudder.

We walk to the far side of the tennis court, still technically on Canadian property though it's outside the living quarters. Then, hunching low to the ground, we run across the road and leap into the brush. From here I can see the bright lights of our guardhouse. There are two guards on duty, chatting quietly and smoking. Spotlights illuminate a radius of about a hundred feet all around the entry gates, but beyond that, shadows from the huge trees we're now hiding under create a deep and impermeable darkness. We begin moving slowly through the brush directly opposite the gates.

I'm impressed, if completely terrified, to see our guards stop talking and gaze across the road as if they've heard something. I'm fairly certain they can't see us, but it's not a reassuring thought. I've seen the pile of dead cobras and kraits they produce most mornings. They'd like nothing better than a little random target practice. One of the guards comes out of the house and walks to the edge of the light, staring into the darkness. He slings his rifle off his shoulder and holds it in his hands, his finger resting lightly on the trigger. Angie pulls me down to the forest floor, and we sit there for what seems like an eternity. Finally, the guard calls something to the one who remained in the guardhouse, and after a final look in our direction, heads back inside.

We start moving again, keeping low to the ground.

"What is this about, Angie?" I demand as soon as we reach the corner opposite the edge of our compound and are out of earshot.

She turns to me, her eyes glistening in the moonlight. "You need to trust me," she says softly. "It's important."

"We could have been killed back there."

"But we weren't." She attempts a smile, but even in the gloom, I can see it's a struggle. She bites her lip and turns away, heading down one of the roads that leads out of the diplomatic enclave. I watch her, unsure whether to follow. I tense as a nearby bush rustles ominously. I've never been down the road in this direction, and even in daylight, I know it's dangerous to leave the enclave. But surely we'll hit the perimeter wall and have to turn back. It's not fair that she expects me to trust her with no explanation. More troubling than our current life-threatening situation, however, is the realization that I do trust her. I sigh as I hurry to catch up.

There are no more buildings in sight, but the road just keeps going, with forest on one side and low-lying bush on the other. I wonder why we haven't reached the wall and get the sinking feeling we're already outside the enclave. Strangely, I'm enjoying being out in the night air. It's cool, and I don't think I've ever seen so many stars. Every once in a while, we hear noises from the undergrowth. One time a mongoose scurries across our path, but for the most part, the quiet is as complete as the emptiness of the landscape.

"Why haven't we hit a perimeter wall?" I ask, stopping to shake a pebble out of my sandal. "Are we still in the enclave?"

"No." She pauses to wait for me. "We left the enclave ages ago. Everyone thinks we're so well guarded, but there's only a wall on the side that faces the city. From the villages, you can walk right in."

"We're not supposed to leave the enclave, Angie." She knows this as well as I do, though it's obviously too late to worry about that now.

"Live a little," she says lightly. "Sometimes you have to take a few risks."

I try to read her expression in the moonlight, but she quickly looks away. The gesture is so unlike her that my breath catches with a premonition that I may have more to fear from her tonight than anything lurking in the darkness.

We continue on the road, which eventually turns into a dirt path angling up a hillside. The brush gives way to grassland, and I imagine there might be a good view of the enclave in the daylight, though from this angle we can see only distant lights through the curtain of trees. The path is narrow, so Angie leads and I follow, pausing every once in a while to look out at the changing landscape. In the distance are some dim flickering lights.

"What's that up ahead?"

"A village," says Angie. "We won't go into it, but we'll stop just above it."

The path begins to head up more steeply, and we breathe heavily as we climb over ground that is increasingly rutted with rocky outcroppings. I'm watching my feet, trying not to trip, so I don't notice that Angie has stopped until I bump into her. She points ahead to where dozens of huge creatures loom out of the darkness. Sharp tusks jut out from upturned jaws like spears, and hair bristles out of hunched backs.

"Monsters," I whisper, my heart thudding.

"Wild boar," she whispers back.

"They're going to eat us?"

Angie shakes her head.

"They're gentle?" I ask, trying to imagine their toothy jaws spreading into friendly smiles.

"No, they might kill us," she says. "They just won't eat us."

I give her an annoyed look, which is lost on her in the darkness.

"They're territorial," she whispers. "We need to back up. Slowly."

I creep backward several feet and trip, crashing to the ground.

"Slowly and *quietly*," Angie hisses as several of the beasts begin advancing toward us.

Keeping my movements slow so I don't further antagonize them, I rise and decide to face forward this time – even if it means I can't keep an eye on the predators. *What are we doing out here, anyway?*

We descend a ways, then leave the path to walk across the hillside directly parallel to the herd, but below them.

"We can cut back up when we get beyond them," Angie says, her voice still barely above a whisper.

We begin climbing uphill again and have to stop talking because it's much harder going this time. There's no path, and we're ascending more steeply. It seems like we climb for close to an hour before we finally hit the path again and, sometime later, the summit.

"Where are we?" I ask.

"The foothills of the Himalayas," says Angie, and I can hear the satisfaction in her voice. "The view is awesome. I wish you could see it in daylight."

I look down at the clusters of flickering lights. "Are they fires?" I say.

"And lanterns," she replies. "Sometimes, when my life seems too hard or complicated, I come up here and watch the villagers going back and forth, the little kids walking for miles to fetch a bucket of water and carrying it all the way home, kids our age with stacks of firewood on their heads that weigh more than they do. It kind of puts things in perspective."

There's something in her tone that makes my mouth go dry. "Why are we here, Angie?"

"I'm leaving," she says quietly, like she doesn't want to shatter the beauty of the night.

"What do mean, you're leaving?" I try to keep the note of panic out of my voice.

"They bombed two of our embassies in Africa. We just got the news tonight."

"What does that have to do with anything? We're nowhere near Africa."

"They think Islamabad will be the next target."

We're silent for several minutes. I think Angie is giving me time to process, but the truth is, I can't. I don't know if I should be feeling sad that they just suffered massive bombings on another continent. *Did people die? How bad was it?* Maybe I should be worried that they think Islamabad is a target. Their embassy is a stone's throw from my bedroom. It doesn't take a genius to work out those implications. But all I can think about is that's she's leaving. I made the stupid mistake of letting myself care about someone again. After everything I've been through, you'd think I'd have figured it out by now. You can't count on anyone to stick around. All relationships are transient. Only fools let themselves get attached.

"I'm so sorry," she says, and I'm glad it's too dark to see her clearly because I know she's crying.

"It's okay," I say, even though it isn't. But it's not her fault. I sink down to the ground, and when she collapses next to me, I put my arm around her.

"It's not the end of our friendship," she sputters through heaving sobs. "If things calm down, they might send us back. We can stay in touch. E-mail and chat online."

I pat her back and watch the flickering lights in the valley below.

I don't tell her I've given up on long-distance friendships. In fact, after tonight, I may have given up on friendship completely. I don't want this to be any harder for her than it already is, but I can't lie to her either. I know her dad didn't bail on her, but she's a rotational kid, like me. She's been through the grief of losing friends, the agony of starting over. Sooner or later, like me, she's going to realize that relationships always end.

"Nothing lasts forever," I say. "Don't worry about it."

I stop listening as she spends several minutes telling me how often we'll write, what days we'll Skype, how we're going to manage the time difference. Finally, she peters out and looks at me. I haven't shed a tear. She probably thinks I'm in shock, that I can't make sense of this abrupt severing of our bond. But it's the opposite. Deep in my heart, I knew this would happen. It always does, and now that it has, I just want it over quickly. I stand up and start walking.

"Don't be angry, Emma," she calls after me. "Please, don't be angry."

"I'm not angry," I call back, but I don't slow my pace. I hear her footfalls behind me as she runs to catch up.

She makes a few more attempts to get me talking, but I don't respond. Eventually she gives up, and we walk in silence. Pink streaks of light appear on the horizon as the sun begins to rise. We stay on the path this time and pass near the village, skirting a cluster of simple mud houses. Women are already outside starting the cooking fires. A few pause to watch us pass. Children carrying empty buckets and jerricans join the path and descend with us. The braver ones say *salaam,* and we answer politely.

It must be almost time for school when we get to the crossroads at the edge of both our compounds, and I wonder if anyone has noticed I'm missing. I look at Angie. It's the first time I see her face clearly since this long night began. Her eyes are puffy and still brimming with tears, while my own are as dry as the landscape that surrounds us.

"I'll e-mail you," she says.

I nod because I know she will. I don't promise to write her back. I want to thank her for being my friend, but the words stick in my throat, too trivial to express what I feel. She steps forward and hugs me, and I hug her back, fiercely, like I can stop this day from snatching her away. Yet in the end, I pull away first, turn without another word, and run all the way home.

CHAPTER 24

The school is like a refugee camp after a cataclysmic event. Those of us left search for the faces of friends in every cluster of students. More than half the school population, including teachers, is gone. The superintendent is the rare exception, and he waits in the parking lot, greeting kids as they arrive, trying to fool us into thinking it's business as usual.

I've lost the person I least wanted to lose, and I'm grateful to Angie for letting me make that discovery in private. There are many kids in tears as they get the news on arrival. I wonder about Jazzy and look for her when I walk into the upper-school quad.

"What are *you* doing here?"

I'm startled out of my personal misery by an unfriendly voice.

Aisha is standing with her princessy friends, eyeing me like I'm a lower life-form. Of course, all of *them* are present and accounted for.

"Shouldn't you be on a plane by now?" asks Aisha,

walking forward to confront me.

I hate her with a white-hot fury, and I relish the reprieve from sadness as I round on her, fists balled at my sides.

"I refused to leave, Aisha," I sneer. "I just knew you'd be devastated without me."

"Believe me, darling, I would have managed somehow."

"Maybe," I say as if I'm giving it some thought. "But your boyfriend wouldn't."

For a minute, I think she's going to slap me, and I wish she would because I'd be more than ready to hit her back. In the same instant, we both notice Mustapha striding across the courtyard toward us. Aisha takes a step back and turns to him, her face wreathed in a smile.

"Mustapha, look who hasn't been deported yet," she says in a cheery voice, like we've just been exchanging fashion tips.

"Aisha," says Mustapha, smiling indulgently. "No one was deported. They were evacuated."

"Oh, that's right," she exclaims and turns her cold eyes back to me. "They left when they realized they weren't wanted. So, where's your little friend? Angie, wasn't it?"

I don't know if it's hearing her name spoken aloud by this hateful girl or the overwhelming realization that Angie really is gone and that this girl and her friends are whom I'm left with, but I have to get away. Fast.

I do my best not to run as I rush to the nearest girls' washroom. I'm relieved to find it empty and go into a stall and lock the door. Leaning my head on it, I take deep gulping breaths, fighting the nausea that competes with tears busting to get out. The outside door opens. *Damn.*

"Emma, are you in there?"

Mustapha?

"Emma, come out. I want to see you."

This is a girls' bathroom. He can't come in here.

I jump as he raps on the stall door.

"Just come out so I can see you're okay. Then if you want me to leave, I will." His voice is soft and cajoling. *Is there a female on the planet who could resist that voice?*

I come out.

He gives me a searching look, and I don't even realize I'm crying until I feel the hot wetness on my cheeks. He steps forward and pulls me into his arms, and it's exactly where I want to be. I rest my face on his chest and wrap my own arms around him. It's comforting and safe, and then it changes. I don't know how it changes, though I know enough about biology that I could probably work it out, but suddenly we're kissing. Not sweet, friendly kisses either. His tongue is in my mouth and mine is in his, and it's like we're trying to devour each other. It's *so hot*. And for once, I'm not talking about the weather.

He pulls away first, but he holds my head in his hands and looks deeply into my eyes. I can just feel that this is the moment where he'll declare his undying love, and I'm ready to do the same.

"I can't do this," he murmurs.

That wasn't quite the declaration I was expecting. But before I have time to respond, we're kissing again. I'm a little confused now, but it's no less passionate. The bell goes for first class, and with a groan he pulls away again, giving me such an intensely longing look that my entire body trembles. I'm pretty sure there are birds singing just for us and a crescendo of music in the background.

"Emma."

"Yes," I say, and I'm not sure what I'm saying yes to, but at this moment, I can't think of anything I would deny this beautiful boy.

"This can never happen again," he says, and giving me a last longing look, he turns and walks out.

I slump to the ground, and it goes through my mind that I'm sitting on the floor of a public bathroom, which is totally gross, but I can't get up. My heart gradually slows to something approaching normal, but my mind is racing, replaying the last few moments. The heat that suffused my body at Mustapha's touch has left me quivering, but I force myself to my feet, using the stall door for support. I take a long shaky breath and avoid the mirrors as I walk out. I think one look at my puffy, tear-stained face would finish me.

The classrooms are completely empty when I arrive in the upper-school courtyard. I imagine there's a reasonable explanation, but I allow myself a few minutes to fantasize that everyone, particularly Mustapha and the ice princess, has been abducted by aliens and are right at this minute undergoing invasive medical procedures that will leave them emotionally scarred for life. But unfortunately, I remember that my siblings and the few people I do like would also have been abducted, which is a total buzz kill.

When I walk into the middle-school quad and find those classrooms also empty, I figure there must be an assembly. I could go along to the theater. Or not.

CHAPTER 25

Mr. Akbar is standing outside the greenhouse as if
he's been waiting for me.

He holds the door open as we walk into the
building, and I fall in step behind him as we weave
through the maze of greenery to our spot at the back.

"I just put on the water," he says. "You have arrived
at the right time." He settles contentedly into his chair
while I crouch over the brazier and begin adding
spices to the water. I settle on the ground next to it
and breathe in the comforting smell of cinnamon and
cloves.

"My friend left," I say.

"It's hard to say good-bye."

"I'm used to it. I do it a lot." I hear the hardness in
my own voice.

I take the tea from the shelf and shake some into the
kettle, replacing the lid.

"I was stupid to make friends with her in the first
place. I didn't even want to be her friend."

"One who is burned by milk blows even when given buttermilk," says Mr. Akbar gently.

I think about this for a minute. I wonder how old Mr. Akbar is. He looks way too old to be working. Maybe they don't have retirement age here.

"Do you have children?" I ask.

"Nine living, three have passed on."

He doesn't sound sad. *How can he just accept losing a child?* On the other hand, Dad ditched me without a backward glance.

"Do you miss them?"

"My children?"

"Yeah."

"Raawiya, my youngest, was fourteen when she died. She was like you. Always asking questions." He smiles as if the memory pleases him.

"How did she die?"

"The question, I think, is how did she live? And she lived well. She loved and was loved."

I add the milk and watch it bubble before I take the cups off the shelf and pour tea, first for Mr. Akbar and then myself. I take the chair opposite him, and we sip in companionable silence. How different this is from having tea with Mustapha's mother. I'd like to talk about Mustapha, but I don't know what I could say. I don't want Mr. Akbar to stroke out from the shock that I kissed an engaged Muslim boy in the girls' bathroom. I don't want him to think less of me.

"Do you ever wish Raawiya hadn't been born?" I

regret the question immediately. I think he might mistake my meaning, but he looks sympathetic rather than angry.

"You mean because I lost her?"

"Yes." I blow on the tea and don't look at him as I wait for his answer. It's slow in coming, and I hope he's not reliving the pain of losing her. I sneak a furtive glance, but he just seems lost in thought.

"If we never move forward, we can never enjoy Allah's blessings. The world is sorrow but also happiness."

"I'm not sure I can get through this year without her," I blurt. I think this confession surprises me more than Mr. Akbar, though I don't know if I'm more shocked by my own total lameness or the fact that I've admitted it.

There's another long silence as we sip tea, and I look at the flowers around us. The plant nearest Mr. Akbar's bench wasn't blooming last week. Now there are so many tiny blue flowers it's difficult to see the green of the stem and leaves. I wonder that so much can change in a single week.

"It is when we feel ourselves most alone that we discover we are among friends," says Mr. Akbar.

I look at his wizened hands as they wrap round his small cup, and I wish I could just stay in this greenhouse with him for the rest of the year. I'd happily do an independent study in botany. I could learn a lot from him, about making things grow – but he's dead wrong about the friend thing. If I could bring myself to tell him about Mustapha, maybe he'd realize how wrong he was.

"I have to get back to class."

He looks at me for a long minute. "Wait," he says. "I have something for you."

He takes an empty jar from his shelf and heads off into the undergrowth. I follow, curious. We pause at a tap, and he fills the jar half-full before he carries on. Finally, we stop in front of the frilly orange plant.

"You remember its name?" he asks.

"The Red Bird of Paradise."

His face cracks into an enormous, nearly toothless grin. I grin back.

He takes a small worn jackknife from his pocket and flips it open. I notice how gently he holds the plant as he saws off a small branch that holds a single flower. He pops it in the jar and hands it to me.

"Change the water every few days. When the roots get this long," he says, showing me with his fingers, "you can take it out of the water and plant it in a pot. Winter is coming soon, so you want to take care of it inside this year. But in the spring, you can plant it in your garden, and when you leave, you can take it with you. Do you remember what I told you about this plant?"

"That it can grow anywhere."

"That's right. Its flowers look fragile, but its roots grow deep."

"But I won't be able to take it with me. They don't let you take plants through Customs."

"All you need is a seed," he says. "A single seed properly cared for will flourish wherever you plant it."

I take his offering and head out to my first day at my new school without my new friend. I don't have theater class and I don't see Mustapha for the rest of the day, which means he's avoiding me. It's a small school, tiny now, and you don't *not* see someone unless you're trying. I'm relieved and disappointed at the same time.

I eat lunch with Tahira and Leela, who are so overly kind that I almost cry again, but I manage to hold it together. Tahira reminds me I'm still invited to her brother's wedding, which sounds like it's going to be a complicated event stretching over several days. We make plans to go out on the weekend to buy me some "appropriate clothes." I get the impression I'm going to need at least four different shalwar kameezes, and I try to share their enthusiasm for the outing.

Johan seems to be missing Jazzy and invites me to sit with him in math class. It turns out he, Leela, and Tahira are in most of my classes now because sections have been combined due to lack of students and fewer teachers. Some electives have been canceled entirely, and I have a moment of hope when I think maybe there won't be any theater class, but those kinds of things never work out when you want them to.

On the bus ride home, I listen to Mandy chattering happily with the remaining kids about the new structure they're going to add that day to Secret City. She asks me to join in the construction work, but I decline the offer.

Vince is in the back, talking quietly with Michelle. He invites me to go swimming with them after school. It's a pity-invite, but well-intentioned. I turn down their invitation too, though I don't have other plans.

I hold Mr. Akbar's gift in my lap and gently finger the scalloped edge of the petals. It's hard to imagine something so fragile and dainty could have such a determined will to survive. It reminds me of two other lives that have that same determination. I remember how the reality of their burden lightened my own, and I selfishly wonder if it can happen again. Maybe they feel as much like outsiders as I do. Maybe they can teach me how to keep living from one day to the next. Suddenly, I know what I'm going to do when I get home.

CHAPTER 26

I've been sitting in the underbrush just beyond the garbage dump for over two hours. I'm starting to feel
this is a very bad idea. They may be the only people
in my neighborhood more sad and desperate than I am,
but that's hardly the basis for a meaningful friendship.
I don't even know if they'll show up. I rock up on my
heels trying to ease myself into a more comfortable position. This is a waste of time. My butt is sore, the smell
of the trash is giving me a headache, and I just noticed
a freaking-huge spider on a nearby bush. I shift away
from the spider, keeping an eye on it in case it should
suddenly pounce.

I hear the rattle of their bike over the gravel road a
good five minutes before I see them. The girl hops off
the handlebars before the bike has fully stopped and
clambers up the heaping mound of refuse while her
brother props the bike against a tree and unties an
already half-filled bag from the back. I move out from
the bush slowly so as not to startle them. I try to look

casual, but I'm stiff from sitting on the ground, so I stagger the first few steps, which is either a dead giveaway I've been lying in wait or suggests I'm stoned. I'm not sure which they would find more alarming. I give them a toothy smile, but like last time, they respond with unblinking stares.

"*Dost*," I say, pointing to myself like Jane in a *Tarzan* movie. According to my Urdu dictionary, this is the word for *friend*, though from the reaction I'm getting, it would appear I said, "Clear out or I'll call the cops." The boy stands immobilized at the foot of the trash, watching me with the same wary attention I gave the spider. His sister is descending as quickly as safety will allow, given that she could bring the whole foul mountain crashing down on her brother.

"Emma," I say, thumping my chest again.

Still watching me, the boy directs a curt comment to his sister. She looks at me anxiously but stops moving.

"Esfandyar," he says, thumping his own chest. He points at his sister. "Mehri."

I feel like he's handed me a gift, and I get misty-eyed until it occurs to me I hadn't imagined our encounter past this point. I don't know what to do next. *What am I doing here?* It's not as if we're kindred spirits just because I am a friendless loser and they survive on other people's garbage.

But I can't leave.

Slowly, so as not to startle them, I walk over to the garbage dump. I'm gratified to see they don't scuttle away at my approach. Leaning into the trash, I dig out an empty pop bottle. I carry it to their plastic bag and pop it in. I look at them out of the corner of my eye to see if they'll stop me, but they're both still staring at me, transfixed.

"Don't worry," I tell them, even though I know they can't understand. "You're not going to suddenly have a bunch of foreigners competing with you for the best trash." I lean in again and dig out a couple more bottles.

Esfandyar says something to me, which might be "Go away" but could just as easily be "Rock on," so I just smile at him and keep digging. He says something else, which I ignore, but when he grabs my wrist, I have to stop and look at him. He takes the plastic bottle I'm holding and throws it back on the pile. He says something and dramatically shakes his head. Then he picks up a glass bottle and nods.

I grin. I think I may have just failed trash picking 101, but he's taking the time to teach me, so he hasn't totally given up. Mehri has gone back to work at the top of the pile, and with my newfound expertise, Esfandyar and I continue picking away at the bottom. Ten minutes later, their bag is full. I hold the bike steady while Esfandyar ties the bag on the back. Then he holds the bike as Mehri climbs on the handlebars.

"*Shukria*," says Mehri before they ride off. I know this is the word for *thanks*. I also know I should be thanking them, because at this moment, the knot that has twisted my stomach since I arrived in this country feels like it's starting to unravel.

CHAPTER 27

My heart is thumping as I approach the theater. I haven't caught a single glance of Mustapha since The Kiss. I'm actually very impressed with his disappearing act. I was never so invisible when I was trying. I wonder if he's even still here. Maybe he transferred to an all-boys school, somewhere high in the Himalayas where the only eligible females are yaks and mountain goats.

I've rehearsed what I'm going to say to him a hundred times. I really wish Angie were around to run through it with me, though. There's no one left I can talk to. Leela and Tahira are still being especially nice, but they'd write me off as a skank if I told them what I'd done. Kissing is a much bigger deal here, like having sex would be back home.

But maybe I can just put this whole episode behind me. When I see Mustapha, I'm going to be totally cool and nonchalant, like I kiss boys in bathrooms all the time. I take a deep breath before I push open the theater doors, and there he is. I don't mean "there he is down at the front with the class where he's supposed to be." I mean "there he is lurking in the gloom at the back of the theater, inches from my face."

"Oh crap," I say.

Okay, that wasn't exactly the opening line I'd rehearsed.

"It's lovely to see you too, Emma."

"What are you doing here?" I squeak.

Still not the nonchalant attitude I was going for.

"I take theater class at this time. You might recall we rehearsed a play together."

Obviously, he's practiced this whole first meeting with a little more success than me, but it's not too late to recover.

"You kissed me," I blurt.

Okay, that's it. Kill me. Kill me now.

"Yes," he says. "Sorry about that."

Sorry? Does he mean "sorry, you really suck at kissing"? Or "sorry, my lips fell on you by accident, I thought you were someone else, like my girlfriend"? What the heck does sorry *mean?*

"Listen," he says, sounding totally relaxed and reasonable. "Can we just forget the whole thing? I'd still like to be friends."

Now I'm pissed. That was totally *my* line, almost word for word what I'd practiced back in my bedroom. It's also a total lie. If I'd had the chance to say it, I wouldn't have meant a word of it, but I *so* wanted to be the one to say it.

"Whatever," I say and push past him, walking as fast as dignity allows to the front of the theater.

Ali and Faarooq come over to me immediately, and I prepare myself for another confrontation. I know Faarooq already hates me. I wonder if Mustapha's told him about The Kiss.

"We're very sorry about Angie leaving," says Faarooq sincerely, and he awkwardly pats my arm.

Ali nods miserably, and I realize I'm not the only one who's missing Angie.

"That's right. She's a great girl. We're all going to miss her," says Mustapha, coming up behind me. I feel the hairs on the back of my neck rise.

We don't have time to discuss it further because the teacher calls the class to order and tells us that since a lot of students are missing and some groups will need to recast their skits, we have the rest of the week to practice. I'm not surprised to see it's a different teacher than we had last week. The cherub must have been American. This guy looks like he'd rather be doing anything but teaching theater. He has a pile of papers in front of him that he's clearly planning to grade while he pretends he's giving us more time out of the goodness of his heart.

"We may as well relax," says Mustapha, walking over and plopping down on a chair in the front row.

In my opinion, he's way too relaxed already, but as Faarooq and Ali walk over and sit down on one side of him, leaving the seat on the other side for me, I'm faced with a dilemma. Whatever lingering doubt Mustapha might have that I'm totally freaked about The Kiss would be confirmed if I don't sit next to him. I have to get through the next eighty minutes acting like I don't want to crawl in a hole and die.

I walk over and sit down.

"So, what have you been up to?" he says.

You mean, other than making out with you in the bathroom?

"Not much," I say.

"What did you do yesterday?"

I give him a look, and in spite of the dim lighting, I'm pleased to see him turn slightly crimson.

"After school," he adds hastily.

"I picked through trash."

"Really?" He grins and shifts in his seat so he's angled toward me. "Did you find anything interesting?"

"A few glass bottles," I say stiffly. "They're worth more than the plastic ones."

"Worth more for what?" he asks.

"Money." I assume that's right, though until this moment, I hadn't really thought of that. Maybe they use the bottles for something.

"You're hard up for cash, are you? You should have said. I could spot you a few rupees."

He's laughing now. I crack a small smile and seriously hate myself. To prevent myself from completely falling into some lust haze and climbing into his lap, I decide to tell him about the trash-picking children. I talk about the first time I saw them and how I'm trying to win their trust.

"I wish there was some way I could help them," I finish, and I realize for the first time how much that's true.

"You should talk to Aisha," he says.

I should talk to the ice princess about helping poor kids? It's a jaw-droppingly stupid idea. I turn to him and roll my eyes.

"I'm serious," he says. "Her mother runs Dosti, a volunteer organization that helps the trash-picking kids. *Dosti* means —"

"Friendship," I finish for him.

"Very good. You speak Urdu." He sounds genuinely impressed, and I get a little rush of pleasure, which is so lame, but I'm starting to think he's like my kryptonite. I can't *not* like him.

"A few words," I say truthfully. "So, what does her mother do exactly?"

"I'm not sure, different things. But I know Aisha volunteers at a school for these kids two afternoons a week. You could go with her."

"I could also chew off my own arm, but I don't think I'm going to do that just now. Thanks, anyway."

"You said you wanted to help." He says it like a challenge, and I think it would actually show more willpower to resist him, but the fact is, I'm intrigued — and not just because I want to help these kids. It's also the idea of Aisha doing something that isn't evil. It's like when Darth Vader turns out to be Luke Skywalker's dad. It screws with the balance of the universe, but you have to see it for yourself.

"I'll think about it," I say, and for most of that evening, I do little else.

CHAPTER 28

I'm sitting in a car next to Aisha, and the world has not stopped spinning.

Yet.

I still haven't figured her angle. When Mustapha brought us together yesterday to discuss me going with her to the trash-pickers' school, she was almost pleasant. It's obvious she's taking me only because Mustapha asked her, but strangely that only makes her seem more human. She can't say no to him either.

So here we are in her car on the way to the trash-pickers' neighborhood. Alone. Well, not quite alone. Her driver and a heavily armed bodyguard are sitting in the front seat, and I'm pretty sure neither of them would hesitate to shoot me if I do anything to upset her, like suggest she maybe shouldn't have given me a gold-embroidered shalwar kameez to wear into a neighborhood where the dress is worth more than most people's yearly income. Especially since she insisted I wear it so I *don't* attract attention. Oh, no, I don't stand out at all: blonde hair, blue eyes, and a million-rupee outfit.

Maybe she's trying to get me killed.

"How long have you been volunteering?" I ask politely.

"Since ninth grade. My mother started the organization with some friends about eight years ago. They work mainly with Afghan refugees, but some of the trash-picking kids are poor Christians as well."

The Christian thing doesn't surprise me. We employ a lot of Christians at the embassy for the same reason. It's hard for them to get work in other places.

"There are two children who pick through trash near my house," I say.

"Yes, Mustapha told me."

"Do you think we might see them?"

"Maybe. We can ask about them, if we don't."

We're on the outskirts of town. Though it's a different area than the diplomatic enclave, it's a strange coincidence that both foreigners and refugees live on the margins. I guess they're as unwelcome as we are.

"Do all of the children go to school?" I ask.

"No, most don't. And those who do only come for two hours at the end of their workday. It's as much time as their families can spare them."

We leave the paved road and head down a heavily rutted dirt track. Single-room mud houses hem us in on both sides, and a rivulet of water meanders down the middle. We have to swerve several times to avoid hitting small children scooping the muddy, oil-smeared water into buckets. We jerk to a halt several times as suicidal goats and chickens dart in front of the car. A fine sprinkling of reddish dust coats everything, both living and not.

We pull up outside a single-storey structure that is virtually identical to all the others, but through the open doorway, I notice there are kids inside, sitting on rusted metal chairs. The room is small, about the size of my bedroom, and dark, even though it's still light outside. Aisha waits for the driver to come around and open her door. The bodyguard jumps out first and walks into the classroom, giving it a careful once-over.

As soon as Aisha climbs out of the car, it's like she's a rock star. The kids inside the building spill out to greet her, and more kids materialize from nowhere, crowding her and grabbing her hands. The children are filthy, but she doesn't seem to notice their matted hair and the grubby hands stroking her tunic as if it's a magic cloak. She laughs good-naturedly and speaks to several individually. I wait for the telltale signs that she's only pretending to be human, the curled lip and disdainful stare, but they don't materialize. She might actually care about these kids. They obviously adore her.

I get a lot of shy curious stares, but no one approaches me as we leave the guards outside and go into the makeshift classroom. Children keep piling in, squeezing two and three to a chair, and several settle themselves on the floor. We're full to bursting, and what little light was filtering in through two small glassless windows is almost entirely blocked by the faces of the children who peer through them.

Aisha gives a direction to one of the older boys and he disappears briefly, returning with a kerosene lantern that he loops over a hook on the wall. There's a single small table at the front of the room. Aisha puts her water bottle on it, picks up a long thin stick, and taps it lightly in her hand as she speaks.

She gives me a long introduction in Urdu, which inspires several giggles and makes me wonder what she's saying. The only word I understand is my name. When she's finished, the entire group stands up, and Aisha raises her stick like a baton and leads the class in a chorus of "Good afternoon, Miss Emma."

It's totally cute, and I wonder when she had time to teach them that. I say "Good afternoon" back, which sends them into paroxysms of laughter, for some reason. Then a girl around Mandy's age comes forward, takes my hand, and leads me to one of the less broken chairs at the back of the room.

"I can stand," I say to Aisha, who's writing words in chalk on a board at the front. "There aren't enough chairs as it is."

"It's not our culture," she says firmly. "You're a teacher, a guest, and older than them. You sit."

I sit down and attention turns, more or less, back to the board, though I'm clearly a distraction because many of the children cast furtive glances at me as Aisha organizes herself at the front.

"I should have mentioned," she says as an after-thought, "if I tell you to run, you must do it immediately. No questions. And if you hear a bang or gunshots, get down on the floor."

I look at the roomful of shyly curious children and give her a skeptical look.

"We're not in any danger from them," she says. "But there are some who don't like what we're doing here. They don't want us empowering these children. If they learn to read and do basic math, it will be harder for people to cheat them and their families. Not everyone is happy about that. And the ones who don't object to what I'm doing would still want to kill *you*. One less infidel fast-tracks them to heaven."

"Thanks."

"It's not what I believe. Necessarily. But a lot of people do." She turns back to the board. She's certainly bossy enough to be a teacher.

She says something about Mehri and Esfandyar at the start of the lesson, and I'm grateful she hasn't forgotten them. From the children's excited reaction, I can tell they know who they are, and one of the window children is dispatched presumably to look for them.

Aisha's teaching style is straight out of a textbook on how *not* to teach, complete with the stick that she raps on the table if any child falls behind in the unison repetition of letters and sounds. I can't figure out why one of them doesn't snatch the stick out of her hand and crack her over the head with it. By the end of an hour, I'm sitting on my own hands so I don't do it. When she walks to the back of the room and hands it to me, I wonder if she's read my mind.

"Math," she says. "Your turn. They know their numbers to fifty and can do double-digit addition and single-digit subtraction. Begin where you like."

I take the stick and walk with it to the front of the room. Brandishing it above my head, I watch thirty or more sets of eyes grow huge before I toss the stick out the open doorway. There's a heartbeat of silence as fear turns to confusion, and then a brave boy at the back snickers and the whole class erupts into laughter.

"Get up," I tell them.

Of course, they don't understand, so I have to mime what I want them to do, pretending to sit on an imaginary chair and suddenly leaping to my feet. This causes more hilarity, but none of them moves. I have to do it three times before someone at the back catches on. However, when I walk out of the classroom, they all follow without being asked. By this point, they don't want to miss what I'm going to do next.

Aisha's guard begins to object, but Aisha holds up her hand to silence him. So it's one crazy white girl, a breathtakingly beautiful Pakistani princess, an ever-growing number of mud-spattered children, several stray dogs, a bodyguard, and a driver who spend the next hour walking through the village adding and subtracting everything from chickens' eggs to cooking pots.

By the time Aisha and I are back in the car, there are so many villagers crowded around us we can only roll forward an inch at a time, much to the grumbling of her driver. Aisha and I are now both rock stars, and we keep waving until I think my hand's going to drop off. We're close to the end of the village when Mehri appears at my window, running alongside the car. I roll it down and put out my hand. Mehri takes it in both of hers, and we grin at each other like long-lost friends. Aisha tells the driver to stop.

Mehri says something, which I don't understand.

Aisha translates. "She says she'll come to your class next time. Her father has never allowed her to go to school before, but Esfandyar has convinced him."

"That's wonderful," I say and give her a big smile so she gets the spirit, if not the words.

"*Dost*," she says, touching her chest.

"Friends," I agree and touch my own.

We clear the town and drive in silence, staring out our windows, each lost in our own thoughts.

"I didn't want to bring you," says Aisha, turning to me. "Mustapha said I really hurt you with that comment about your friend leaving. I only agreed to bring you because he said it would take your mind off her, and I felt I owed you that."

I nod.

"But these children," she says, "their misery isn't here for anyone's distraction."

"I know that."

"Yes," she says. "I realized that tonight. I hope you'll come back. I think we make a good team."

I smile at her and she smiles back.

"You know, you're going to have to lose the stick," I say.

"That's the trouble with you foreigners," she grouses. And for a moment, it's the old Aisha. "You always think you know better." She gives me a reproving look, but even in the dwindling light, I can see the sparkle in her eyes.

CHAPTER 29

I'm not surprised when they send us home early on Friday. After keeping us late last Friday, they probably want to be extra sure we make it home before the post-prayer demonstrations. It's still weird to me that the result of attending a service of worship is to march around chanting death threats to a bunch of people you don't even know. Anyway, last week's evacuation of half the school population has everyone on edge, so it's a relief to leave.

What's surprising is that Mustapha is waiting for me outside my classroom when we get dismissed. He falls in step as I walk to my locker, and my heart starts skipping for joy, even as I firmly remind myself that he's taken.

"How did it go yesterday?" he asks.

"Not bad. It turns out your girlfriend isn't that heinous after all."

"You're too kind. How did she win you over?"

"Haven't you talked to her about this?" I open my

locker and begin piling books into my bag. The amount of homework we have to do at this school is insane.

"Yeah, she said it went well. Actually, I was thinking – since you two are friends now – maybe you'd like to come to my party tomorrow night."

"What party?" I stop loading books and turn to look at him.

He shifts his feet and flushes. "The one you weren't invited to when you thought my girlfriend was heinous."

"Oh, I see." I turn back to my book bag, throwing in the last few items and zipping it shut. "So this is one of those last-minute, bottom-of-the-barrel afterthought invites." I try to keep my voice light, but it hurts that he would have a party and not invite me until I passed the Aisha test.

"Yeah, pretty much." I look up at him and he grins to take the sting out of it. "So, will you come?"

"I don't know." I slam my locker closed and hoist my ridiculously heavy bag over my shoulder. "Is this going to be one of those drinking too much, doing things you won't want to remember in the morning, and vomiting in the rhododendrons kind of party, or is it more of a sitting in your games room watching you boys play Nintendo party?"

"Well, technically, alcohol's illegal in this country. . . ." He slides his hand under the strap of my bag, grazing the bare flesh of my arm, and lifts my bag up, tossing it effortlessly over his own shoulder. "So it's probably more likely to be the Nintendo-type party."

"Well, it does sound really exciting," I say sarcastically, trying to ignore my thumping heart and the flutters in my stomach caused by the nanosecond our skin touched. And now he's carrying my bag. *How romantic is that? Could I be more pathetic?*

"Will your mom be there?" I ask. I start taking slow, deep breaths to try to slow my heart.

"Do you want my mom to be there?" He sounds surprised.

"Not really," I say in a neutral voice. If we're going to get married, I'll have to get used to his mother.

"My parents are in Paris, but my Aunt Faatina will be chaperoning, if that's what you're worried about."

"Yeah, right," I smirk, having found my cool. Deep breathing really *does* work. "I'm a sixteen-year-old North American girl. Making sure we're properly chaperoned at a party really is my top priority."

"So you'll come, then." He looks so hopeful that my heart starts bouncing around again.

"Are Tahira and Leela invited?" I stall as we start walking toward the parking lot.

"Do you want me to invite them?"

"Only if you want *me* to come."

This is so wrong. I'm totally flirting with him. *What is wrong with me?*

"Then they're absolutely invited."

He is totally flirting back.

But he's with Aisha.

"What about Johan?" We've reached my van now,

and I rest my hand on the open door, trying to look casual. Unfortunately, I forgot that metal heats to a zillion degrees in this country, and I quickly drop my charred hand to my side.

"Yeah, he's invited."

"You invited Johan before you invited me?"

Reality check. He invited me only after I made friends with Aisha.

"I'm sorry." His eyes cloud with concern. "Do you want me to un-invite him? I will. Just say the word."

"You're shameless." I laugh, reassured of his undying love. "You can't un-invite people just to get me to come." Except Aisha. He could definitely un-invite Aisha.

Aisha, my new friend.

I am a truly bad person.

"So, you will come?"

"If Leela and Tahira agree and you don't un-invite anyone, I'll come."

He leans forward and I raise my face, certain that this is the moment he'll seal the deal and our lips will meet in hot passion.

He chucks my bag onto the front seat of the van and steps back.

"See you tomorrow morning, then."

"Your party is in the morning?"

"No, but you're going shopping with Tahira and Leela to buy clothes for Tahira's brother's wedding. Faarooq and I are chaperoning."

"*You* are chaperoning *me*," I say in disbelief.

"Not just me," he says defensively. "Faarooq will be there as well. You didn't think you girls could go trailing through markets on your own, did you?" He sounds genuinely incredulous.

"Gee, let me think about that," I snap. "I'm not in elementary school. I'm not brain-dead. So yeah, I did think we could go shopping without seventeen-year-old boys tagging along."

"Well, you can't," he says firmly. "Anything could happen. If Tahira's mother were free, you would go with her, but she isn't, and you can't go on your own."

"You can't tell me what to do," I say heatedly.

He raises one eyebrow and doesn't answer.

Obviously, in this situation, he can tell me what to do.

"Whatever." I heave myself into the van, turning my face away from him.

Only after a few more seconds of fuming do I realize that for the first time in several days, I don't feel like kissing him.

Progress?

"Emma."

I turn to look at him, still standing at the van's open door.

"What?" I snarl, looking down at him from my sparkling new tower of indifference.

"I'm really looking forward to spending the day with you tomorrow," he says, beaming his heartbreaking smile.

And the tower crumbles.

CHAPTER 30

"**Y**ou can't wear that."

Tahira and Leela have both come to the door to get me, and they're united in their horror at my loose-fitting T-shirt and jeans. I already cleared it with my mom, so I don't know what they're going on about. *Do they think I look too slovenly?*

"You need to completely cover your arms," says Tahira.

"And your bottom," says Leela.

"My *bottom?*"

"Definitely," agrees Tahira. "You need a long-sleeved, loose-fitting shirt that covers your bottom and loose pants that don't show off your legs."

"You mean, I need to wear something that looks exactly like a shalwar kameez?" I say, trying hard not to sound irritated, even though I had the same conversation two days ago with Aisha and am getting a little sick of feeling like my body is something to be ashamed of. At least she came prepared with an outfit. I know if Angie were here, she'd make a joke, and the whole thing would seem funny rather than annoying.

"A shalwar kameez would be perfect," gushes Leela. "Do you have one?"

"No," I say. "That's why we're going shopping. Remember?"

"Well, let's go look at what you do have," Leela says soothingly, squeezing past me into the house. "I'm sure you have something suitable."

Fifteen minutes later, we're sitting on my bed, sweating in spite of the AC. Clothes that have been pulled from the closet and drawers lie in scattered heaps around the room.

"You really need some new outfits," says Tahira. "You don't have *anything* appropriate."

"The T-shirt actually was the best thing she has," says Leela, her voice betraying her amazement. "Everything she owns is so . . ." She struggles to find the right word. "Tight."

I sigh and don't bother defending myself. I've never considered myself a slutty dresser. Until now.

Footsteps pound up the stairs, and I have a second to consider that things are about to get a lot more embarrassing before Faarooq and Mustapha burst into the room.

"What's taking you girls so long?" demands Faarooq. "We don't have all day for this, you know. I have to help Mustapha set up for his party."

"She has nothing to wear," says Tahira before I can stop her.

I stand up and move to the doorway, hoping to prevent the boys from entering. I am not going through my wardrobe again with Mustapha.

He looks past me at the chaos of the clothes. "Where's Vince's room?" he asks with an amused expression.

"Down the hall," I say warily. *Is he going to go tell Vince that his sister dresses like a skank?*

Mustapha disappears from the doorway, and I push past Faarooq to follow him down the hall.

"Vince isn't home," I say.

Mustapha knocks lightly on Vince's door, and when there's no reply, he opens it and walks in. I stand in the doorway and keep an eye on him as he goes over to Vince's open closet and begins rifling through his clothes.

"What are you looking for?" I ask.

He doesn't answer as he pulls out several shirts, holds them up, and returns them to the closet. Finally, he pulls out one of Vince's dress shirts, a dark gray, long-sleeved cotton shirt. Mustapha smiles in satisfaction and tosses it to me.

"Try it on," he says.

"I am not wearing Vince's clothes." I glare at him.

"Try it on," he repeats evenly.

I sigh for the second time and shrug into Vince's shirt. It's miles too big. My hands are trapped inches from the end of the sleeves, and the bottom of the shirt brushes the tops of my knees.

"Satisfied?" I ask, starting to take it off.

"Wait." He walks over to me.

Stopping just in front of me, so close I can feel the heat off his body, he begins doing up the buttons. I would object, but my breathing has suddenly kicked into overdrive and I need to concentrate on not hyperventilating. He finishes the buttons and steps back, surveying the effect. I'm pretty certain no part of my figure is discernible. He reaches forward and rolls the cuffs of the sleeves so my hands emerge from the ends. Then he stands back again, and his eyes sweep over me. I'm suddenly glad the shirt is so loose.

"Perfect," he says.

I don't say anything because my breathing is still messed up, and now I'm dealing with a rise in body temperature as well.

We hear the others coming, and I step guiltily into the hallway like we've been doing something we shouldn't.

"Emma, that's perfect," shrieks Leela, grabbing both my hands and spinning me around. "Aren't you clever to think of it."

"Mustapha," I mumble in the same instant I feel him come up behind me, his body giving off little shock waves.

"Can we finally go now?" grumbles Faarooq.

I'm happy for the shift in focus. We head downstairs and pile into Tahira's SUV.

We're going to Rawalpindi, a city just ten miles – but light-years – away from Islamabad. We leave behind the quiet tree-lined roads and enter into a chaotic jumble of narrow streets. Beggars lurch haphazardly out of alleys and bang on the car windows, trying to get our attention. Slow-moving rickshaws and throngs of people and livestock prevent us from moving quickly. When the driver eventually stops, I'm not sure if we've arrived somewhere or he's just given up.

"We should have covered her head," says Mustapha. He and Faarooq are sitting in the seats behind us. I turn round to see Mustapha looking worriedly out the window.

"You're right. We should have thought of it," says Leela. "Did you have a shawl, Emma?"

"I'm not a ninety-year-old grandma, Leela," I snap and immediately feel badly.

"Maybe we could make that our first purchase," says Leela to Mustapha.

"All right," he agrees, "but we should leave her in the car until we get her head covered."

"Are you kidding me?" I crane round in my seat to glare at him. "I am *not* staying in the car."

Faarooq and Mustapha exchange looks.

"Maybe we should try a less crowded bazaar," says Faarooq.

"But this is where the best shalwar kameezes are," objects Tahira.

"And there's the most amazing fabric shop," says Leela with authority. "I buy *all* of my fabric here, and they have a wonderful tailor."

"Look," I say. "I don't need to make a fashion statement. Can we just get this done?"

"Exactly," says Faarooq, and for a minute it feels like we're on the same team, until he continues. "She doesn't need to look *nice*. She just needs to look *appropriate*."

Leela, Tahira, and I all object at the same time. Leela's aghast at the suggestion that looking good isn't the most important goal of the outing. Tahira feels her brother has suggested I'm less than beautiful and demands an apology. And I've had enough of being told there's something wrong with the way I dress.

I roll down the window and crane my head out, wondering how hard it would be to get a cab home from here. I did see some yellow cabs at the edge of the market when we drove in, but there are none nearby, and my view down the street is blocked by half a dozen beggars and twice that many children crowding around me, demanding money and treats. I really want Angie. I want to be with someone who gets me and doesn't think I'm *inappropriate*.

Mustapha leans forward and yanks me back in as Faarooq sticks his hand through the seats and puts the window up.

"All right," says Mustapha, "we've come this far. We're all going to get out of the car, go to Leela's fabric shop, Tahira's ready-made shop, and then we're going home. And we will all stay together and try not to draw attention to ourselves." He looks at me when he says this, as if it's my fault.

The driver gets out of the car first and opens the door for us, scrutinizing the crowd like a Secret Service agent on a presidential detail. The boys scramble out and stand on either side of me, which is totally embarrassing, and I'm sure it just makes me more gawk-worthy.

Leela leads the way into the crowded market, which consists of narrow cement walkways between open one-room shops. I'm determined to get this outing over with as quickly as possible and get home, but as we leave daylight behind and make our way into the dimly lit interior of the market building, my irritation dissolves under the onslaught of sights and smells. The pungent spices are intoxicating, and I can't stop myself from pausing to examine the variety of things on sale. Pickled snakes, monkey skulls, perfect replicas of Viking helmets, stone-inlaid jewelry and weapons, intricate handmade carpets and wall hangings, vibrant painted crockery, and fabric – woven, embroidered, batik – the choice is overwhelming. I keep stopping in awe, picking things up and gushing worse than Leela ever does. I am expecting Mustapha or Faarooq to scold me for slowing us down, but when I look up, eyes shining, to show Mustapha an ornate silver pendant with a leaping lion carved into the inlaid blue stone, he's smiling.

"It's the same blue as your eyes," he says.

"Can you ask the trader how much?"

Mustapha starts a long conversation with the merchant, which I'm sure goes far beyond the price of the pendant, but finally he turns to me and tells me he can't get him down below fifty dollars because it's an antique. I put it back, smothering my disappointment, and as we carry on, I'm quickly swept up in the excitement of just looking at things. Finally we come to Tahira's shop, and I have to admit even the shalwar kameezes are beautiful. Despite Leela's advice, I choose a plain one, in earth tones, that I could wear in the squatters' settlement without feeling totally overdressed.

When we move on to the fabric shop, though, I allow Leela to talk me into two amazing lengths of cloth, one silken batik and another embroidered with tiny geometric diamonds. I even pick up a gorgeous woven shawl, despite my insistence I don't really need one. By the time we're ready to leave, more than two hours have passed, and I can't stop smiling. I know it's just retail therapy, but it's like the weight of the last few days has eased and it's such a relief to have fun for once.

We're almost back at the entrance to the market when we hear the shouting. At first, I don't pay attention. It's just one more voice among many, but when I notice people stop what they're doing to stare behind me and then at me, I realize something's up. I slow down, but Mustapha puts his hand on my elbow and firmly propels me forward. I look back and see an old man behind us, coming closer. He looks enraged, and I wonder what we've done to upset him. It's only then that I realize he's shouting in English and I can actually understand what he's saying. Faarooq nudges me to keep moving.

"Infidel!" shouts the man. "You will burn in the fires of hell for eternity. Who are you who touch the unbeliever? Strike her down, or you will bear her fate."

My heart bangs in my chest like a caged bird trying to escape. It's impossible for the five of us to make quick progress through the crowded market. I think he's gaining on us. *Does he have a weapon?*

"Keep moving," hisses Mustapha. "Don't look back."

"Your skin will burn black and melt from your bones!"

I stumble and fall against a counter of embroidered cushions, knocking several to the ground. Looking up at the trader who's come around to the front to retrieve them, I try to apologize, but he stares right through me.

Mustapha helps me to my feet. I pause for a moment to catch my breath, but all I can see in every direction are dark unreadable eyes. *How many of them want me dead?*

Tahira and Leela walk just ahead of us. Tahira looks back at her brother, her face fearful.

"Keep walking," says Faarooq.

"You will drink the oozing pus of your own flesh!"

"Be quiet, old man!" shouts Mustapha.

"Leave it, Mustapha," says Faarooq.

"You dare to say no? You want to share the fiery grave of the harlot?"

"You don't know anything." Mustapha stops and faces the man. We all stop, and I'm torn between horror, admiration, and a desperate fear he will be hurt.

Faarooq grabs his arm and pulls at him. "You're putting the girls in danger," he says urgently. "We have to get them out of here."

"Your blood will spill at the gates of hell as your body is lashed with iron rods!"

The blood is pounding in my head. I feel like I'm going to throw up. I'm no longer holding my packages. I don't know where I dropped them.

Mustapha turns away from the man and again urges us on. Finally, we emerge into the sunlight, and the car is where we left it. The driver rushes forward as he registers the distress on our faces. Faarooq says something to him in Urdu, and the driver runs to the car, throwing open the door so we can scramble inside. Only when he's closed it again do I discover Mustapha is nowhere in sight.

"Mustapha," I gasp.

"Don't worry," says Faarooq. "Someone called a policeman. Mustapha stayed back to give a statement." Faarooq says something to the driver and we pull away from the curb, inching forward through the crowd that has doubled since we arrived this morning.

"What are you doing?" I shriek. "We have to wait for Mustapha. We can't leave him!"

"I have to get you girls to safety," says Faarooq calmly, turning around in his seat to talk to me. "He's meeting us at a nearby hotel. Don't worry. It's very nice, and air-conditioned."

"I couldn't care less about the hotel," I scream,

unable to rein in my rising hysteria. "Stop this car at once!"

Faarooq furrows his brow and looks at Leela for support.

"I think we should wait for him," she says.

"Fine," he sighs. He speaks to the driver, and we roll to a stop.

"Are you going to go back for him or am I?" I ask. I really hope he volunteers because just the thought of going back makes me feel queasy again.

"He won't be happy I left you alone," Faarooq grumbles. But after giving more instructions to the driver, he hops out of the car and disappears into the market.

It's twenty minutes later before they reappear. By then, the three of us have imagined about a zillion different ways they could have been murdered. I'm weak with relief to see Mustapha unharmed and can't stop grinning at him, which, given the ordeal we've all just been through, seems a little crazy. He gives me a surprised look but then smiles back.

CHAPTER 31

"So, you were really worried about me?"

We're sitting around a table in perhaps the most beautiful hotel I have ever seen, quite likely the most beautiful in the world. Admittedly, I'm still freaked from our morning, and – after the crowded, garbage-strewn streets of Pindi – my standards may be lower than normal, but from the multicolored, mosaic marble floors to the stained glass skylight a hundred feet up, this place is amazing. And it's so effectively air-conditioned I pull my new shawl out of one of my shopping bags, which Mustapha had the whole time, and drape it over my head and shoulders.

Faarooq nods approvingly.

"I wasn't worried about you, Mustapha." I flush, fidgeting with the fringe on my shawl. "I was more concerned for that poor, delusional old man."

"Really?" he says with a smirk. "You were concerned about the man who wanted to see you burn in hell?"

"Well, you're a big strong boy," I say, dabbing my lips with my napkin. *Did I mention I'm drinking a real cappuccino?* Not the best cappuccino I've ever had, but at this moment, it tastes pretty damn fine. "You were hardly in danger from a little old man. Or were you?"

"You think I'm *buff*," he grins.

"I didn't say *that*."

"You did, actually," says Leela, looking searchingly from me to Mustapha and back again.

Tahira nods, and she and Leela exchange glances.

"Emma, they'll be bringing our food soon," says Leela. "We should wash our hands." She pushes out of her chair and stands up. She takes my hand, which is one cultural weirdness I'm still getting used to. Leela and Tahira often hold hands or link arms. Strangely, you never see a boy and a girl doing that in this country, so maybe when two girls do it – or two guys, for that matter, because they do it too – it's just a natural need for connection. However, at this moment, it feels more controlling than chummy.

I'm surprised when Tahira doesn't join us in the bathroom, and I get the distinct feeling that she and Leela have some kind of agenda.

"What's up between you and Mustapha?" she demands as soon as the door closes.

I stop halfway to a stall and turn to face her. "Nothing." I honestly don't know the answer myself, and she's not the person I want to explore this with, though with Angie I would.

"I know you think Angie was the only one who cared about you," she begins, like she's just read my thoughts.

"I don't think that," I cut in.

"Tahira and I care about you just as much. You should trust us. You should trust me." She takes my hand again and squeezes it. "I might be able to help."

"He kissed me," I blurt, realizing only after I've said it how much I wanted to tell someone.

"No!" gasps Leela.

I immediately regret telling her. "It's no big deal," I say hurriedly.

"Of course it's a big deal," she says, her face creased in concern, like I've just confided to being molested.

"Really, it's not. It was just a kiss."

"There is no such thing as *just a kiss*," she says, though I'd be willing to bet she's never been kissed. "And besides," she goes on, "he's engaged."

I was wondering when that would come up. Now that it has, I'm curious to see how long it will take her to realize what a slut I am.

"He had no business taking advantage of you like that. He needs to be spoken to. I'm tempted to do it myself, but I think it's better if Tahira talks to Faarooq. Faarooq will straighten him out."

"No," I say hastily. *God no.*

"It didn't mean anything," I say, trying to sound

reasonable. "And he already apologized."

"But he's *still* flirting with you," she points out.

I don't answer, and her comment hangs in the air.

"I'll talk to him myself," I say finally. "Tonight, at his party."

Leela doesn't look convinced. I brush past her and head for the door anyway. She reluctantly follows me, but I stop short just outside. Mustapha is lurking in the hallway. I really hope he didn't overhear our conversation. Leela comes out and gives Mustapha a decidedly unfriendly look.

"What are you doing here?" she asks.

"Just washing my hands," he says smoothly.

She hesitates, perhaps because Mustapha makes no move to return to the dining room.

"We'll be right along," he says. "I just need a word with Emma."

"I think you've had enough time alone with Emma, don't you?"

I take a step back as the two square off. Mustapha is as awkward, casting nervous looks in my direction, as Leela is resolute, her cold gaze never shifting from his face. I watch with morbid fascination as his color rises and wonder where the superficial girl with the bangle-mania disappeared to.

I suspect Mustapha's wondering the same thing.

"I just need a minute," he says, attempting a winsome smile. But his voice cracks, spoiling the effect.

"It's okay, Leela," I say.

She continues to glower at Mustapha. "One minute," she says. "I'm timing you." She stalks past him into the dining room.

"I better make this fast," he says with a smile, relaxed now that she's gone. I wish he wasn't so sure of himself, but I can't stop myself from smiling back, even though it'd be so much cooler to be all reserved and standoffish. Leela's totally right. He's practically engaged, and he *said* we were just friends.

"I know that man in the market scared you, even if you'll never admit it." He pauses, like he thinks maybe I will admit it. But he had it right the first time.

"I didn't want *that* to be the thing you remember from this day because it's not the thing I'll remember. I really enjoyed being with you, Emma." He stops again.

I don't know what to say. The guy in the market was scary, but the rest of the day was good – great, actually. I enjoyed every minute with Mustapha, but he still has a girlfriend.

"So I got you something else to remember this day by." He reaches into his pocket and pulls out a small felt-covered box. He opens it, and there resting on a white silk cushion is my leaping lion pendant. My heart leaps right along with it. I look up at the beautiful boy who is now holding the pendant, so gently, just like he's holding my heart, and when he leans in to fasten it around my neck, my only thought is that I wish he would kiss me.

"I think our time must be up," he says.

"Maybe," I say, but what I think is, maybe our time is just beginning.

CHAPTER 32

"Mom will be home any second."

I glare at my brother as he stands with one foot out the open doorway.

"She isn't here now." I state the obvious. "I have somewhere to go tonight too, you know." I don't add that although he always has somewhere to go, this is unprecedented for me. It would be a good argument, but even I'm not that pathetic.

"You have the driver," he says in such a reasonable voice it makes me burn. "And you're going to a party. It's not like it's a big deal if you're a few minutes late. If I don't go now, I'll miss my ride. Michelle's friends are already waiting for me at her place. They'll leave without me."

"So what? Then you and Michelle can stay home and make out. It's what you're going to do anyway. What difference does it make where you do it?"

He exhales loudly. "You're not being fair, Emma. I agreed to you having the driver tonight. You can go the minute Mom gets here. Text her again. I'm sure she's on her way."

"I texted her five minutes ago. She was waiting on a call from Canada but said I should go ahead."

"Well, there you go. Why are we arguing?"

"Because she said *I* should go ahead, not *you*!"

"She'll be here soon, and I can't wait. I'm already late." He slips out, shutting the door firmly behind him. I consider running after him and dragging him back in, but the fact is, one of us has to wait, and I do have the driver. But I am worried about how long Mom's phone call will take. I slump into the living room and flick on the TV.

An hour later, I've put on my makeup and tried on a dozen or so combinations of shirts and jeans, with Mandy belligerently ensconced on my bed, watching. By nine o'clock, when I realize I'm going to have to put her to bed, I'm in no mood for the bedtime-story argument.

I sit on the edge of my bed and try Mom again on her cell phone. Mandy is wriggling into the pink T-shirt I just gave her. It was a gift from Mom on my last birthday, but I've never worn it. I don't wear pink, which Mom would know if she'd ever once gone shopping with me. My call goes straight to voice mail and I close the phone, not bothering to add another message to the four I've already left.

"You need to get your pj's on," I say, helping Mandy pull the tee down over her belly.

"It's too tight," she says with disappointment. She walks to my full-length mirror and examines herself in profile.

"You're not quite the right shape yet," I say, coming to stand behind her. "Let me help you get it off."

"I wish I looked like you. It's not fair."

"You do look like me," I say truthfully. "You just haven't stretched up yet."

"I'm fat." Her jutting lower lip is starting to quiver.

"You have baby fat. It's not the same thing."

"Mom was supposed to put me to bed tonight. She promised."

"I know." I stand behind her with my hands on her shoulders, and we look at our reflections.

A tear spills down her cheek, and I hate my mother with a blazing passion. It's not enough that she's ruining my plans. Mandy's just a little kid. Mandy still thinks parents can be counted on. I look at my watch for the sixth time in as many minutes. Right now, I should be in the car almost at Mustapha's. Ahmed, our driver, has been waiting downstairs for more than an hour.

"I want to stay up till she gets home," Mandy sniffles.

"She'll be angry if she gets home and you're not in bed," I say, though truthfully I don't think she'll care if Mandy's still up or not. My real concern is that I've spent the last hour doing a little more than getting dressed and feeling sorry for myself. I've come up with a backup plan. I feel guilty just thinking about it, but I can't get it out of my head.

If I can get Mandy to sleep, I'm going to the party. I'm going to leave her alone in the house and just go. I tell myself that nothing bad can happen. The embassy guards are just outside. If she's asleep, she can't get into any trouble – and Mandy's a sound sleeper. She never wakes in the night, and I'll be gone only a few hours.

Mom said I could go to this party and I *need* to go. I have to talk to Mustapha about our relationship. Mom's the one who gave The Ghoul the night off. She promised she'd be home in plenty of time, and now she's not even picking up her phone. I tell myself all this and still I know it's wrong to leave my sister. I cross my arms as a shiver runs through me. *Is it fear or anticipation?*

"Will you finish Angie's story?" She struggles out of the shirt as I lift from the bottom.

"I can't," I say. It's hard to believe it was only ten days ago that Angie started that story, less than a week since she left.

"Angie said you would finish it."

"Angie said a lot of things."

Like that she would be a friend I could count on. I blink back tears, fold the shirt, and walk over to my dresser, laying it down on the top. Mandy follows me and picks it up, taking it with her as she walks to the door. She stops in the doorway and looks back at me. Her eyes glisten.

"She said sisters always come through in the end."

"I'll read you a story," I say.

"Forget it." Mandy turns and walks out.

Her footsteps recede down the hall, and as I sink down on my bed, I hear her go into the bathroom and brush her teeth. As usual, she doesn't shut the door, so I have to listen to her pee. She leaves the bathroom, forgetting to flush or wash her hands. It's all so ordinary, but I feel this great chasm has opened between us. Maybe it's just the guilt over the betrayal I'm planning, or my inability to provide sisterly guidance by finishing a story about the nature of boys, but I feel there is nothing in me that can give her comfort at this moment. When I finally get up and go into her room, she has turned off her own light and is under the covers.

"Mandy," I whisper.

She doesn't answer. I cross the darkened room and stop next to her bed. Her eyes are closed and her breathing is deep and even, but I'm almost sure she's just pretending to be asleep.

"Mandy," I say again in a slightly louder voice.

Still she doesn't stir.

"I'm sorry," I say. "For everything."

Her breathing doesn't falter. *Are people really that still when they're sleeping?* I lean over and switch on her night-light, then pick up the pink T-shirt she's dropped on the floor, fold it, and put it in her dresser drawer. Going over to the AC, I try to check the temperature, but can't make out the numbers in the dark. I look back at my sleeping sister one last time before leaving the room, careful to leave the door just slightly ajar, the way she likes it.

I hesitate at the top of the stairs, and for a moment, I think I'll do the right thing and stay home. But Mustapha's gift is around my neck, and I feel the weight of it like his touch. Before I can change my mind, I sprint down the stairs and out the door. Ahmed is standing in the carport and doesn't look surprised to see me climb into the car. He listens politely as I explain where he should drop me and that I'll call him when I want him to come back. He must know that my mom isn't home yet, as he's the one who has to pick her up. Maybe he thinks Guul's still here. It's probably more than he can imagine that I would leave Mandy alone in the house. He doesn't say anything as we pull out of the driveway. When we stop at the gates, I wait nervously for an objection from one of the guards. They keep track of our movements. Surely they know there is no one left in the house with my sister, but they wave us through and go back to smoking their bidis.

As we cruise down the road and are waved through the next gate that lets us out of the diplomatic enclave, I take a deep breath, but I don't know if it's one of relief or anxiety.

CHAPTER 33

The vast lawn of Mustapha's compound glitters with a zillion fairy lights. Chairs and round tables are set up randomly in the grassy area between his house and the swimming pool. A long banquet table, heaving under plates of food, is at one end, and what looks like a dance floor has been constructed at the other. Dozens of teenagers are milling about, talking or sitting at tables eating. There's no sign of any adult chaperones. I scan the crowd for someone I know, and it feels like the first day of school all over again. For a moment, I think Angie might magically materialize at my side, but instead it's Leela who gets up from one of the tables and comes over.

"We thought you weren't coming." She links her arm through mine and leads me back to where she was sitting. "Tahira has to be home at ten, and I'm staying over at her house, so we both have to leave soon. It's been no fun anyway. All of Tira's brothers are here," she continues, lowering her voice as we near the table, "and they won't let poor Tira out of their sight."

"Look who's finally arrived," says Leela brightly as Faarooq stands up to fetch another chair so I can join them. There's half a dozen kids at the table I don't recognize, but I know who Tahira's brothers are without being told. They surround her like fortress walls.

Tahira looks pathetically thrilled to see me and orders Faarooq to put my chair next to hers, which forces one of her scowling brothers to shift. I plop down next to her and surreptitiously look around for Mustapha.

"There's a dance floor," whispers Tahira in a voice that lets me know this is somewhat scandalous, which I suppose explains why no one's dancing. "There's alcohol too," she confides.

"Really? Where?" I match her disapproving tone so she doesn't know how much I'd like to get totally wasted right now.

"The bar is inside," she says suspiciously.

Perhaps I'm not quite the actress I think I am.

"Do you know where Mustapha is?" I ask.

"I think he's inside as well," she says even more suspiciously.

Booze and Boy in one location. I definitely know where I need to be. Now I just have to extricate myself from my righteous companions. But I need to sound cool and casual.

"I need to go to the bathroom," I say and jump up, knocking over my chair.

Okay, not as cool as I was hoping for, but the bathroom excuse was inspired.

"I'll go with you," says Leela.

Damn.

"Me too," says Tahira.

Are you kidding me?

"You can go when you get home, Tahira. We're leaving soon," says one of her brothers.

I feel a sudden rush of warmth for this overbearing, brutish boy.

Leela stands up with the gracefulness that eluded me earlier and pulls Tahira to her feet. "We need to go before we get in the car," she says. The air becomes thick with barely concealed dislike as all three brothers eye Leela and exchange glances among themselves.

Leela stands her ground and raises a heavily bangled arm to adjust the drape of Tahira's dupatta in a proprietary way.

Tahira's oldest brother gets to his feet. "I'll walk you over," he says. "I should say good-bye to Mustapha."

Leela links one arm through mine and the other through Tahira's and hustles us off, leaving the brother to trail after us. When we get to the house, Leela actually does head for the bathroom, and since it was my idea, I have to go along. All three of us go in together, which Tahira's brother seems to think is totally normal, and he mumbles something about going to look for Mustapha.

The bathroom is almost as large as my bedroom, with

a full-size vanity, an upholstered bench, a double sink carved from gleaming marble, and a sparkling toilet and bidet.

"Sit down," Leela says to me, pointing to the vanity bench. But because it's the only nice place to sit and I'm the only one in jeans, I hop up on the wide marble counter next to the sink.

Leela orders Tahira to the bench, and taking a large wad of toilet paper to protect her hands, she puts down the toilet cover. She damps a second wad to wipe it and a third to dry it. After thoroughly washing her hands, she perches on the edge.

I chew on a nail. I have a pretty good idea what's coming. I don't think Leela knows exactly what happened between Mustapha and me this morning – even after she specifically told me to end it – but she can't have missed our outrageous flirting through lunch and on the car ride home.

"We thought you might need some help talking to Mustapha," begins Leela.

"No," I say, biting down hard on a cuticle. "I've got it covered."

"You really like him, don't you?"

"Yeah." It crosses my mind to lie, but I just watched her take down Tahira's three brothers without breaking a sweat. She's my new hero, and I'm a little scared of her.

"Then you should declare yourself," she says.

I drop my hand from my mouth and stare.

"He and Aisha haven't had the *Mangni* yet – that's the formal engagement ceremony – so technically he can still get out of it. Isn't that right, Tira?"

"His parents made a commitment," Tahira says, choosing her words carefully. "Not honoring that commitment is a very big decision."

"But he could do it?" Leela persists.

"He could," says Tahira. "He should still have his parents' permission –"

"But there would be no shame," Leela interrupts.

"What about Aisha?" asks Tahira.

Leela makes a sweeping motion with her hand at the mention of Aisha. "What about her? She's never given you a moment's thought, Tira. She's a spoiled snob."

"We just have different friends," says Tahira, though we all know Tahira's neither pretty nor stuck-up enough to fit in with Aisha's crowd.

"Tira, you can't say a bad thing about anyone, can you?" says Leela affectionately.

"Aisha isn't so bad," I say, shifting uncomfortably on the cold marble. Whatever Leela thinks, I can't pretend Aisha deserves to have me wreck her life.

"The point is, if you and Mustapha love each other, it's not fair to anyone, even Aisha, to pretend you don't," insists Leela. "Would you want to marry someone who was in love with someone else?"

She has a point. Maybe I'm rescuing Aisha from making a bad marriage. But if that's true, I'd have to believe Zenny rescued Mom from a bad marriage too. I hop down from the counter and check my makeup in the mirror over the sink. I don't want to think about this anymore. I turn back to them and lean on the counter, my arms crossed over my chest.

"Some families do allow love matches," Tahira concedes.

Tahira's brow is ridged with worry, but Leela's eyes shine triumphantly. She stands up, crosses the room, and hugs me. It's an Angie move, and it immediately makes me tear up. I close my eyes for a moment and try to pretend it is Angie, but Leela smells of jasmine, which Angie never did, and Leela is about a foot taller. *Well, who isn't?*

"You go after what you want," Leela whispers. "Don't let anyone stop you."

But what do I want? I wonder, as we leave the bathroom together. Tahira's brother is standing vigil outside the door. *Has he been there the whole time?*

"They really need to find a hobby," says Leela under her breath as she looks at him irritably, but Tahira just smiles as if she's genuinely happy to see her brother.

It takes all kinds.

I say my good-byes because they're heading home, then go in search of Mustapha.

CHAPTER 34

I try the games room first because it seems the most likely hangout. Ali lounges on the floor exactly where he was last weekend, and I'm pretty sure he's playing the same game. I don't know the boy he's playing with, but Johan is half-reclined on the couch behind them, watching. He looks up cheerfully when I walk in and raises an almost empty bottle of some amber liquid, whisky or something like it. I'm not an authority on alcohol.

Johan gets unsteadily to his feet and weaves over to me.

"Can I offer you a drink?" he asks. He sounds surprisingly articulate for someone who's obviously had too many himself.

"Sure," I say, taking the bottle. "Are there glasses?"

"Glasses?" His brow furrows exactly as it does when he's called on in math.

"Maybe in the dining room? Do you know where that is?"

"Certainly," says Johan, pointing vaguely in the direction of the ceiling, which seems an unlikely spot, but as he staggers to the door, I figure I may as well follow.

He crosses the hall to the huge double doors that I know lead to the dead-animal room. I try to warn him, but he's already pushed them open and stumbled through. I really don't want to go in there, but he's too drunk to leave on his own. I look down the hall in both directions, hoping Mustapha will suddenly materialize, but he's nowhere in sight. After a moment's hesitation, I join Johan and the animals.

The room is in almost total darkness, the only light coming from the hallway and filtering in through tall windows along one wall. In this half-light, the room is even more sinister than last week. Shining eyes peer out from the shadows, and I think I see movement behind the ottoman where I remember a forlorn herd of mouse deer.

"Shhh," says Johan, putting his finger to his lips. He tiptoes past me toward the hallway. I think he's going to make a break for it, and I'm right behind him. No way am I staying in this room alone to get attacked by a herd of zombie mouse deer, but Johan closes the huge doors and we're left in the silver glimmer of moonlight.

"Are you crazy?" I hiss as the zombie mouse deer shift restlessly in the corner. I keep them in my peripheral vision as I scowl at Johan.

"Do you like me?" he asks, leaning – or, to be more

accurate, falling back – on the closed doors.

"At this moment," I snap, "I'd have to say no. Now move so we can get out of here."

"I like you," he slurs.

Oh my God. I'm trapped in a dead-animal room with zombie mouse deer and a crazy Swedish boy. *Where the heck is Mustapha?*

"Can I kiss you?"

Jazzy was right. This boy really is dense.

"Johan," I say as sternly as I can under the unblinking stare of dozens of eyes. "You're wasted. Now step aside and let me out of here."

"Jazzy left," he says. And as if that single statement releases the last bit of resolve holding him up, he slumps down to the floor, his head flopping back against the door. His eyes shine with tears in the eerie nightglow.

"Oh, Johan," I sigh. I walk over to him and slide down beside him, taking one of his hands.

"I was going to ask her out, you know?" His disembodied voice echoes in the darkness. "I've been wanting to for over a year, but you don't just ask a girl like Jazzy out. Did you know she has thirteen piercings?"

"Thirteen, huh?"

"And three tattoos."

"Wow."

"She's like an Amazon or something. Nothing scares her. So different from me. But I had this whole plan worked out."

I'm really afraid he's going to start crying.

"Tell me about it," I say, and the mouse deer, from their resting place behind the ottoman, lean in to listen.

"I was going to ask her to this party. Tonight was going to be our first date."

How long was this party planned before I was invited? I really *was* an afterthought.

"Do you think she would have said yes?" he asks, his voice cracking.

I smile into the darkness, and the mouse deer smile back.

"I think she would have," I say.

We sit quietly, hand in hand, side by side, and when Johan's head slides sideways, settling on my shoulder, I don't ask him to move. Gradually his breathing slows and deepens, and I realize he's fallen asleep or passed out. Whichever it is, he's going to have a wicked headache in the morning, but the heartache will be worse. It's that thought that has me still sitting there thirty minutes later, when Mustapha finally shows up.

I blink as the harsh overhead light fills the room. Mustapha glares at me, his hand still on the light switch.

"Am I interrupting something?" he demands.

By now, Johan's whole body has slid into my lap, and I imagine we probably look like a romantic couple, like Romeo and Juliet after she downed the poison and before he offed himself. And I can understand how Romeo thought she was really dead and not just sleeping because Johan's a total deadweight on my legs. I've lost all feeling below the hips, and I'm in no mood for a jealous scene.

"Help me get him to a couch," I order.

I'm starting to worry about how long I've been here. My confidence that Mandy won't wake up and I can slip back home undetected is disintegrating with each passing minute.

Mustapha crosses the room and heaves Johan off me a little more roughly than necessary, but I'm so grateful to be freed that I don't comment. He half-carries, half-drags him to the sofa in the middle of the room and drops him down, arranging his legs and putting a pillow under his head.

"What's going on here?" he asks, turning to look at me struggle to stand up on tingly legs. He doesn't offer to help.

"That's exactly what I'd like to know," I snap. "Do you even have a right to ask me that?"

"What are you talking about?"

"What exactly is going on between you and me?"

He blinks. I can almost see the anger seep out of him as he contemplates my question. Coming over to where I'm now leaning on the doors, he reaches out and lifts a strand of my hair, curling it round his fingers. It looks blonder, paler, against his skin.

"I don't know," he says, letting the strand drop. "There is something between us. Every time I'm near you, I want to touch you."

"Do you love Aisha?"

It's a coward's question. What I really want to ask is if he loves me.

"I've known Aisha all my life." He runs a hand over his eyes. "She's smart and beautiful. And she's kind, though you may not have seen that. She'll make a good mother. A good wife."

"But do you love her?" I search his eyes, trying to read the answer.

"You're different from anyone I've known." I don't know if he's deliberately changing the subject or just following the course of his own reasoning. "I never know what you're going to do next. You're . . . " he hesitates, "so unexpected."

It's not the answer I want, but somehow we're kissing and I'm not certain he's the one who started it.

We jump apart when his landline rings.

"It's after eleven," says Mustapha. "Who would call this late?"

We both look at the phone as the ringing persists, but he makes no move to answer. Finally, it stops and he reaches for me again.

"Wait." I press my hands against his chest and take deep, slow breaths, trying to clear my head. *Is this really what I want – sneaking around, jumping every time the phone rings, stealing someone else's boyfriend?*

The phone starts ringing again. Johan shifts around on the couch and groggily opens one squinty eye.

"I'm going to puke," he says. And in that same instant, the door behind me bursts open and Aisha rushes into the room, followed by a smaller-than-usual entourage of girls, and Ali.

Aisha stops just inside the door, and whatever announcement she was about to make dies on her lips as she looks at Mustapha and me, no longer entwined but only inches apart.

Ali waits a beat to see if she's going to say anything before he blurts out the news that has brought them racing to find us.

"There's rioting in the town," he says, looking from Mustapha to me. "And bombing. We can't get any news on TV, but we shouldn't panic. It may not be that bad." He looks directly at me, his eyes soft with concern, and I wonder why.

Then, all at once, I know.

CHAPTER 35

I try phoning Mandy on the landline, but no one picks up. I let it ring and ring as tears stream down my face, and my heart threatens to burst from my chest. Even Mandy can't sleep through a bomb blast. *Why doesn't she pick up?*

I try Mom's and Vince's cell phones, even though Ali tells me that cell phone coverage has been shut down. It's a security measure to make it harder for the rioters to communicate as they rip through the streets, leaving burned-out vehicles, looted shops, and dead bodies in their wake. Ali doesn't know if rioters have made it inside the diplomatic enclave, but someone did. A truck filled with explosives blasted into the wall of the American embassy, right next to our home. There's no news yet on the injured and dead.

How could I have left her alone? The selfishness of it seems unbelievable, like the actions of someone else, someone I don't even know. I have to go to her. As I sit on the sofa next to Johan, inches from his puke, all

I can think about is that somehow I must get to my sister.

A cup of tea materializes from nowhere. A servant mops round my feet, and I gag as a wave of nausea makes vomit rise in my own throat. Aisha sits on the edge of the sofa, rubbing my back.

I need to get out of here.

Ali and Mustapha talk in hushed tones. Television service has been cut. News is sketchy and unreliable. They say the rioting is the biggest concern. *If the bomb killed people, they're already dead, too late to save, but how many more will die in the riots?*

I take a sip of tea and my stomach recoils again. I stand up on wobbly legs and fall back down, putting my head between my knees. Aisha holds back my hair, obviously thinking I'm going to throw up. She croons meaningless words of comfort.

I stand up again, sway unsteadily, but manage to keep my footing as I slowly advance toward the door. Mustapha is immediately at my side, taking my arm. Aisha takes the other.

"Do you need to use the washroom?" she asks gently.

"No." I take another shaky step, but now they are not so much supporting me as holding me back.

"Where are you going?" asks Mustapha. Based on the tone of his voice, he knows the answer. "There's rioting in the streets," he says, as if I've been deaf to every word they've been saying rather than feeling each of them pierce my flesh like nails.

"I have to go home," I say. But I stop walking because he holds my arm and has frozen at my side.

"Let go." There's a strength in my voice that's unfamiliar.

"I can't let you go. There's nothing you can do. I'm sure your family is safe. Your mother will take care of things."

"My mother is not home," I say, looking into his eyes and wondering if he can see in my own the enormity of what I've done to my sister.

"It's just Vince and your sister?" he asks, surprised.

"Not Vince."

"Well, your servants, then," says Aisha, trying to sound confident, but I can hear the doubt creeping into her voice. "They'll make sure nothing happens to your sister."

"No servants." I look at her directly so she cannot mistake my meaning.

"You left your sister alone?" It comes out as a whisper but reverberates off the walls as all eyes turn to me, accusing.

"I left her alone," I confirm. "Now I have to go back to her."

"It's too dangerous," says Mustapha, making one last effort to be the voice of reason, but his tone is pleading. I've already won.

"You can't stop me." I look up at him, and I almost feel sorry for him as he struggles between doing what he thinks is right and what he knows is inevitable.

"I'll drive you," he says.

"No." Aisha and I speak as one voice.

"You can't get there on foot, and I can't send you with a driver. I'm not putting a servant into danger." Now that the decision has been made, his voice is determined, fearless, and all at once, I have a vision of the man he will one day become. No matter what else happens tonight, I wasn't wrong to love this boy.

"Then I'm going too," says Aisha, and we both whip round to stare at her.

"No," says Mustapha. "I can't let you do that, Aisha."

"And I can't sit at home while you go out and risk your life, Mustapha."

I step away from her as she moves between him and the door and seems to rise up to his height.

"Well, you're going to have to, because you can't come," he asserts, also seeming to grow to his god-creature proportions. "I won't allow it, and you know your father and mine would never forgive me if I let you put yourself in danger."

"*My* father has never said no to me," she scoffs. "And as for your father, if I'm going to live in this house, he will have to get used to my nature."

If I wasn't so desperate to get going, I would almost enjoy this battle. Aisha is every bit the haughty princess I've always known her to be, and I've never liked her more.

"Mustapha," I say urgently. "We don't have time for

this. Aisha is too bossy to take orders from anyone, not even you, so deal with it. No offense, Aisha."

"None taken," she says, still glowering fiercely at Mustapha.

She takes my arm and together we hurry from the house with Mustapha trailing in our wake. We head across the lawn toward a massive garage I hadn't noticed before. There are only a few teenagers left sitting at tables. I wonder if most have gone home, or if they're inside trying to get some news. We walk past several servants, who greet Mustapha in subdued tones.

Walking into the garage, I'm amazed at the fleet of vehicles to choose from. There are two uniformed servants, obviously drivers, sitting at a desk just inside the doors. Mustapha has a brief discussion with them in Urdu. There's obviously some disagreement about him taking a car out alone, and I wonder if they fear for his safety or their jobs. Finally, one of them takes a set of keys off a hook next to the desk and reluctantly hands it over.

We walk over to a black midsize SUV with tinted windows.

"It's bulletproof," says Mustapha, no doubt trying to be reassuring, though until he says it, I hadn't even considered getting shot at.

Aisha climbs into the front next to Mustapha, and I get in the back, happy to have the feeling of being alone. I couldn't bear the effort of making conversation right now. I run through all the ways I'm going to be a better sister if I can only get home to Mandy and find her unharmed. I try to quell images of what might happen to her at the hands of angry rioters.

Mustapha has another discussion with the guards at the gate. It goes on for so long I start wondering whether I could scale the perimeter wall. Mustapha finally raises his voice and the discussion is finished.

The gates open, and as we turn onto the quiet jacaranda-lined street, I marvel at the deceptive peacefulness of this beautiful moonlit evening.

CHAPTER 36

The streets are deserted as we drive down the wide boulevard that crosses the city from Mustapha's neighborhood to the diplomatic enclave. He takes a different route than my driver. It's more direct, and I wonder if he's unaccustomed to keeping a low profile or just sacrificing caution to speed. I feel exposed on the empty streets, but at the same time, there's a sense of safety in the wide open spaces. We'd be able to see people coming from a distance, though I'm not sure what we'd do about it. We pass through several red lights, barely slowing down, and although we hear sirens in the distance, there are no police waiting to pounce on us for traffic violations. They have bigger problems tonight.

A shadow lurches out from behind a tree, and Mustapha screeches on the brakes as Aisha gasps. We all sigh in relief when we realize it's only a calf that's lost its mother in the darkness. We're a long way from the farms on the outskirts of the city, but on a night like tonight, farmers will join the urban poor in the rioting. I don't even want to consider what chaos drove this poor creature so far from home. It stands confused in our headlights. As Mustapha slowly drives around it, we hear shouting and what sounds like gunshots. Mustapha stops the car again and kills the motor as we listen for the direction of the noise.

"I thinking it's coming from down there," says Aisha, gesturing just ahead of us and to the right.

"I don't think so," says Mustapha. "I think they're behind us." He points in the opposite direction.

We listen for several more minutes before the awful reality dawns on us. Mustapha and Aisha are both right.

"We need to get off this road," says Mustapha urgently. "We're too exposed."

"Maybe we could outrun them," I suggest.

"We can't go forward. We'd be driving right into them."

"If we make a right at the next corner, we might be able to get behind them," says Aisha.

"It's our best chance," Mustapha agrees. He starts the motor and we slowly advance.

Aisha leans forward, watching intently out the front windshield for signs of movement. I'm on my knees, looking out the back window. We turn onto a narrow road flanked by small cement-block shops. It's only a block away from the gleaming, high-towered boule-vard, but it's a step back in time. Corrugated iron shutters are pulled across storefronts and secured with padlocked chains. There are no streetlights here and no lights in any windows either. It's as dead as any ghost town. I shudder.

The noise of voices is getting louder, and we can hear the stamping of many feet.

"I think we're driving right into them," murmurs Mustapha.

"But I can still hear them behind us as well." Aisha's voice quavers, and sweat breaks out on my forehead in spite of the car's AC.

Craning to see through the darkness, I spot them the second they come round the corner, hundreds of them, marching forward like an army. The ones at the front pause briefly when they catch sight of us, like they're trying to make sense of what they're looking at. But the seething mass behind presses them onward. They carry weapons, farm tools, thick wood-handled hoes and scythes. All at once, they raise them above their heads and begin to run.

"They're chasing us!" I shriek.

Mustapha doesn't need more information. The car leaps forward and I fall back in my seat. I struggle to put on my seat belt as we take a sharp turn and I'm slammed into a side door. I crawl across the seat, grappling again for the belt, but another turn slams me against the other door and I tumble to the floor.

"Stop!" Aisha screams.

Mustapha brakes instantly. I'm grateful to be on the floor because otherwise I'd be through the front windshield. I climb onto the seat and wish I hadn't. We're surrounded. White-clad Islamists close in on us not more than fifteen feet away in both directions, cutting off any hope of escape.

"Down there." Aisha points down an alley that is surely too narrow for our car and only feet ahead of the approaching army, but Mustapha doesn't hesitate.

Our tires squeal and the car skids, ricocheting off the corner of a storefront as Mustapha takes the turn too fast. He shouts what I think are curse words as the car fishtails. A sickening crunch of metal rings out as we sideswipe another building, but finally he regains control and we roar down the narrow laneway.

"Right!" Aisha shrieks.

Mustapha turns again.

"Stop!"

I've been on the floor since the last turn and decide to stay put this time, but Aisha flings open her door and jumps out.

"We need to hide," she hisses.

I *am* hiding, in a bulletproof car, which seems like a much better idea than whatever she's got planned. I don't move.

My door swings open and Mustapha reaches in, trying to haul me out, perhaps thinking I'm frozen with fear or haven't heard Aisha's insane instruction. I prove harder to haul than expected.

"Aisha, she's stuck," he groans, which is just stupid. I'm holding on to the far door handle with all my might.

He leans in farther and puts his arms completely around my chest and yanks hard. It is *so* not where to grab a girl, and I gasp as I release the handle and let him drag me backward from the car. I land on my butt.

"Quickly," says Aisha, helping me up.

We crouch low, as if it's going to make a difference, and run from the car into a building. Once inside, I realize it's a covered market. There are rows of stalls and shuttered stores in an organized grid. A few bare lightbulbs hang from the ceiling, providing some light.

Mustapha looks back to see if we've been followed. "They're not here yet, but we need to hide. They'll see the car and come looking for us."

"Why are they chasing us?" I ask, but I know the answer. I'm white, an infidel, and female; Aisha and Mustapha are rich and helping me. We're screwed on so many levels.

"Do you think they saw her?" asks Aisha. Perhaps my question has prompted her to reflect on their chances of getting away if they turn me over to the crowd.

"I don't think they could have seen who was in the car," says Mustapha as we walk quickly through the market, looking for a place to hide. "The fact that we're driving such an expensive car would have been enough to anger them."

We've passed numerous closed-up shops, and I'm still trying to figure out what kind of market this is. There isn't the usual smell of rotten vegetables and freshly slaughtered animals that permeates the food markets.

There's no smell of spices either. Finally, we come to a shop that has an open storefront, with several empty tables in the middle and two closed wooden counters along the back.

"We could hide behind those," I say, and we all walk back to check them out.

They're not a great hiding place. We can crouch behind them and not be seen from the front of the shop, but someone would only have to walk to the back and we'd be in plain view. Mustapha crouches down next to one of the counters and lifts the padlock on a sliding wooden door.

"If I got the crowbar from the car, I could get this open," he says.

"Mustapha, you can't," Aisha gasps. "They weren't that far behind us. They could be at the car by now."

"Let's keep looking," I say. "We'll find a better hiding spot."

"We won't," says Mustapha grimly. "This is as good as it gets. I'm going back for the crowbar."

"Even if we get the lock off, they'll see from the outside that it's unlocked," Aisha argues.

"Not if I lock it again after you're inside." He stands up and walks around to the front of the counter.

Aisha shoots me a look.

"What are you saying, Mustapha?" I challenge.

"I have to keep you two safe."

Aisha sinks back against the counter and rests her hand on it for support.

"No," I say. "It's my fault we're in this situation."

"I'm not arguing," says Mustapha. "My decision is final."

He stalks off, but Aisha chases him to the front of the store.

"Please, it's too big a risk," she implores, pulling at his arm.

"Aisha." He stops and turns to her. "The only risk I can't take is losing you." A look passes between them, and Aisha drops her hands. "Hide behind there until I get back." He quickly disappears round the corner.

Aisha stands in the center of the room. I go to her and lead her by the arm to the back. She follows like a sleepwalker, her face twisted with anxiety.

CHAPTER 37

Mustapha's been gone a few minutes when we hear angry shouting nearby. Aisha and I exchange frightened looks. I wish I could understand what they're saying. There are two, maybe three voices, and they're having some kind of argument. For whatever reason, they've stopped just a few feet from where we're hiding.

Our fear turns to horror when we hear a new voice. Mustapha.

Aisha clutches my arm, digging her fingernails painfully into my flesh, and looks at me with huge eyes.

"What are they saying?" I whisper.

"They're asking him what he's doing here, who he's with."

We listen as Mustapha responds to their questions. I don't understand his words, but I hear the desperation in his voice and the increasing anger in theirs.

"He says he's alone," whispers Aisha, "but they don't believe him."

The shouting continues. The fury of the interrogators escalates by the minute, and Mustapha's voice becomes frantic as he tries to make them believe his lies.

Suddenly he's cut off in mid-sentence by a terrible thud, followed by a second thud. I don't have to see to know it's his body hitting the ground.

"We have to help him," I whisper urgently. I try to stand, but Aisha pulls me back.

"If they see you, they'll kill you both," she hisses. She crawls away from me until she's at the far end of the counter, then, taking off her dupatta, which she normally wears around her neck like a scarf, she drapes it over her head, pulling it tight so her hair is completely covered. She looks back at me and gives me a small nod before she stands up and rushes forward.

I lean around the counter for one brief look, and the scene in front of me is both horrific and startling. Mustapha lies on the ground in a pool of his own blood, and Aisha has prostrated herself, forehead pressing against the floor at the feet of three bearded men. I slump back against the counter and close my eyes, but the image of the proud beautiful girl at the feet of men who look no different from the farmers I see along the roadside every day is seared into my memory. As I replay the image, I see that one holds a hoe, dangling at his side, the sharp blade still dripping.

Aisha's voice is one I have never heard from her before, or imagined her capable of. I don't understand her words, but the tone of humility as she pleads for

Mustapha's life transcends language. As she babbles on, I hear an occasional word from the men, angry at first but gradually softening as her hot wet tears weaken the foundations of their hatred.

Finally, I hear footsteps recede and I sneak another look. Aisha is sitting tensely over Mustapha's body, her hand resting lightly on his chest, perhaps reassuring herself he's still breathing. The men are nowhere in sight.

"I think they're gone," she says in a low voice.

Mustapha lets out a feeble groan and his eyes flutter open.

"How did you get rid of them?" I ask, my voice betraying my awe.

"I told them he was my brother," she says, standing up and picking up the crowbar that has been discarded on the ground. She goes behind the counter. "I said he was taking me shopping to buy things for my trousseau. Help me, I need clean towels to stop the bleeding."

I follow her behind the counter, wondering why she would expect to find towels here, but sure enough, when we break the lock and slide open the door, we find neatly piled towels of every size and color.

"This is the towel market," she says, carrying a hand towel back to Mustapha. He's half-risen to a sitting position and I feel a rush of relief. But when I get closer, I see the wound on his head, its edges gaping open to reveal tissue and skull beneath, and I think I might faint. When it occurs to me how much worse it will be for my beautiful little sister if she falls prey to these hate-filled men, the blood pounds in my ears so loud I can barely hear Aisha's terse instructions as she folds the towel and presses it against the wound.

"Hold this," she orders.

I replace her hand on the towel as she takes off her long dupatta and winds it tightly around Mustapha's head to hold the towel in place.

"Good god, Aisha!" he says. "Does it have to be so tight?"

"Don't be a baby," she chides, but her voice shakes with emotion.

"We need to get him to the car. Can you drive?" she asks.

"I have my learner's permit."

"Well, that's more than me, so you'll have to do your best."

We lift Mustapha and, supporting him between us, shuffle him out of the store. He's more wobbly on his feet than I was when I heard of the bombs, and he stumbles and almost falls a few times as we guide him down the dim corridor toward the entrance.

"Just a little farther," Aisha croons.

I'm terrified the men will come back, but whatever Aisha said must have satisfied them because when we emerge from the building, there's no one in sight. But what we do see is almost as frightening: our car a smoldering wreck. Unable to break the bulletproof windows, the rioters must have doused it in kerosene, inside and out, and set it on fire. I want to cry in frustration, but this is no time for tears, and as I look at Aisha, I see she's come to the same conclusion. Her eyes have the hard sharpness of fresh-cut emeralds.

"We need to take him back inside," she says. "One of us will have to go for help alone."

"No," croaks Mustapha, but even he knows he's no longer in charge.

We make the slow journey back to the same store and walk Mustapha right to the back, lowering him behind the counter. Aisha pulls out a pile of towels, laying them on the ground as a makeshift bed. Mustapha refuses to lie down, even though it's obvious he's going to pass out before long. Aisha's dupatta is already soaked with his blood.

"I should go," I say. "You should stay with him."

"You don't know your way around town," she argues, but it's halfhearted. We both know it has to be this way. "They'll kill you if you get caught," she says.

"Then I won't get caught," I bluster, turning away so she can't see the fear in my face.

"No one should go," rasps Mustapha, collapsed against the wall, his eyes closed. "We should wait here until morning."

"You need a doctor," I say. "And I still have to get to my sister. I'm just sorry I got you two into this."

"Well, personally, I knew you were trouble the first time I saw you," says Aisha, managing a small smile.

"Right back at you." I try to smile, but it's a shaky effort.

We walk together to the front of the store. As Mustapha croaks out my name from behind the counter, we both stop.

"I'll wait here," says Aisha.

I give her a grateful look before hurrying back to Mustapha's side. He's still slumped against the wall where we left him, but his eyes are open, looking at me intensely.

I kneel in front of him. "You need to lie down," I say, trying to press him down to the nest Aisha made.

"I have to tell you something," he says. He winces as he shifts to a more upright position so he's level with my eyes.

"Tell me later," I say. "I'll be back."

"No," he gasps, but I don't know if it's in pain or with the urgency of what he wants to say. He closes his eyes again, and I wonder if he's passed out.

His breathing is ragged, and I put my hand on his chest, reassured by the steady pulsing.

His eyes snap open and he looks at me with the forest-green depth that only he is capable of.

"I've never felt about anyone the way I feel about you –" he begins.

"Not now," I cut him off.

"I've loved Aisha my whole life," he continues, as if I haven't spoken. "I never questioned whether I wanted to be with her. It's just the way things were. And I was happy."

"Okay. I get it."

"But that day you leaped into my arms . . ."

"I tripped," I say indignantly, and I catch his playful smile before he winces in pain.

"And you looked up." He grimaces with the effort of speaking. "It was like being struck by lightning. The feeling. You can't imagine."

"I think I can." I smile and gently stroke his creased brow, wishing there was some way I could take back the last few hours.

"I think I love you too," he says.

"You know, I'm not into polygamy," I quip, but we look into each other's eyes and a whole lifetime of conversation passes between us. Conversations we will never have. I know what's coming next.

"My life is here," he says. "Aisha is my life. You should know that in case you have to make a choice."

"A choice?"

"Between your own safety or coming back for us."

"I know you belong with her," I say, realizing in that moment that I've always known.

He closes his eyes again, and his breathing gradually slows down. I take him in my arms and gently shift him onto the pile of towels. He groans, but his eyes stay closed.

I kneel beside him, leaning down close to his ear. "I *promise* I will come back, for both of you."

CHAPTER 38

I stand in the cool night air next to the smoking carcass that was our vehicle and try not to think of the rage and hatred that went into slashing the tires, pouring the kerosene, and throwing the matches. The acrid smell of burnt rubber makes my eyes water, and I'm reminded of women I've seen in the past few weeks who've had their faces burnt off by husbands and relatives. *If they can do that to women who share their lives and faith, how much easier will it be for them to set fire to me or Mandy?*

To walk away from the building that suddenly feels like a sanctuary takes all of my willpower. I have only a vague idea of the direction of the diplomatic enclave, and first I must find my way back to the main road. The sound of sirens carries through the stillness, but it's a distant call, and for that I'm grateful. I have no more desire to confront the dour, heavily armed military than I do the militants. I just want to go home.

As I leave the front courtyard of the market, I pass close to a pack of dogs sleeping by the roadside. A huge mastiff that looks straight out of a gothic horror flick lumbers to his feet and trots after me. Strangely, his attention doesn't surprise me. I've always had a thing with animals. They're drawn to me and I to them. For years, I begged Mom for a dog, but she never gave in. Too complicated, she said, with the many moves and different quarantine regulations.

I look down at the mostly furless beast keeping pace with me. His skin is stretched tightly over jutting ribs, and both ears have chunks bitten out of them. On another night, I might wonder what diseases he carried and begin concocting plans to get him to a vet, but tonight he just seems a suitable companion, as luckless as the rest of us who find ourselves alone and unprotected in a hostile land. I give him a brief smile as we steal down the laneway, keeping to the shadows.

At the first crossroad, we stop and listen. Turning right will take me in the direction of the enclave, but from that direction I hear sirens. I remember my night walk with Angie. If I go beyond the main road in the other direction, I can perhaps find a path that will skirt the front wall and take me into the enclave from the unfortified side. I wonder how similar my devious scheming is to the others who have gone before me tonight. *Did the bomber sit with his fellow jihadists, plotting the various ways they could infiltrate my world? How could I have left my sister to face them alone?*

I turn left and speed up, breaking into a steady jog. My scruffy friend lopes along, easily keeping up. He seems happy to be with me. Perhaps he thinks we're going to my home, where a solid meal awaits him. Or he plans to pick over my bones when I'm caught and killed. I give him a sidelong look, but he wags his tail and I weave close to pat his head. He licks my hand, which is gross but also comforting. I wipe it on my jeans when he's not looking.

A light goes on in a house we're approaching. My heart jumps, and I run flat-out to get past it. I keep going till I'm well beyond. My side aches and I really regret not taking up running before tonight. It seems shortsighted not to have developed such a basic survival skill. When no voice calls after us, I slow down again, holding my side. I don't look back to see if anyone has come out of the house to observe the strange spectacle of a pale, fair-haired girl with her scabby cur running through the night. I imagine we would look more like minions of the devil than two comrades chasing our own salvation.

We're only a few yards now from the main boulevard, and I move toward it cautiously, loath to step into the harsh glare of the streetlights. But I have to get across the boulevard if I'm going to have any hope of finding a side road into the enclave. I wait in the shadow of a house for several minutes, straining my ears to pick up any sound that might indicate the jihadists are nearby. The silence is thick and ominous. There are no cars, no voices – none of the sounds that would be normal in a crowded city, even at night.

I plunge into the street and move quickly, running across the road, hopping up on the wide landscaped median, dodging trees and flowering bushes, and stepping down onto tarmac again. Only a few more yards and I'll be back on another side street, once again cloaked in the darkness. I sprint the last few feet under the last bright light.

It's then I hear them.

I don't know if they've been lying in wait the whole time. Perhaps they were on their way home and came upon me by chance. As the four of them step into the harsh brilliance of another streetlight less than a block away, I see they are not much older than Vince, though their hard expressions make them look ancient. I stop so abruptly the dog bumps into my calves. His whimper is not from the collision but from the fear that passes from me into him like an electric current.

It's a moment frozen in time. They stare at me in shock. And in my terror, my body turns to stone, unable to take advantage of these few precious moments when I might secure a head start. I can only stare back.

One of them breaks the silence with a laugh that is so harsh, so unlike any laugh I've heard in my life before, that it penetrates my frozen consciousness and empowers my immobile limbs. I run.

I run like I've never run in my life before, my legs churning, my chest heaving, a searing pain in my gut. I

trip several times, once falling, but I barely notice the
rock that tears through my jeans, gashing my knee, as
I stagger to my feet and keep running. I hear the click
of nails on pavement as my dog runs with me, and the
slap of leather sandals that tells me they're not far
behind. I race for the safety of darkness. If I can get back
to the narrow side street, there are places I can hide,
sheds in front courtyards, empty street stalls. They laugh
and shout as they make chase, as if we're playing a game.
I'm sport to them, exotic quarry, and my body shakes
to be this close to their evil, but I don't slow down.

As I hurtle back toward the darkened streets I
emerged from, their voices get closer. They're gaining
on me. My small advantage is that I know these streets,
and as soon as the darkness surrounds me, I veer left,
leaping a low wooden fence into a front yard where I
noticed animal pens earlier. I dive behind one. My heart
pounds as cold sweat drips down my back. I curl myself
into a ball, pressing my body into the foul-smelling dirt
that is home to more than one species of animal. I pray
that no part of me can be seen above the low wooden
cages and duck my head lower, hoping my blond hair
isn't glowing in the slivers of moonlight.

The men's voices come near, and for a second, I'm
certain I've been found. They sound as if they're just
beyond the fence of my yard. A sheep bleats, but I'm
grateful for the cover of its noise so the men can't hear
my ragged breathing. Finally, their voices move off.
Apparently they hear nothing worth investigating. I stay

nestled in my hiding place long after the last sound of their receding footfalls. The dog, with a cunning born of years on the streets, crouches silently at my side. The darkness covers us like a warm cloak, and I wish I could hide till morning, but I've already endangered too many lives tonight, and if there is ever a time to *make things right*, this surely is it.

Slowly, keeping low to the ground, I move across the front yard, ducking from one animal pen to the next until I reach the fence. I look down the street in the direction I believe the men disappeared. I look the other way toward the boulevard. Both directions seem to hold their own dangers, but I decide to try the boulevard one more time. I step over the fence. And hear a noise. A rustling so soft it could be a mere shift in the atmosphere, but my dog hears it too and growls low in his throat. The hairs on his back rise up, as do mine.

He charges across the road, barking at a heaping pile of refuse, and two men step from behind it, smirking. I've been tricked. The other two are nowhere in sight, but it's hard to feel happy about the prospect of being murdered by two people instead of four.

They look warily at the dog that stands between us, snarling and snapping. One man is armed with a twisted iron rod that he likely picked up on the roadside somewhere, but the other has a scythe. Its sharp, angled blade designed for farmwork suddenly looks custom-made for beheading infidels. The dog crouches low, ready to spring.

I won't have a better opportunity. I turn and flee, throwing every ounce of my being into the desperate race. I have no doubt it's my life I'm running for, and perhaps not just mine. They're not immediately behind me, and I falter when I hear a yelp, but seconds later, my dog is back at my side, then bounding ahead of me. We fly across the pavement into the harsh light of the boulevard. For the third time tonight, I leap the same curbs, dodge the same bushes, disregarding the branches that tear at my arms and face as I go for the shortest routes through the greenery.

We run for the narrow street on the other side of the boulevard. I don't know this street, but in my mind, I picture darkened alleys and hiding places. This time, I won't move until I'm certain they're gone. We're over the median and almost across the second stretch of wide road when a hand that feels every bit like a demon claw clutches my hair. Momentum carries my attacker tumbling onto the pavement on top of me. I grunt under his weight as I struggle to roll out from under him.

He grabs my wrist, dragging me to my feet, and shouts something back to his partner. He holds my arm aloft in victory. The dog stops a few feet ahead of us, watching anxiously. I notice he's bleeding from the head, and the fact that they hit him fills me with a hatred I wouldn't have thought myself capable of. I want to hurt them as surely as they want to hurt me. The second man reaches us and leans forward for a minute, his hands on his knees, panting loudly. I'm not the only one who was tested beyond their limits tonight.

As his breathing returns to normal, he stands upright and laughs, and I recognize the sound; it's no less chilling the second time round. Reaching over, he grabs my hair and twists it in his fist with a viciousness that brings tears to my eyes. He pulls my head toward him, and I suddenly realize his intention. I twist away, but his tongue pursues me like a parasitic worm trying to burrow into its host. His breath is foul and I think I might vomit in his mouth, but suddenly he's wrenched away, taking with him a chunk of my hair. He's lying on the pavement, pinned under my dog, and I'm free to run again, but I am riveted by a vision more horrific than any I have seen tonight.

The second man, raising his scythe high above his head, brings it down in the powerful fluid motion of a seasoned farmer – onto the neck of my dog. The blade slicing through flesh and bone makes a sound of despair and I fall to my knees, too late, throwing myself across my fallen friend. He makes but the tiniest whimper before his body goes limp. The wetness of his blood mingles with my own tears soaking my shirt. I hold his head in my hands, searching his eyes for some hint of life that would deny what I know to be true, but his staring eyes express the shock we both feel that a creature so badly treated by humans throughout his life could be brought down by his own undaunted loyalty.

I look up at the two men looming over me, and for a moment, I think maybe this life will be enough and they'll leave me in peace. But their looks of shock are fleeting and quickly replaced with leering grins as the one with the cruel laugh drags me away from my dog, throwing me back onto the street and dropping down next to me to reach for the zipper of my jeans. I kick and claw and bite. I don't just want to escape now; I want to kill them. His laughter dies on his lips as I gouge at his eyes. He smacks me across the face, but I hardly feel it. The second one kneels on my chest and tries to grab for my hands. I twist up and bite his arm, tasting blood. I grimace in satisfaction even as he wraps his hands around my throat. I struggle for breath and use the last vestiges of it to scream. I continue to thrash, though all my limbs are now crushed under their combined weight. Amid the anarchy of our life-and-death struggle, we don't hear the approach of the jeep until we're pinned in its headlights.

CHAPTER 39

The shock and dismay on the men's faces is almost laughable as they stare into the headlights. They look back at me as if I might offer a solution to this interruption. A gunshot close enough to scare all of us confirms their worst fears, and leaping off me, they scuttle away into the night, leaving their weapons on the ground.

I pick up the scythe, still dripping with blood, and roll up onto my feet, ready to run or continue the battle. I'm not sure myself which one I'm hoping for as rage and anguish course through my body. I stare into the headlights, loosely swinging my blade and feeling a grim pleasure as it catches the light.

"What are you doing here?" A man's voice barks out in perfect English.

Though the tone is not friendly, I'm so relieved to find someone speaking my language that I give up the idea of flight, at least for now. As he steps into the light of the jeep, I see he's wearing army fatigues and sporting enough weapons to start his own war. He also has a rifle pointed right at me.

"I'm trying to get home," I say. "I was visiting a friend, and he was driving me home when we got caught in a demonstration."

I don't tell him the other less innocent details about deserting my sister.

"Where is this friend?" he demands.

"I left him at the towel market. He's hurt. I need to go back to him quickly."

"Drop your weapon," he orders.

I consider his request. If he's not going to help me, I'll need it to protect myself. I don't doubt for a moment that I would use it.

"Will you take me back to my friend?" I challenge.

"Don't you know it's dangerous to be out tonight? The only place you're going is back to our headquarters."

"No," I say with a steely calm. "You take me to my friend and then the Canadian compound, or I'll go by myself."

"That's out of the question," he says firmly. "The diplomatic enclave is closed. You will come back with us to headquarters. You'll be safe there until things are sorted out."

He takes a step toward me, his rifle still cocked. I raise the scythe.

"Be a good girl now," he says in a placating tone. "You're not safe out here by yourself. Let us help you."

"No," I repeat. "If you won't take me where I want to go, then I'm not going with you. You can help me, shoot me, or let me go."

He takes another step forward but lowers his gun and reaches out a hand in a gesture of conciliation.

"I won't go with you!" I shout, backing away and wondering if he'll bother to pursue me if I run.

Suddenly another voice calls out from the jeep. In the glare of the headlights, I can't make out anything more than a dark shape climbing down and striding toward us, but as he steps into the light, I recognize his tall lean build, the thick mustache, and his gaunt hawkish face. Everything around us drops away like extraneous props on a stage. I look into his shadowed eyes and I wait.

Without looking away, he speaks in Urdu to the first man, then he gives me a curt nod and walks back to the vehicle.

"Come on, then," says the first man impatiently.

"I said no," I say harshly, though my anger is no longer at him. For the second time, The Hawk has failed to acknowledge our connection.

"Hussain has spoken for you. We're taking you where you asked."

I look at him in surprise and let the scythe fall to the ground.

"What did he say?" I need to know.

"He said he knows you."

"That's all?"

"He also said you are a strange girl," he adds. "At least he got that right."

I follow him to the jeep, and he directs me to climb into the backseat. The two soldiers already there scoot over to make room. The Hawk sits in the front, his eyes fixed on the darkened road ahead, but as I pass, his gaze flickers in my direction so briefly I wonder if I've imagined it.

"Shukria," I say to his impassive profile.

Not turning in my direction, he gives the slightest of nods, but it's enough.

I stare out the window as we make the short ride back to the towel market. Every shadow seems to move with malicious intent, and several times I'm sure I see my attackers, but I don't ask the driver to stop. My blood lust has leaked away as my imaginings turn back to what I might find when we get to my sister. If anyone has hurt her, or even tried, in the way they went after me tonight, my life will be over. I alone will carry the responsibility for her suffering. The madmen roaming the streets tonight will be only instruments of my selfishness. And I won't be able to live with that. I stroke my damaged throat, close my eyes, and I tremble.

Leaping from the jeep before it's come to a complete stop, I race into the market, trusting the military will be on my heels.

"Aisha, it's me!" I shout before I even reach the shop. I don't want her to be frightened when she hears me coming.

She's at the front by the time I get there, her face crumpled and tearstained.

"He's been unconscious for at least thirty minutes," she whimpers. "He's lost so much blood."

"He's going to be okay, Aisha." I try to sound confident, but I can't meet her eyes as we run behind the counter and I take in the gray, inert body on the floor. I drop to my knees and put a hand on his bloodstained face. I'm reassured by the warmth of his skin, but there is so much blood it's hard to imagine this can end well.

The army guys appear and immediately speed up when they see us, either because we look so freaked or because Aisha, even bedraggled, is probably the most gorgeous girl they've ever seen. Together they pick up Mustapha, and they're surprisingly gentle for such hard-faced men.

The Hawk rounds the corner last and starts asking Aisha questions. English-Speaking Guy has stayed in the jeep, so I have to follow the next few minutes without the sound track. There seems to be some disagreement about the best way to carry Mustapha, and they put him down while they argue. I'm just on the point of grabbing Mustapha's ankles and dragging him to the jeep when they manage to come to some resolution and lift him exactly like they had him the first time.

Aisha wants to go straight to a hospital, but I convince her we'll get better service in the enclave. I'm thinking of Mandy's best interests and not Mustapha's, and I only hope I can help him when we get home. Every embassy has a clinic and doctors on call, though the Canadian clinic is no better equipped than a regular doctor's office. But now that I'm past the immediate crisis of bringing help for Mustapha, I'm desperate to get to my sister.

The streets are quiet, and the only other vehicles we see are military. I wonder if the demonstrations are over. It's almost two o'clock in the morning. I suppose even jihadists have to sleep. When we get to the enclave, The Hawk and English-Speaking Guy both get out of the jeep to argue with the guards on the gate, who clearly don't plan to let us in. English-Speaking Guy wasn't lying about the enclave being closed. Finally, the entire pack of guards comes over to the jeep to stare in at me. I really wish I could do something that would be more worthy of their scrutiny than just exist in all my weirdness, but it seems good enough for them. They return to their posts and wave us through.

CHAPTER 40

We see the flashing lights of emergency vehicles when we're still blocks from the Canadian compound. Approaching from this direction, it's impossible to see if the violence targeting the American embassy has damaged us as well. My heart twists with anxiety, and I'm almost grateful when we slow down for a roadblock. I take the opportunity to jump out and run while The Hawk begins another heated negotiation with a guard to gain entry. I hear Aisha call something after me, but the only thing on my mind is Mandy.

No one stops me as I dodge past fire trucks, ambulances, and military vehicles of every description. The guards at the Canadian compound take a gazillion years to unlock the gates, but it gives me a moment to look around. From this vantage point, I can't see any damage to our compound or to the Americans'. I'm tempted to walk around the far wall so I can actually look down the street at the full length of their compound and not just the corner that's visible from where I'm standing. But I have other priorities.

I dash through the gates, cross our carport, and run up the front path to our house. I pause a nanosecond at the door to promise Allah, the Fates, and anyone else who's listening that I will be a totally reformed, loving sister and an obedient daughter if I can just find my sister unharmed. I don't even get my hand on the doorknob when Mandy flings open the door and leaps into my arms.

The tension spills out of me so fast I almost drop her as I bury my head in her hair and breathe her in – baby shampoo, sweat, and something else that's all Mandy.

"I'm so sorry." I hitch her up to eye level so I can see her whole beautiful face when I say it.

"Are you crying?" she asks, her eyes round.

"Oh my God," cries Mom, bursting out of the house and throwing herself on me. "We thought you were dead, or worse," she sobs.

I manage to shift Mandy to one arm and put the other around Mom. Vince is right behind her. He doesn't try to hug me, keeping a safe distance so as not to get hit with flying estrogen, but he gives me a goofy, relieved smile.

"Where were you?" demands Mom, pulling away to look me over. I'm pretty sure this is the part where she tells me I'm grounded, if not disowned, and I try to think up a believable lie. "I'm so sorry," she sobs. "I'm so sorry."

Clearly she's got her facts wrong. She must think I was kidnapped or something. She steps back, examining me carefully from head to toe, like she can't believe her good fortune to have me returned without having to shell out a pile of dough.

"I'm so sorry," she says again, grabbing me. "I shouldn't have taken the conference call from Canada. I should have been here. I knew how much you wanted to go to that party, but I thought Vince would stay, or I didn't think. But when you didn't come home tonight, I thought I'd lost you too."

In the midst of my sympathy and guilt, I'm reminded of that other night when she cried with this same desperate abandon. I look past her to Vince and know he's also remembering the night we failed her. I hug her tightly as Vince walks forward, puts an arm around her shoulders, and gently pulls her off me.

"I'll take Mom inside," he says. We share a smile, both of us grateful for this second chance. They hobble into the house.

I hesitate. Aisha and Mustapha should be here by now. I wonder if they couldn't get through the roadblock. With Mandy still clinging to me like a koala, I head out to our gate to look for them and find Aisha arguing with our guard.

"This idiot won't open the gate!" she shouts.

I cringe, but the guard lets the insult roll off him and eyes Aisha defiantly. I'm impressed by his ability to protect our compound from uninvited princesses and almost regret having to tell him to open the gates. The second they're open, Aisha flounces through, hissing something in Urdu to our guard that I'm really glad I don't understand.

"How is he?" I ask. Now that I've found Mandy totally fine, I feel even worse about what happened to Mustapha.

"He's breathing," says Aisha.

"Right," I say. "Well, just let me talk to my mom."

I'm halfway through the door, Aisha right on my heels, before I remember how upset my mom just was. I put Mandy down.

"Why don't you wait with Mustapha," I suggest to Aisha, who stares at me and stands her ground. I try to stare her down but she doesn't blink. Together we stomp into the house.

I find Mom at the kitchen table, her face puffy from crying. She's holding a cup of tea and staring off into the distance with a glazed expression. Vince is leaning against the counter behind her. Trying to block Aisha's view into the room, I give him a questioning look. He shrugs.

"Mom," I say, "I know this isn't the best time, but I have this friend outside with a gaping wound in his head. He got it when he was trying to get me home safely, and he needs a doctor."

Mom springs to her feet, her eyes shining. "I'll take care of it," she says fervently. Maybe I wasn't the only one wishing for a second chance.

She punches numbers into her cell phone, and we all listen as she orders an ambulance from the American clinic next door. I'm relieved to hear that one has been standing by in anticipation of their own casualties and can be dispatched immediately. Mom puts down the phone and turns to Aisha.

"It's taken care of," she says and gives me a squeeze on the shoulder as she rushes past me out of the room.

"Do you want a cup of tea?" I ask Aisha.

"Shouldn't we get back outside?" she asks, her tone slightly indignant.

"Knowing my mom, Mustapha's halfway to a clinic by now, but you're right, we should check on him."

Once outside, we see the ambulance has already arrived. I hold Aisha's hand as we watch Mustapha get loaded into it. He's still unconscious, which is probably a good thing. Paramedics hook up an IV while Mom runs around bossing people, like she picked up a medical degree on summer vacation. Not a single person tells her to back off.

"Your mom's *amazing*," breathes Aisha.

"Yeah," I agree, with a hint of sarcasm but – strangely – no bitterness.

Aisha decides to get in the ambulance with Mustapha, which is just going around the block to the American embassy. They have the best-equipped clinic. It turns out they also have a lot of bored medical personnel, since everyone leaped into action when the bomb went off, but there were no major injuries to attend to. The truck bomber who attempted to crash the embassy's front gate didn't get farther than the huge cement barrier that runs down the middle of the road. And there weren't enough explosives in the truck to do serious damage anyway. Someone didn't do their homework on this one.

At the last minute, Mom decides to go in the ambulance with them to make sure they don't have a problem getting into the American compound, but just as they're closing the doors, she shrieks at them to stop and jumps out. She's on me in two quick bounds and pulls me into a fierce hug.

"Things are going to change around here, Emmy," she promises.

I cringe at the name I haven't heard since I was younger than Mandy, but I hug her back and enjoy the moment.

I go inside and find my brother and sister still in the kitchen, drinking tea. I collapse into a chair, and Vince slides Mom's cup across to me.

"She won't really change," I predict, wincing as the cold tea slides down my sore throat.

"Don't be so sure," Vince replies. "You should have seen her tonight. She was out of her mind when she thought something might have happened to you."

I want to tell him that something *did* happen. But then I realize he's not the one I want to say that to.

"Was she here when the bomb went off?" I ask.

"No, but Guul came running from the servants' quarters when he heard the blast. He got to Mandy before she even got downstairs. Right, Chipmunk?"

"I went into your room, and you weren't there," says Mandy accusingly.

"I know." I reach across the table to squeeze her arm. "I promise you I'll never do that to you again."

Like Mom said, there are going to be some changes around here.

"So Guul, The Ghoul, is a hero," I say.

"You need to stop calling him that." Vince says.

The phone rings, and Mandy and Vince exchange glances.

"Dad's been calling all night," says Vince.

"Then I guess I better answer." I get to my feet and walk to the phone. Before picking up the receiver, I look across at my sister, whose head is drooping toward the table. "Mandy, don't fall asleep on me. I have a story to tell you tonight."

"*Tell* a story?" she asks, immediately straightening up.

"Absolutely. It's about a little girl named Mandy who could stop time. I finally figured out a use for that power."

I wink at her sweet shining face, then I pick up the phone and talk to my dad.

CHAPTER 41

Light is filtering through the curtains of my bedroom window, but I have one final thing to do tonight. I talked to my dad for over an hour and spent another hour finishing Mandy's story. We both reveled in the power of the little girl who stopped time so her older sister could get home to her. Of course, I no sooner finished that story when she demanded an ending for the wolf story as well. Only when I confided that I needed to call Angie did she agree the wolf could wait.

Now that I'm alone, I feel a flutter of anxiety that Angie won't be as anxious to talk to me as I am to her, but it's a chance I have to take. Sitting on the edge of my bed, I resolutely punch in the number she sent me in her first e-mail, the first of at least a dozen e-mails that I never answered. I try to remember why it was so important to me to sever our friendship and wonder if she'll give me a second chance.

She picks up on the first ring.

"Emma," she says before I can tell her who it is.

"I'm sorry," I blurt. I've wanted to say it for too long to wait another minute.

"It's been all over the news," she says, her voice cracking. "I've been trying to call you all night, but I couldn't get through. God, Emma. I was so scared."

"I should have answered your e-mails. I want to stay friends, Angie. We have to stay friends. You were right about everything." Tears are flowing down my cheeks.

"They didn't know the extent of the damage –"

"Well, not everything," I interrupt. "Mustapha doesn't like me the way you thought –"

"My dad tried to get news through his contacts –"

"I did like him. I even ran out on my sister to go to him –"

"But no one could tell him anything –"

"I shouldn't have left her –"

"I was so worried about you –"

"But after he kissed me –"

"What?" she asks.

"What?" I echo.

"Did you say Mustapha kissed you?" she squeals excitedly.

I smile into the phone. "Twice, but it didn't mean anything. He's totally into Aisha."

"You have to tell me every detail," she demands. "Don't leave anything out."

I punch up the pillows on my bed and lie back to get comfortable.

"It's kind of a long story," I begin.

"I'm not going anywhere," she says. And this time I believe her.

CHAPTER 42

I hurry across the field, pulling my sweater more tightly around me. I never would have thought I'd be cold in this country, but just when you think you have things figured out, there's one more surprise in store. Frost is on the ground now, though it's usually melted by midday, and the leaves are changing color like they do in Canada. In Canada, however, it happens a few months earlier. It's been a lot of years since I've been in a country that had anything close to winter. Last night, Guul built a real fire in the fireplace while Mom unpacked boxes of ornaments, and we decorated the tree all together, just like a family.

The greenhouse feels almost too hot, so I shed my sweater as I make my way to the back. The water is already boiling, and Mr. Akbar is in his chair. He smiles happily when I emerge through the foliage, and I set about making our tea with a confidence born of experience.

"The Americans might return next semester," I say, shaking the cinnamon into the boiling water. This is always my favorite part of our ritual, when the smell of spice first mingles with the scent of flowers. Many years from now, I will smell this same scent, perhaps in a market in some exotic country or in the home of a Pakistani friend, and I'll be transported back to this moment.

"It would be good if they return," says Mr. Akbar. "You'll see your friend."

"I have other friends," I say, looking at him fondly. "Besides, I'll see Angie in a few weeks. We're meeting in Thailand for New Year's."

"How are your plans going for *Basant*?"

Basant is this huge festival in February, where everyone goes outside and has kite wars.

"Amazing," I gush. "We've raised over a hundred thousand rupees. I never would have thought the kids at this school would pay that much money just to enter a kite-flying contest. At this rate, we'll be able to start building the trash-pickers' school by spring."

Mr. Akbar smiles in satisfaction. The contest was his idea.

"I still think we should get Aisha into a kissing booth, though," I say. "She's being such a priss. It would totally solve the rest of our money problems."

"Aisha is a good girl," says Mr. Akbar firmly, his eyes twinkling.

"But it's for charity, Mr. A. Surely Allah would look the other way if it's for a good cause."

I hand him his cup and settle in my chair.

"Besides," I continue, "Mustapha would never allow it. He'd pay off every guy who signed up *not* to kiss her. She keeps her virtue, Mustapha can play the hero, and we get our hands on his cash. Everybody wins."

Mr. Akbar laughs. "You will see your father at Christmas?" he asks, changing the subject.

"Yeah. I'm spending a week with him and Zenny in Manila. It'll be weird, but I'm looking forward to it, and I'll see some old friends."

"And what will you tell them about Pakistan?" he asks, taking a sip of his tea and stroking the petal of a flower that has grown over the back of his chair.

"Fishing for compliments, Mr. A?"

He smiles and puts down his cup, takes pruning shears out of his pocket, and turns away to trim the overhanging branch. Settling back, he takes another sip of tea and gazes out at the vista of his kingdom, color and life spreading in every direction.

I think about his question and the one right answer. No matter how often the landscapes change, that question never does. After so many moves, I wonder how it could have taken me this long to understand it. The answer isn't in the beauty of a tropical setting or the squalor of a refugee camp. It doesn't change if the buildings are ramshackle, with garbage on every street corner, or if the manicured lawns front gleaming mansions. The answer is not a place.

"Mr. A?" I call his attention and he turns to me, his deeply rutted face as familiar now as the creases in my own hand. "I'll tell them it's paradise."

URDU WORDS*

"Aap ka naam kya hai?" – "What is your name?"

Achcha – I see, Okay, Good

Assalam Alekum – Hello

Basant – Kite-flying festival usually held in February

Bidis – Cigarettes

Bindi – The decorative spot on a woman's forehead

Bindya – Decorative wedding jewelry worn on the forehead

Daal – Lentil curry

Dost – Friend

Dosti – Friendship

Dupatta – A scarf worn along with a shalwar kameez

Jhoomers – Ornate earrings, sometimes attached to a
   nose ring

Khuda Hafiz – Good-bye

Kurta – A long loose shirt

"*Kya aap Angrezi?*" – "Do you speak English?"

Mangni – The betrothal ceremony

Mullah – A religious leader

Salaam – A typical greeting

Shalwar Kameez – A South Asian outfit that consists of
   a long tunic over coordinated pants

Shukria – Thanks

"*Wa Alekum Salam*" – A polite response to a greeting,
   such as, "Peace be with you"

*The translations provided here are loose and not literal.

ACKNOWLEDGMENTS

I think every new writer will acknowledge that their book, specifically their first, was the work of many, and I'm no exception. In fact, I'm nervous of thanking anyone for fear I leave someone out. But I wouldn't be enjoying this dilemma if it weren't for the faith, labor, and patience of my writing team.

First, I'd like to thank my wonderful agent, Andrea Cascardi of Transatlantic Literary Agency, who took a risk on me and devoted many hours to improving my work and teaching me the business of publishing. I'd also like to thank my author friends at Mig Writers, who critiqued and encouraged in equal measure: Andrea Mack, Carmella Van Vleet, Christina Farley, Debbie Ridpath Ohi, and Kate Fall.

There are many current and former colleagues at Tundra Books who had a hand in making this book a reality. I can't name them all, but I'd like to mention Kathryn Cole, who first saw its potential, and Sue Tate, who I hope continues to see mine. I'd also like to thank Kelly Jones for her attention to detail.

This is a book about many things, but at its center is the importance of family, and there's a reason for that. I'd like to thank my sister, Catherine Allen, who always believed in me; my brother Rob Laidlaw, for his words of wisdom on making a career in the arts; and my brother David Laidlaw, for always being there when the going got tough.

Like Emma, I'm a global nomad. I've unpacked my life in many countries and made new friends – only to pack up a few years later and start the process again. So finally, I'd like to thank my fellow traveler of more than thirty years, from my first adventure in Nigeria to my most recent in Indonesia, the person who has made every foreign land feel like home, always my first reader and my last, my husband, Richard Bale.

ABOUT THE AUTHOR

Born in Philadelphia, S.J. LAIDLAW spent most of her childhood in Toronto. From an early age, she loved reading and writing stories. After completing an undergraduate degree in English, with the dream of becoming a novelist, she ventured to Africa as a volunteer teacher. There she discovered that her students needed as much support and guidance outside the classroom as in it, so after three years, she returned to Canada to complete a graduate degree in clinical social work. Since then, she has worked as a counselor in many countries and has led workshops for parents and educators on raising and working with third-culture children. *An Infidel in Paradise* is her first book.